W9-DAW-956

The Vegan
A Novel
Andrew Lipstein

Lipstein challenges our morality with a brilliant tale of guilt, greed, and how far we'll go to be good.

Herschel Caine is a master of the universe. His hedge fund, built on the miracle of machine learning, is inches away from systematically sapping profits from the market. His SoHo offices (shoes optional, therapy required) are ready for desperate investors to flood through the doors. But on May 12, his mind is elsewhere—at his Cobble Hill townhouse and the dinner party designed to impress his flawless neighbors. When the soiree falters, Herschel concocts a prank that goes horrifically awry, plunging him into a tailspin of guilt and regret. As Herschel's perfect world starts to slip away, he clings to the moral clarity he finds in the last place he'd expect: a sudden connection with his neighbor's dog.

A wildly inventive, reality-bending trip, *The Vegan* holds a mirror up to its reader and poses a question only a hedge fund manager could: Is purity a convertible asset? The more Herschel disavows his original sin, and the more it threatens to be revealed, the more it becomes something else entirely: a way into a forgotten world of animals, nature, and life beyond words.

Andrew Lipstein, the author of *Last Resort,* a novel that "you'll think about . . . for weeks after you read the last pages" (*Los Angeles Times*), challenges our ideas of contemporary morality (and morality tales) in his scintillating, provocative second novel.

Andrew Lipstein is the author of the acclaimed first novel *Last Resort* (FSG, 2022). He lives in Brooklyn, New York, with his wife, Mette, and son, August.

Farrar, Straus and Giroux | 7/11/2023
9780374606589 | $26.00 / $35.00 Can.
Hardcover with dust jacket | 208 pages
Carton Qty: 24 | 8.3 in H | 5.4 in W
Brit., trans., 1st ser., dram.: Trident Media Group
Audio: FSG

ALSO BY ANDREW LIPSTEIN

Last Resort

The Vegan

The Vegan

Andrew Lipstein

FARRAR, STRAUS AND GIROUX • NEW YORK

Farrar, Straus and Giroux
120 Broadway, New York 10271

Title page art by Cecilia Zhang

Library of Congress Cataloging-in-Publication Data
ISBN: 978-0-374-60658-9

Designed by Gretchen Achilles

Our books may be purchased in bulk for promotional,
educational, or business use. Please contact your local bookseller
or the Macmillan Corporate and Premium Sales Department
at 1-800-221-7945, extension 5442, or by email at
MacmillanSpecialMarkets@macmillan.com.

www.fsgbooks.com
www.twitter.com/fsgbooks • www.facebook.com/fsgbooks

1 3 5 7 9 10 8 6 4 2

dedication TK

After all, the sky flashes, the great sea yearns,
we ourselves flash and yearn

— JOHN BERRYMAN

The Vegan

Chirp. Gong. Ding-ding. Ocean waves, ding-ding.

The alerts were coming more frequently now, sounding from the overhead speaker system every few seconds. Something was happening, a lot of activity even for market close. It was perfect timing, a blessing; this barrage of sound was just the kind of quirk Foster might appreciate. I was always looking for ways to underscore our nerdy kind of brilliance, our rejection of the old maxims. In fact I'd had a banner made: *Toto, I've a feeling we're not in Greenwich anymore.* Milosz, my partner, told me to take it down. I knew he was right because he said anything at all. Milosz gave what could be called *an opinion* about twice a year. He spoke only facts, facts that could be backed up with more facts, a chain of unimpeachable logic that I assumed culminated in either the meaning of life or the number zero. They say the best person to start a quantitative hedge fund is someone who can both manage the hell out of other people and master any sort of math thrown their way. Milosz and I were that person, divided in two.

I hurried across the trading floor to the speaker, fiddling with some knobs as Peter, our receptionist, watched patiently. *Do you want me to turn it off?* he asked. I laughed, I couldn't help it, my performance adrenaline was already spiking. *Louder*, I said, and he tapped at his computer. *Chirp, ding-ding. Cash register sound.* It was a bit loud, that was okay. But a cash register alert was too on the nose—what did that one stand for, anyway? I told him to change it ASAP. I turned around and saw Asja, Yuri, and Jake, three of our associate-level researchers, hunched over a table; their posture, their furtive glances, made them look like teens copying homework. I was about to send them back to their desks when I noticed the scrawl on the blackboard. It was a seemingly simple algorithm they'd been discussing for weeks, often for hours at a time, always with a piece of chalk in hand, although they never made a mark lest they disturb such an elegant formulation. *Why don't you three go to the board and have a lively discussion about the, uh*—I drew my finger in a circle until Yuri said, *The Baum-Welch algorithm.* He didn't mind that I could never remember the name, he was glad to teach me something new. *Right*, I said, and smiled. I looked at my watch, 4:01, and then at the door, where I saw Foster standing, his suit jacket over his arm, his hand flattening his hair. I renewed my smile and strode over, pointing to Peter and delivering our tired joke about gearing up the light show. He was game, Peter, his laugh sounded nothing like vocational obligation.

I opened the door and gave him my hand.

Ian? I asked, as if I didn't know what he looked like.

The great Herschel Caine. He didn't wait for an invitation to walk in; actually, I had to move out of his way.

Let's head to my office, I said, stepping past him. I preferred we not loiter, I hardly knew who he was. Well, I knew almost everything about him, I'd scoured the internet—just not what exactly he was doing here. He wanted to invest, that was what he said in his email, but he had a way of phrasing things— *I'll be in the area Monday, might I stop by?*—that suggested conspiracy. And was it just a coincidence that he was also invested in Webber? That part didn't make sense. We had nothing in common with them, the whole point of our firm was to be the antithesis of Webber; in fact Milosz and I often made business decisions by asking ourselves what our old employer *wouldn't* do. Of course I'd never say anything of the sort in a pitch, let alone mention Webber Group, unprovoked, by name. This wasn't just because no investor wanted a David in a sea of Goliaths—they all wanted a Goliath with an excess return slightly higher than that of the other Goliaths—it was because vindication and the associated passions simply weren't the stuff of moneymen. They preferred to hear something more along the lines of *We've discovered a quantitative scheme that, we believe, once perfected, can generate untold wealth.* This line I knew by heart; it was my opener no matter the audience, a nice balance between supper club restraint and carnal greed—Wall Street's stereotypes for WASPs and Jews united at last.

I turned around to find him staring at the floor, as if to make a point of not seeing anything he shouldn't. This only fed my paranoia, that he was so attuned to our need for secrecy. Actually I hoped he'd glimpse enough to see we weren't another Dockers-and-beige-carpet hedge fund, some isolated *campus* with priority parking spots. We had designed our office for creativity, for thinking; we surrounded ourselves with plants: not ferns or cacti but fiddle-leaf figs, variegated strings of pearls, wandering Jew, *Monstera obliqua*. We had no dress code, official or implicit; employees were encouraged to come as they were. *Yuri was our case in point: he didn't even wear shoes, and I frequently found strands of his long, dry hair around the espresso machine or on the coffee table with the art books. It was with this mindset that we chose to rent three thousand square feet in SoHo, on Wooster off Broome, even though we could have spent the same amount for thirty thousand up Metro-North. It was why we mandated (and paid for) once-a-week therapy for each of our fourteen employees, myself included (Milosz was a harder sell). You had to be careful, though, not to fall on the wrong side of the obnoxious-tech-startup divide, so we forwent the furniture so modern you dared not sit on it, the murals, the liquor (I doubt our researchers even drank), and decided on Vintage seltzer over LaCroix.

Still or sparkling? I asked. He leaned in, he hadn't heard. I told Peter to turn the alerts down and, with my hand on Ian's back, shepherded him into my office.

Some people here think it sounds like a song, I said, walking behind my desk. *Some say it's like listening to a cartoon. But I think if you really pay attention, it starts to sound like language.* He nodded and gave a perfunctory smile—rather, a smile meant to convey that it was perfunctory. Fine, so it wasn't such a profound thought. I would have thought someone with a master's degree in English from Harvard (earned at age forty-two, no less) would appreciate the grace note, but apparently he had more straightforward tastes. *It sounds funny, gimmicky even, and yet, every time you hear, say, a studio audience clapping, that's our algorithm telling us there's a public stock that's more than sixty-two point five percent likely to rise at least two percentage points by market close.*

He gave a more genuine smile now. *If only 62.5 were 100.*

Of course, I said. And that's why we hear a sound at all. Because we need someone with ears—albeit someone quite smart with ears—to hear that studio audience clapping and walk over to a computer and do something I certainly don't understand, something they could have spent a dissertation on, something that, applied differently, might have made a real difference in the world, but instead it's being used here, in this office, to generate guaranteed profits for people who are already too rich. I sat down, held my palm out, inviting him to do the same. *Well, that was some kind of introduction. Let's start over.*

Ian Foster, he said. Nice to meet you. But perhaps I shouldn't waste more of your time. By the sound of it you're basically printing money, and money is all I come with. He didn't sit. Was he for real? I took him in, matched him against all those preening men I'd met at Webber, at business school—no, surprisingly the best fits were from college; yes, he was a bit immature, insecure, he wasn't at home in the world. He couldn't act natural so he withheld himself, became someone else, covered his unease with affectation—like that hand, his right, which swam in front of him constantly.

Well, we're not printing money just yet. We still need to raise enough to buy the printer. But once we've got it, once we can cover the ink and maintenance fees, et cetera, I promise I'll let you walk out of here. In fact I'll stop returning your calls.

Ah, taking a page from the RenTech playbook. Renaissance Technologies was one of the first hedge funds to use quantitative modeling, and still is an industry paragon. Decades ago, their Medallion Fund became so lucrative they kicked out their own investors, and now only employees and executives reap their unprecedented returns. *You know I met Jim Simons, he said. Who hadn't?* I acted impressed. *But let me be a bit more up front. I'm here to invest, yes, but I'm also here as a favor to a friend, Colin Eubanks. You know him, I assume?* I nodded, as if it were some name that fell on my ears now and again—my dentist, my wife's ex-fiancé—and not the Colin Eubanks whose support the firm needed to survive, $220 million, money he'd guaranteed was ours, guaranteed not in a promissory note, which I would have preferred, but with a firm hand on my shoulder and intense eye contact one night at the Harvard Club, a venue I didn't know was taken seriously—let alone by British financiers who hadn't attended Harvard—at least not $220 million seriously. But he was serious. I believed that, I'd already rewritten the clinching line of my boilerplate pitch: *To date we've filled out most of a fund of $400 million,* a line that had helped generate almost the additional $180 million, though this was all uncommitted, and assumed people wouldn't drop out. They would, I knew how this went, I'd gone through the fundraising cycle end to end four times at Webber. But of course pitching Webber to investors was an entirely different proposition: *In this market? You want tried and true.* Webber had beat the market seventeen years out of the past twenty, and usually by a good margin. We, Atra Arca Capital Management, had beat the market zero years out of zero; we were exactly the kind of risky proposition I'd spent my past life warning investors against: a firm that relied on numbers and numbers only, a quant hedge fund that was truly a quant hedge fund, and not what firms like Webber claimed to be—a quant hedge fund wrapped in rationale. We didn't want rationale, we wanted to build a black box so opaque, so dense with algorithm and data—50 petabytes of it, computed at 105 teraflops, eventually (we already had the servers, $1.5 million worth, so said the insurance we took out on them and the information they would hold)—that none of it could be explained, not with words or numbers or even overly abstract schemata (the currency of overeducated researchers). Yes, it was sexy, and investors loved to love it, but when it came to putting down a check they wanted to see historical returns, hopefully decades of them. In other words, I was plenty aware of the stigma, and it was my mandate to prove we were not just a room full of PhDs, data servers, and chalk. Hence the name Atra Arca, which means *black box* in Latin, a detail I thought might serve me well in meetings just like this, with people of the Ian Foster sort, the *learned* sort, the sort who, if they didn't know Latin, at least revered it.

Colin, I said. *He's a good man. And I'm intrigued: What's this favor?*

Oh, he said, as if he hadn't guessed I'd ask. *Colin has superb taste, great instincts. But sometimes he needs help pulling the trigger.*

Right, I said, and smiled. *So you want a bit of due diligence. We'd start with an NDA, of course.* A bluff of my own. The only nondisclosure agreement we had was for employees; it was needlessly punitive and meant for people who'd know our strategy inside and out—not something that would ever be on offer, even to Colin.

He waited a beat. *No NDA*, he said. *I'm not here for due diligence. I'm not a numbers guy, I trust I know even less than you about*—the hand wave again—*all of this. And I'm not some fink, not that I've never been called that in so many words. It's just that . . .* Now he began talking at great speed, words that were mostly for himself, I could tell by the way he lit up, the self-sneer he couldn't hide, he obviously enjoyed having a captive audience. He spoke about regulation, finance in the eighties, *Den of Thieves* and *Barbarians at the Gate*, books I grew up on that now seemed so outdated I doubt anyone in the office had even heard of them—and he clearly had a keen mind, his sentences were clever, unexpected, I found myself laughing, a real laugh, which I didn't get every day, at least not at work. *And every other character in these books is either tall, thin, and silent, or short, fat, and egregiously loud. No, I don't think things are so cut and dried, and, likewise, I don't know why exactly Colin trusts me. Probably because we think alike, so with me he gets an objective version of himself. So let's say that's why I'm here, to be Colin when Colin's somewhere else. And we'll proceed with that.* He gave a quick nod, an abrupt end to his little soliloquy, and suddenly it felt like our meeting was all but over. Did he only need to be listened to, humored, flattered? That I could do. He smoothed his hair again, looked for his coat and found it already on his arm. I was going to say something, wind the meeting down with some formality, but that didn't seem to be his way; from now on my only purpose with him was deference. He made to leave but stopped at the door. *I have to ask: Why Atra Arca?*

Ah, it means black box. As in—

No, he said. *I know that. But I'd think it would be* Niger Arca. *Atra is more . . . gloomy, dismal even.*

Really? I'd used Google Translate. I'd confirmed it with a friend. A Hail Mary: *Do you know why they call economics the dismal science?*

Something about population growth, limited resources—no?

Exactly. To profit in any market you have to take from others. But that predator-prey mindset presumes intent, which we've taken out of the equation. Only our algorithm knows why it does what it does, and so the dismal science is kept in a box.

He laughed. He shook his head. *Herschel,* he said, *that's evil.*

I bought a six-pack at a grocery store outside the office and drank one in the Uber back to the house. I needed some sort of reset before the big dinner; that meeting had left me disoriented, in a mild stupor, as if I'd just woken up. When Ian left I'd felt good, that I'd done well, but by the time I myself left, about thirty minutes later, I wasn't sure precisely what I'd done well *at*. I almost called Colin but thought better of it, when we'd spoken last week he'd made clear, in so many words, that he'd commit when he was ready. It didn't help that there was a swarm of protestors just outside the office: next door was some tech company that had recently signed a deal with China that would, somehow, enable them to expand the tracking and surveillance of their Uighur population. They booed me as I entered the black SUV, even though I'd obviously come out of a different building, further proof that their protest was just an outgrowth of a more generic frustration; I was wearing slacks, that was the problem. They weren't radicals, they just wanted to feel alive; their animus wouldn't change the world outside, it only expressed a void within. I could forgive the young ones, they didn't know how the world worked, but on those my age, almost two decades out of college, I let my spite exhaust itself, I needed it out of the way. After all, it was the twelfth of May.

May 12. Franny and I had used the date as shorthand more times than we'd ever admit to the evening's guests. It was, by this point, a code name for our mission, one we'd been planning for months, a feat that would guarantee that our life here in Brooklyn, in Cobble Hill, would be all it needed to be:

we would make new friends, best friends, in our late thirties. And we would do this by showing our neighbors, Philip and Clara (née Miller) Guggenheim (yes, that one; his great-great-etc. had founded the museum), that we were not only just as interesting as they were, but fun, good people, married with kids on the way, next year if everything went to plan, which they were shooting for, too—an intimate detail revealed on just our second rendezvous a few weeks ago, as both couples lounged in the narrow, shared courtyard that separated our (nearly identical; I'd found their floorplan on StreetEasy) brick townhouses. The similarities were uncanny: Jewish husband, gentile wife, none of us actually religious; we'd bought our homes within two months of each other; Franny a furniture designer, Clara an interior designer; husbands runners, wives in book clubs; both couples shopped at Trader Joe's despite being rich. Even our differences were complementary. Outside the office there was nothing I liked talking about less than finance, and Philip was a film director (and actor, but only in his own movies), my secret (I don't even think Franny knew this) dream profession. And their dynamic perfectly counterbalanced ours. Whereas Franny was our chief executive officer, it was clear from the first time we met that Clara was beta to Philip's alpha. It wasn't so much that there was an imbalance between them, just that their personalities produced a natural equilibrium: Philip was the consonants, establishing order, setting terms, and Clara the vowels, sliding through the indeterminate middle, applying her apparent vagaries to a neatly prescribed life. For the past few weeks, when we saw that they were outside, we would come up with an excuse to join them—claiming that the gardeners didn't water the lilies enough but we were happy to do it, or noting that it was the only hour of the day when our thin patch got direct sun. We clicked, there was no denying it, but their social life seemed more than full (practically a dinner party a week, it appeared) and we wanted to be much more than casual acquaintances. We wanted, we needed, to impress them.

May 12 was also, not by coincidence, the night we were having over Franny's freshman roommate, Bertie "Birdie" Barnes, a prominent British playwright, in town under the pretense of the opening of a friend's show, but really because she was finalizing her (second) divorce and needed something to do—hence the contacting of old, lost connections. Birdie and Franny had been inseparable at Brown for exactly one semester; since then their relationship had consisted of a phone call every few years (albeit one that lasted half the day). I'd never met her but had the impression we wouldn't share much common ground; Franny used the term *outsized* whenever she described her. But this was a perfect opportunity, kismet, Birdie was the whole package, a posh accent and a dazzling career in the arts, the idea came to Franny and me at the exact same moment: yes, May 12 would also be the night we'd finally invite Philip and Clara into our home. With Birdie's charm coloring the evening, they would witness firsthand our lives, our taste, Franny's artistry; while they ate they would sit on her trademark chair, the one featured in *Architectural Digest* not six months ago (did Clara subscribe?). The invitation was delivered offhandedly, as if Franny had just come up with the idea. *Yes*, Clara had said right away, *that would be lovely*. Franny gave me the news that night as though she were recounting a special at Paisanos; from then on we agreed, tacitly, to play it cool.

When I got home I found Franny in the kitchen wearing

her teal linen dress, her hair shorter than I'd ever seen it. In fact she was trying and failing to tie it back while frowning at her laptop, which sat dangerously close to the lit stove. On the screen was an email written in her assistant's signature blue font. Franny had worked from home to prepare for the evening, and it now seemed, as I'd expected but did not suggest, that she hadn't been able to balance the two. I noticed steam rising from the trash bin: the still-hot memory of a false start. I stopped myself from asking how it was going, I knew the answer and anyway she was obviously in—as she herself called it—her *do not fucking disturb* mode. If she slid into that gear more often than she liked to admit, still she only did so when necessary, when there was too much to do in too little time. This penchant was so ingrained in her that I'd always assumed it was inherited from her family—until our wedding last year, when I met them, or rather, the few who chose to attend. That our ceremony was to be held in a temple was enough for most to decline the invitation. They were devout Lutherans, all living in or around her hometown, Fergus Falls, Minnesota. She still spoke of them as the spurned do, with vulnerability but also with the conviction that comes from forging a life of one's own. Even her accent, an indistinct composite of Northeast modulations, had been fully scrubbed of its quasi-Scandinavian roots. But unlike most every transplant I'd met from that part of the country—all of whom seemed to view their lives through the eulogizing lens of their families—Franny had something indelibly *New York* about her. It was as if she captured the spirit of the city, embodying all those threadbare sayings. She unironically believed in the concept of *making it*, which both moved and inspired me, probably because to her it wasn't a concept. She had nothing to fall back on, she couldn't imagine any other life for herself than this one; for her, failure did not mean settling for something more realistic—there was no such thing.

I went up to the shower, taking another beer with me. Even in the bathroom I could smell the meal, a menu we'd finalized the night before: escarole with pancetta and hen of the woods, sweet potato and sage ravioli in parmesan broth (the idea shamelessly cribbed from Frankies, an Italian restaurant up the street), and bone-in pork chop saltimbocca (ditto); this last item had been subbed in at the eleventh hour for a needlessly complex and desperate beef Wellington.

After I got out, just as I was rubbing the mist from the mirror, I heard an unusual sound, a sort of siren. My first thought was that it was the new security system, which I'd nearly forgotten about despite the fact that it was almost as expensive as our home insurance. I opened the door and identified the source: Birdie. This was her God-given voice, one I'd previously heard only through a phone receiver across the room. It was clarion, there was no other word for it, I pictured those metallic statues on the covers of Ayn Rand novels. But after I got changed, finished my beer, and went downstairs, I found in our family room a woman who might have been the very inverse of those gilded musclemen. She was round and short, her hair ginger but darkened with age, with stubborn curls she forced into a high ponytail. On her person there seemed to be every color, every pattern, every fabric; against all that chaos her face looked like one big pinkish pearl. She turned to me, flashing her emerald eyes—they were so brilliant I inhaled, nearly a gasp.

Hersch-el. Darling. You've absolutely outdone yourself.

I glanced at Franny, whose face had fossilized into a genial smile. I'd seen that face before; she'd been taken conversational hostage. I tried to speak—to say what, I didn't know, I didn't have the slightest clue what she meant—but before I could, she said, walking over to me, *Now listen. You take this.* She disrobed her shawl, jacket, gloves, and sweater, and handed me the pile.

Thanks, I said, and she laughed heartily, a staccato triplet, pulling me in for a hug and then letting go only to appraise me, her hands on my shoulders, as if I were a nephew she hadn't seen in ages. With the weight of her clothes in my hands I nearly forgot it was spring until I made it downstairs to the foyer, where I hoped to take a moment to regain my composure. But I never got the chance; through the glass of our front door I saw Philip and Clara. The dismay I felt at having them witness me in such a disoriented state was washed away by my pleasure in seeing that they too were treating this night as something special: he wore a turtleneck, she a beige blouse and red lipstick, each held a bottle of wine. I opened the door and extended my hand, an awkward enough maneuver, and on top of it I let Birdie's shawl fall to the floor. I bent down to get it but Clara got there first.

Laundry day? she asked, placing it on top of the heap.

This came off a single woman, I said, *and she's still not naked.* They laughed but nervously; as they walked up the stairs I cringed, hearing my words again.

My God, Philip said, *you didn't tell us your friend was Birdie Barnes.* He gave her his hand. *We saw A Feast of Seconds in London, it was this time last year. Loved it, of course.*

Well, that's something coming from Philip Guggenheim, Birdie said. He looked down, a show of humility; he'd done the same when I mentioned *The Phoenicians,* his limited-release but highly acclaimed motion picture of three years ago. *Franny told me all about you two. You know, I once dreamed of getting into the Guggenheim, and now I have, in a way.* She glanced at me and yipped. I tried not to look at Philip's face but couldn't help it, his feigned modesty dripping off to show tainted pride beneath. *I was born to be a painter, that's what my mum always said. I believed her up until I was twenty-four and had given it a go. Yes, some talent—but I digress. Anyway, I have a Carrington in my office,* she said, blinking at him. No, he didn't know what that meant, none of us did. Birdie acted surprised and then told the entire saga, a tale of great love between surrealist artists—Max Ernst and Leonora Carrington—torn asunder by the Nazis, never to meet again. Carrington apparently spent time in an insane asylum, receiving electroshock treatment, and then escaped to Mexico, while Ernst began a marriage of convenience (in Birdie's telling, at least) with Peggy Guggenheim.

I didn't know that story, Philip said. In those minutes he'd retrieved his grace.

Well, Birdie said, eyeing the bottle of wine in Clara's hand. *If I've got any chance of staying up we must pop that open. It's almost midnight in London and, let's be frank, my life is crumbling to dust.* She made a clownish frown none of us knew what to do with; to move the moment forward Franny ushered us into the dining room and handed me a corkscrew.

As we took our seats—me at the head between Philip and Clara, with Franny and Birdie across from each other—Franny apologized for the state of the house. *We're changing everything,* she said. *That is, if we ever get our building permits back.* The city's approval process had been her albatross, it was now the only thing that lay between her and her dreams: a home crafted by her own hand. We had both been thrilled to buy, but as we moved through the closing process we came to realize it was for opposite reasons: I wanted an investment, she wanted something that we'd never sell—that would, eventually, be passed down through generations. It was with this in mind that she'd worked with a contractor to reconceive the space, ditching all the modish effects in favor of something more, as she put it, *permanent*.

I just want a simple, honest home, she said, her eyes softening, or blurring, whatever it was they did when she was seeing something that didn't yet exist. But as she came back to herself, squinting at the other side of the room, her face hardened, a look that had only increased in severity since we moved in. *This house is basically a WeWork. Everything's smart. The fridge is smart. As if we need an app to tell us when the milk's expired. It's like we're trapped in some nouveau riche purgatory, waiting for the gods at the Department of Buildings to look our way.*

Franny wishes our home was carved from a single block of wood, I said.

Birdie looked at me and said something in French I didn't understand, at which only Philip laughed, and not exactly kindly. Franny responded in kind—years ago she'd apprenticed with a cabinetmaker in Paris—and gave me a sympathetic look.

I split the bottle into five glasses and then, as Clara watched, took a sip. I told her I loved it, and then something about the full-bodied flavor, though her smile indicated that wasn't quite right.

No, I said, *I know nothing about wine.*

There's nothing to know, she said, the sort of thing said by people who know just how much there was. *Just don't tell that to my parents, they spend most of their waking hours in the cellar.*

So it wasn't just Philip's family that was rich. I wondered why they didn't get a nicer place, given theirs was the same price as ours. (Again, StreetEasy. And actually it was a bit higher, $3.1 million; even though ours was a two-and-a-half bath to their two, their balcony had an unobstructed view of Manhattan and their living room was, apparently, a sanctuary of light.) *But let's talk about anything else,* she went on. *The market, for starters. We haven't the slightest clue where to put our money.*

I glanced at Philip, who simply looked down; no, he didn't want my investment advice. *I'm hardly the one to ask,* I said. Her look demanded more—didn't people like me fill their funds with just her type? But even without Philip's tacit *No thanks* I would have quashed my instinct to make a pitch; I'd heard too many stories of mixing work and play in just this way. *The S&P would be the most boring place for it, and that's exactly why I'd invest in—*

This wine, Birdie said, her voice rising to break the conversational barrier, *was fabulous.* Was? She'd finished hers; I hadn't even had a second sip. Philip was game, he raised his glass and practically downed it. I took a gulp and so did Franny, but Clara just looked at her husband. Before it became too obvious, Philip put his hand on hers. *Well,* she said, *we have something of an announcement to make.*

Franny cooed, I said *How wonderful* or something just as anodyne, anything to hide my unease; the previous weekend Franny and I had talked for hours about when we'd have children, agreeing, finally, to postpone for six more months. It wasn't ideal—we were both eager to start a family—but in a year and a half the firm would be in a state where I could take some time off, a full two months I'd promised her, we'd bring the baby to Italy, Spain, Morocco. The usual questions were asked, I listened to their answers with a smile, choosing to divert my anxiety, leave enough space to *uncover the upside*, as Magda, my therapist, would say; thinking of her Hungarian lilt comforted me. Their kid would be a year or so older than ours; that didn't mean they couldn't be best friends. Ours might always lag somewhat—a little weaker, a little less smart—risking the development of submissive tendencies, sure, but the upside was much greater: our child would always be challenged, competing in the next weight class.

Well, let's enjoy your freedom while you still have it, Birdie said, lifting her empty glass. *I'm sure the other bottle is just as good, but I think I'll take something stronger.*

And we'll need some food to sop it up, Franny said, excusing herself to the kitchen.

Birdie wiggled the glass and raised her eyebrows at me, like I was waiting on her, like the whole world was. But why did it feel, what—earned? Was it just her accent, her witty little aperçus? Or was it because she never second-guessed herself, never let on a hint of doubt? Whatever it was it arose from her wealth, surely, a lifetime of it, such imperiousness could only be inherited—like the freedom to single-mindedly pursue a career in the arts. Even though Birdie had only garnered success in the past few years, Franny said she'd never had a job, a real job anyway; since college she'd mostly written when she felt moved to and otherwise attended to an apparently packed social calendar. Perhaps I envied her, resented her, even. I never felt empowered to do anything but make money, that being the one glaring lack all through my own childhood. We weren't poor, per se, and yet vacations were riddled with anxiety around eating out, getting our security deposit back. I'll never forget my parents gathering at the dining room table every Sunday night, sorting out their finances in hushed, tight tones.

I'll make you something, Birdie, I said, and followed Franny into the kitchen. I caught up with her at the stove. She glanced at the doorway and said, sotto voce, *She's not normally this, you know, overpowering.* I shook my head and she squeezed my arm, imploring me to remain positive. *She can be good company,* she said. *Great company.* I smiled and looked at the liquor cart. *If I've got any chance of staying up,* Birdie had said. Yes, the booze was enabling her. I searched the fridge for our strongest mixer and took out the black currant syrup. I added it to a tumbler of seltzer and poured on the smallest splash of our cheapest vodka. I added a slice of lemon, squeezing it and then dropping it in, and brought out the drink.

When I sat down Clara asked me what the S&P was, which made me feel better about my uninformed comment about the wine. I talked about mutual funds and indices, reciting the standard recommendations while I watched Birdie. She'd yet to take a sip, she waited until Franny had made it out with the first course. Then she lifted her glass.

To all of you, for having such coherent, respectable lives, she said. *My mum would have been much happier with a daughter like you. All she ever wanted was for me to breed.* She took a drink. *Marvelous, Herschel.*

We started to eat. I was thankful for the quiet, the chance to reset. But it wasn't fifteen seconds before I realized there was too much of it. I looked up to see that Clara had stopped eating, that Philip hadn't even started. He turned to me. *I don't eat meat,* he said, plainly enough that I realized it was something I already knew, he'd told me a week ago, outside in the courtyard.

I'm so sorry, Franny said, glancing between him and me.

It's my fault, I said. *You told me that, but I failed—*

Surely not the biggest surprise, Birdie said. *I didn't eat meat for weeks after I saw* The Phoenicians. *Well, that's a lie. But really, the man had Kristen Stewart served in a stew. Wasn't too ethically ambiguous, now was it?* No, it wasn't. And now it seemed as though, on top of forgetting he was a vegetarian, I hadn't seen the film, which I had.

I separated the art from the artist, I said, lamely. *And also I forgot that simple fact. We'll just give you the next course.* I looked at Franny, my mind was blank.

Ravioli, she said. *Vegetarian.* She got up and went to the kitchen.

The entrée is pork, I said, *unfortunately. But we're happy to pick you up anything you like, we're right by a great Italian restaurant.*

I thought you were neighbors, Birdie said.

Right, I said, swatting away a fly. *We are, I've just had a mental lapse. I'm sure they have those in London, too.* Franny passed a glare as she entered the room.

It's all fine, really, Philip said. *Ravioli sounds lovely.*

Franny set a plate before him. *Sweet potato and sage ravioli,* she said, *in a parmesan broth.*

We all watched as he took a bite. *Wonderful,* he said. *A meal in itself.*

So you're not full-on vegetarian, Birdie said. He looked up. He didn't know about rennet, clearly, or didn't care, that was made obvious by the fact he had ears and had heard the word *parmesan,* like the rest of us.

No, Birdie. I'm not. He kept his eyes on the food, he took another bite. He swallowed, placed his fork down, clasped his hands, and finally looked up at her. *And I trust that even as the writer of* A Feast of Seconds, *you don't think every dinner party should end with someone vanishing into thin air.* It was the perfect retort, a joke strong enough to put everything to bed, but that wasn't his intention, the line came muttered through barely split lips. I saw from Clara's face not just worry but understanding, she'd seen such a reaction before. Was that all it took—his artistic integrity barely ruffled by a stranger? But I was surprised to find that Clara's empathy had made its way into me, too; he was struggling, that was clear, hurt but not wanting to be.

Well, I said, *I hope you wouldn't peg me as a full-on capitalist just be—*

If you must know, that wasn't the original ending, Birdie said, lifting her glass, which was now half-empty. *I had something there that was much better, but a very arrogant, obtuse producer told me he wouldn't do it, it was too close to something Joanna Hogg had done first. I've never even seen her films, actually, but I heard from a friend it was far* . . . She showed no sign of stopping, she was only picking up speed. At this point she didn't need an audience nor did she have one; she was slowly transforming our collective distaste into tedious, flavorless boredom. As I watched her ugly British mouth widen and bend and skew, dancing around her crooked white teeth, something began nagging at me, pulling at me like a child demanding my attention. *Something Joanna Hogg had done first.* That was the line. Unlike Birdie I'd seen Hogg's work. That was what was bothering me, the thought I had to reclaim, it was a scene from a film of hers I'd seen many years ago. It was unforgettable— yes, I saw it now in such high fidelity I could even make out the edges of the screen. A character pretends to faint in order to leave an unpleasant dinner party. The scene had invigorated me then, and even now in recollection, it wasn't only hilarious, it was just lifelike enough, it could happen, it stretched but stayed inside the boundaries of possibility. But then I was shaken out of my reverie, literally; the screen disappeared, and right where its center had been was a glass, shaking. Birdie had finished her drink and wanted another. *One just like it*, she said, now in full focus. I tried dipping one last time back into my thoughts, but before I could, she said, *If you make me make it myself you'll have no liquor left.*

I stood up. I saw that Philip had finished his plate, they all had. I took her glass and walked into the kitchen, where I leaned against the island. In the microwave door I saw my reflection, as dark as obsidian. Outside I heard the first patter of rain; hadn't the forecast said tonight would be clear? I returned to the Hogg scene, the colors of the room suddenly matched that palette, soft and drained but crisp. I laughed to myself, a real laugh; it had to be stifled so they wouldn't hear. It was then that the idea came to me, at once, wholesale, like the ones I have for Atra Arca, a painting too big to see but in pieces.

I turned the music louder. I took off my shoes. I picked up the glass and left the kitchen through the hallway, walking slowly up the stairs—they didn't creak, thankfully, something our broker had pointed out more than a few times—to the bathroom off the master bed. I closed the door and urinated. I washed my hands and opened the medicine cabinet, where I found a bottle of NyQuil and two of ZzzQuil. I didn't know the difference though the ZzzQuil had two cartoon cherries on it. I put one of the bottles in my pocket but it jutted out so I held it in my palm as I walked downstairs. In the kitchen I poured the ZzzQuil into her glass, filling it halfway, and added a few ice cubes. I smelled it. I thought a bit. On the counter I saw two lemons, I quartered them both and juiced every segment. I swirled the cocktail with my finger over and over again. I was just about to go back into the dining room when I saw the bottle of cheap vodka, and put a small splash on top, as before.

As I walked the glass stayed in the center of my visual field, as if my internal camera was stabilized. I delivered it and returned to my seat, where I found the next course, the ravioli. I looked up at Franny, her face was blank, her expression gone, as if she were alone, as if we weren't making eye contact. I winked at her and she reanimated. *We've decided you'd be the one to disappear,* she said.

A fly landed on my hand, I lifted it and it flew away. *What?*

Like in Birdie's play. We were joking about who would be the one to vanish into thin air. I said that with that Cayman insurance you have, it would serve us all if it was you who went poof.

Key man, not Cayman. But even so, you'd have to already be invested in the firm and . . . I trailed off, Birdie had picked up her glass. *Never mind.* Franny followed my eyes to her friend. Birdie took a sip, she let too much in, she coughed, wiped her mouth, tilted her head to the side in mock relief. She swallowed and her eyes lit.

That is— Herschel, it's— My God, it tastes like divorce. I lifted my wine glass, newly filled. She matched, they all did, in silence we drank, Birdie nearly half her glass. *When Franny said Cayman insurance, I thought of my father's pied-à-terre in St. Barts, which is just like the Cayman Islands except it's French— and, well, for people with taste. Not that . . .* I took the time to eat the ravioli, which were delicious, the parmesan broth much more than a gimmick. I savored it, I rarely savor food, but now

I let each mouthful practically dissolve on my tongue. I took a big swig of wine and watched Birdie yap. I blurred her image, her abstracted form was so much more harmless: a symbol, if anything. It was amusing, seeing her head bob up and down, her wrists swivel. I enjoyed the rest of the dish in a sort of solitary state. In some way we were each of us alone.

By the time I finished Birdie seemed to have lost just as much interest in what she was saying as we had. I waited, took advantage of a rare pause and jumped in to change the subject. I spoke about our lone meeting with the previous owners of the house, just after we discovered that they had an outstanding building permit; this was the reason, Franny thought, we were still struggling to get ours through. Franny jumped in, she couldn't help it, she still lost sleep over the incident and had already cultivated a not-quite-accurate impression of the wife, who was German, a professor, and deliriously pretentious. *Vee had no idea! This is for vat? Zee toy-uh-let? No, it did not clugg vonce, vie vould vee need to change zee toy-uh-let?* I egged her on, playing her part in the disagreement: *Frau Schneider, a permit is a permit, and we'll never be able to build our triplex treehouse made of Japanese maple if you don't—* Back and forth we went, until Franny stammered that neither she nor her *hoos-band* had ever taken a shit in their lives. We got genuine laughter from Clara and especially Philip, who I'd worried had turned a bit dour. No, we only needed the right setting, needed that windbag to quiet down for a bit. And now she was more than quiet, she'd all but left the room. Yes, the drink had taken hold, and before I could suggest it myself she said, *Franny dear. I'm terribly sorry but with this jet lag, you know, at my age you just— Well, you are my age but you're much younger, too. Anyway, I don't think I can stay for the pork. Philip can have mine.* She gave him a lazy, nearly flirtatious smile and stood up.

Franny frowned, I matched. I went to get her things and by the time I was back her Uber was just two minutes away. She'd input the wrong address, a block away, she gave Franny and me kisses and then, just like that, drifted out of the house.

From that moment on the night shifted, there was an air of newfound freedom, as if our parents had just left for the weekend. As we finished our meal, the misfortune of Birdie's presence became, in retrospect, comic, in fact all of her little comments seemed funny now; we laughed like we were getting away with something. After dinner we went to the family room and had rugelach with milk and then cognac. The slaphappiness faded, but in its place came real conversation, shared intimacies, Philip talked about the film he was working on, they told us how long it had taken them to get pregnant, even showed us pictures from their ultrasound. Franny pretended to refuse to play the piano, and when she finally did it was lovely, we weren't drunk but had had enough to be able to listen in silence, get carried away. There was no longer a feeling of performance or manners. Clara even admitted to having *low-key stalked* Franny, she was an admirer of her work—to which Franny, never one to miss a window of opportunity, replied that she would love to talk about some sort of collaboration. At this point Philip suggested that we call it a night, that we do it again soon, and we all shared a look that meant *And please let's keep it us four.* As I closed the door Franny and I stood beaming at each other. The night had been, ultimately, a success; we wouldn't have done it differently if we could have. We hugged, we kissed, it was more than a happy kiss;

I became hard and didn't hide it. She told me to meet her in bed and went to the bathroom. I turned off the lights, shut down the stereo system, and finished my drink. In the kitchen I found the ZzzQuil, I brought it up with me to the bedroom, where Franny was, nude, the lights on, her legs spread, her face flush from drink.

The night's saving elixir, I said, sloshing the bottle. Her eyes widened, she laughed, her cheeks wide and plump, it was exactly how she looked in a picture I took when we'd first met. I drank a small sip and then a swig; I needed something to combat the alcohol, which always ruined my sleep. *My God, it tastes like divorce*, I said, my British accent terrible. But she was done with the jokes, she pulled out a condom from the bedside table. I stared at it. My toes gripped the rug. I felt an unusual stroke of gaiety, whimsy even; life was surprising again.

Maybe we start trying, I said. She didn't react, wouldn't allow herself to until she knew for certain I wasn't kidding. I wasn't, I told that to myself and then to her: *It's all we've ever wanted. Why should we wait?* I took off my pants and shirt, my underwear, I stood before her naked, surprised to find that even after such a night, even on the precipice of something so life-changing, I still felt a twinge of shame. I went to the door, closing it slowly, and then turned off the light.

———

I'd never seen Milosz don a tie before, not to mention a suit, if you could call it that. A family heirloom, certainly; I could imagine him shaking hands with Stalin. When had he put the outfit on? He hadn't been wearing it this morning. He was nervous, I could tell because he was making intense eye contact, but at least he shared it equally among everyone in the room, at least it would keep them awake. Seven potential investors, six men and one woman—the wife of a Chinese bottled water magnate—their stares as blank as their Atra Arca–branded notebooks, which had been virtually untouched since Peter arranged them on the conference room table. But how could they be expected to take notes? They'd been plopped into a graduate-level math lecture. Ostensibly he was talking about the market and risk reduction, but really he was expounding on the tenets of machine learning and data—what the term even meant, how there was no such thing as *data* but actually *information* and *noise*, one being the lifeblood of his sort of mathematics and the other a blight, a crop-killing fungus, dangerous not just for its poison but for its invisibility. He didn't put it this way though, didn't care to make things entertaining; instead he opted for variables, Greek letters, formal logic. I myself majored in math and could hardly grasp the symbols he was slashing on the chalkboard. But if Milosz thought he was making sense, the illusion was maintained by everyone present. At Webber I learned that investors can be of any temperament, inclination, or political bent, but they all share one belief: that money is equivalent with intelligence. No matter if their wealth had been created by their father's mother's father—just one-eighth of their genetic pool—and no matter if they had no idea what, actually, we were doing with their investment, they all thought they had an intrinsic understanding of finance, that they could sniff a dollar and pinpoint its provenance, its undertones. So this was flattering to them—this pale, sweaty, poorly dressed Slav who might have been a world chess champion in his past life; this chalkboard full of theorems; this air of erudition. It was why I let him give it a go—yes, he'd asked to do this, explain his work, he loved nothing more than to explain—and also so that my presentation, in contrast, would seem practically erotic. When he moved on to computational linguistics I knew we were almost home. He discussed hidden Markov models—systems we can use to predict the next word in a given text, systems that, in theory, could be used to predict tomorrow's stock prices given today's and all of those preceding—and then made a brief detour into Brownian motion, a subject he thought was overrated; he tried to convey as much, but his emotive range was too limited and anyway the room was half asleep. I thanked Milosz and we all clapped. He couldn't help but blush; he was beaming with pride. When Peter came in with espressos he even allowed himself a congratulatory cup, for him not an everyday treat.

My very appearance at the board reinvigorated the room, I'd timed the coffee exactly to enhance this effect. I needed one myself, by this point I regretted the ZzzQuil, regretted not sticking to my system. I never took a sleep aid two nights in a row, and I made a rule of cycling through them: melatonin (though it always woke me up early), antihistamines, Ambien, CBD oil (hardly did anything), valerian root (ditto), half a Xanax (the gold standard), and NyQuil (the next best thing). This way I wouldn't have the same drug more than once a fortnight, and could stave off tolerance and withdrawal. But I'd had NyQuil just three nights ago, and last night's dose had not only lost some of its magic, it put me on edge, too.

Predicting prices isn't just difficult, I said, scanning the room. *It's impossible. Some firms will tell you that with enough research, with enough understanding of fundamentals, they can predict some winners—or, at the very least, hedge you some risk when they're* wrong. *In my past life I sold such a firm to investors such as yourselves, the kind that was sure to beat the market—and not much else. We hung our hats on covering our management fees and a little more, and then our day was done. I believed I'd spend my life at that firm. That's the truth.*

But then one day at lunch I met a brilliant man in the cafeteria. I understood maybe a tenth of what he was saying but couldn't stop thinking about the small bit I retained. And so the next day we met again. And then the next. And then Milosz and I started to talk at night, too, and texted each other ideas when we couldn't sleep. My wife got worried. Small bit of laughter. *So I showed her his photo; problem solved.* A bit more. *Now we listen to his lectures together when we need to get some sleep.* Bingo.

For such a rational man, Milosz absolutely abhors *rationality, at least when it comes to picking stocks. It's true. Nothing makes him more suspicious than investment strategies based on concrete reasoning. People buy and sell stock for the same reasons they pick their spouse, their profession, the names of their children: circumstance, superstition, fallacies, and whimsy. How can the value of any of the world's largest, most-traded companies change by ten percent, twenty percent in the course of a month without an earnings report or anything else of note? Yes, Milosz abhors people who can tell you why they're buying this stock or shorting that. But we're sure as hell thankful for them. Because every time some* bowtwy *puts his life savings into—*Milosz flagged my attention, right on cue, a better actor than I ever would have guessed. *Sorry. We have a term here:* bowtwy, b-o-w-t-w-y, *short for "bored office workers and the too-wealthy youth." It's a stand-in for all those retail traders scouring Reddit for tips, checking Robinhood thirty times a day. This is our modern-day patsy. Fifty years ago you'd find them in a roadside diner, tell them some sob story about your foreclosed house,* *your sick sister. Now you can write an algorithm—well, not anyone can, hardly anyone actually, but at least one person in this room can—and you can pour into this algorithm ten million gallons of data, and figure out what these patsies, these bowtwys are going to do minutes before they know it themselves.*

By now you're probably wondering: How exactly does it work? Or, more to the point: Why are we asking for money when apparently we can print our own? The answer is data. Milosz has built a machine that's ready to fly, but it needs fuel, it needs data—a lot of it. It needs the most potent, most— Sick of the metaphors? Me too. What we do is track a select set of public companies, matching their price movements in real time against historical data. Our algorithm is trained to find similar patterns and alert us when it can say, "This has happened before." But nothing is ever so simple. Math may be elegant; reality isn't. We can't just match a given stock against one from the past, we need to find hundreds, sometimes thousands, which our algorithm will Frankenstein together to give us something eerily similar to our target. And this, of course, only becomes possible with an immense trove of data to draw from. On your way out, take a look into the room to your right. There you'll find the server space required for such a trove, 50 petabytes in total—enough to store every movie ever made, assuming each was shot in ultra-high definition. Our mission now is to fill those servers with market data—but, as with movies, not all data is good. In fact, Milosz prefers I stop using the word altogether. Information is what we're after, and to this end half of our technical team is dedicated to cleaning and sorting the data we acquire. At other firms, this work usually goes to the most junior researchers, but here it's our secret weapon. We categorize information in a way no other firm can—legally, I mean; it's patented. Milosz's proprietary system all but frees information from the bounds of rigid, right-angled models, allowing our algorithm to make inconceivable connections between drastically disparate sets of information. If it sounds like magic, well, welcome to Atra Arca.

I motioned to Peter, who began passing around copies of our prospectus, a thirty-page document with projections, risk profiles—everything they'd expect and much more, like a one-pager on time and the market, how to warp it, rethink cadence, understand that minutes pass differently throughout the day, that the wrinkles set by man's collective caprices could be ironed out. *If black holes can twist and bend time, it* started, *if God can, why can't a supercomputer?*

I had these made because I have to, because you've received something similar at other presentations you've attended, or will. But I don't want you to think of us as another hedge fund, with an expected return and the like. I run Atra Arca like a technology startup, one that has the vision and talent to build something that doesn't yet exist but soon will, once we have the right resources behind us. And when we do— Here was the moment. I inhaled, let myself hear my own words—*when we've constructed the world's largest repository of good, clean financial information, replete with every modern market movement known to man, every fundamental, every performance indicator and more*—I felt the tears, they never failed, a fact that didn't just make me happy, and confident, it was proof that what I was saying was true, that I was not some salesman but an inventor, someone who might actually change the world—*well, we will then, quite simply, see into the future.* I let it come, a single tear that made it halfway down my cheek before I wiped it away. *Perhaps we'll force the financial world into a reckoning. Perhaps there won't be a single fool left who thinks he knows which stocks to choose. But no matter, by then we will all have become impossibly, unimaginably wealthy.* I clasped my hands and smiled at Milosz, who was furtively looking at the phone tucked in his lap. *Thank you all for coming.* Applause, finally, or at least as much as seven remarkably privileged adults could muster. I had hit all my notes. I had made them believe in me, in us. I had even inspired some of them, that I could tell. And yet, and yet and yet and yet, after they stood up, and put on their coats, and pretended to leaf through the prospectus, after they shook Milosz's and my hands, I knew this batch would yield nothing. If they made eye contact it was fleeting, they departed with polite nods— *polite* anything was the death knell. The only one who even spoke to me was the French-Israeli man, and that was to ask for the bathroom. No, this crowd did not consider themselves tech investors, if they thought the firm's approach was intriguing they still just wanted a standard hedge fund, this was their money after all, something that, even if treated conservatively, could generate enough wealth to enable their kids and their kids' kids to continue living without a whiff of work. Why would they do anything but hedge risk?

I smiled as they walked out, I tried not to care. No, these weren't our top prospects; that was why we'd met them seven at a time. Even if I'd bagged them all, they wouldn't bring me half of what I was going to get with Colin. And once I did, once the ink was dry, I'd shore up the rest of the $180 million, they'd fall like dominoes, I'd only need to set a deadline, put some fire under them.

The last one filed out and it was just Milosz and me. By the way he was erasing the chalkboard, large strokes over territory that hadn't even been written on, I could tell he'd seen what I had. I knew what he'd say, or at least insinuate—that we should reconsider the pitch, especially my half of it—and to avoid that interaction I told him he'd done a great job and went straight to my office.

I sat at my desk and checked my phone, which showed a message from a potential investor and six missed calls from Franny. Before I risked clouding my head further I dialed Colin. He picked up immediately, an auspicious sign. *Monsieur Caine*, he said, even more promising.

Monsieur Eubanks, right. I'm calling because the mail's just arrived, and it seems your signed contract was lost along the way.

He forced a laugh. *You know I wouldn't trust your country's post offices with something like that.*

Well, I wouldn't trust anyone with anything these days, but still business must be done.

You're odd, Herschel. It's why I thought you'd like Ian. I trust he stopped by?

Indeed.

Sharp as hell, isn't he?

So sharp, I said, mindfully unballing my fist.

So he's doing a bit of due diligence on my side, I hope you don't mind. He's got some money of his own, you know. I believe he could put up a million or so. This was half of our minimum, but I'd take it; I'd take anything from someone who was doing *a bit of due diligence* for Colin, or even his laundry.

Well, perfect.

We'll all do great things together, I don't doubt it. But Herschel, I hate to be rude. If this is just a courtesy call I'm running a bit short on time.

Oh, I said. *Well, I've just gotten out of a terrific meeting, delighted to say we now have some Saudi interest, some interest from Beijing, and right here in New York if you'd believe it, and I just thought—* A courtesy call it is. *Well, have fun with Ian and I'll let you know when the contract's on the way. Hate to imagine you panting at the mailman.*

He hates it too, I said. *Talk soon, Colin.*

Click.

I wiped my hand over my mouth down to my chin. I eyed the dregs of my coffee. I picked up my phone and walked out to the espresso machine in the kitchen, where I called Franny. She didn't pick up, but just as I slid my phone back in my pocket it rang.

She started to speak, though I couldn't make her out over the espresso machine. When it finished I told her I hadn't heard a thing. She was annoyed at me, she *ugh*'ed into the phone. *Birdie's at Brooklyn Methodist.*

A church?

Herschel, the hospital.

In Brooklyn?

Please come. Something terrible has happened. She's— She took a moment to reset, she hated being emotional. *She's in a coma, the doctor said it's induced, or maybe it's not induced, I can't—* Again. *We're in the ICU. Room 2019. Will, her husband—or, you know, her soon-to-be ex—he's flying out now. I just can't leave her here alone.*

Of course, I said. *But tell me what's wrong.*

She had a terrible fall last night. The Uber driver found her on the sidewalk, brought her straight here. God, I wish he'd made the trip to Manhattan, I can already tell the staff is . . . Sorry, they're around. She's been here all night. They tracked down Will this morning, he got in touch an hour ago.

She fell? How do they know she wasn't attacked?

They know. I mean, they can tell by the abrasion—the, you know, appearance of her head.

I see, I said. *Well, she was quite tired. And it had rained, hadn't it?*

What?

I'm just— Right, I said, eyeing the finished espresso. *I'll come now.*

———

In retrospect it's hard to believe that my first sight of her brought peace of mind, but it did. She looked serene, even with the bruising: deep shades of green, gray, and purple that covered half of her face. If it didn't quite seem like she was resting then she at least appeared to be in some sort of very deep, rest-like state, a restorative mode, one that was required by severe circumstances but also had an end: a return to her regular self. No, it wasn't until the doctor—a handsome South Asian man with very parted hair—lifted her eyelids to reveal vacant and slightly misaligned pupils that I had to stop deluding myself. It was then that I felt my presence in the room, the weight of my skin and all it contained and the clothes that kept it hidden and carried my phone and wallet, all of it kept aloft by just two legs, each with just one joint—a system that couldn't possibly be sustained for a lifetime let alone a minute more.

I took a seat; Franny followed. This doctor was not the one Franny had already met, though he did have mostly the same questions. He established our relationship to Birdie. He confirmed her age, nationality. He asked, fruitlessly, about her medical history.

Didn't you talk to her husband? I asked.

Unfortunately, I didn't personally, he said, making me aware of my tone. He scrawled something on his pad and looked at Franny, who would receive most of his attention now. *Did she seem off last night? Was she acting, you know, normal?* Franny looked at me. I was too absorbed in Birdie—the doctor hadn't bothered to reclose her eyelids—to help her answer the question. *She was a bit talkative,* she said. *I think there's a lot going on in her life. She's getting a divorce.*

Do you think she may have been under the influence of anything? he asked.

Drugs? No, Franny said.

Well, I said, *she'd been drinking.*

She had three drinks, Franny said. *For her that's nothing.*

I reached for Franny's hand. She turned and we made eye contact. Why hadn't we talked about the ZzzQuil on the phone? Was it something we absolutely had to mention, medically? I waited for a sign, anything, but she hardly moved. At first I thought she was too overwhelmed to remember. But she didn't seem overwhelmed; she'd been here with Birdie for several hours. Then I thought she was acting—albeit giving a performance I didn't know she had in her. And then, finally, I entertained the only option left: that I should reexamine my memory of the very end of the night, or rather what preceded the very end, when we had, for the first time together, unprotected sex. *The night's saving elixir,* I'd said, before drinking some myself. I'd even done an impression of Birdie after she took a sip: *My God, it tastes like divorce.* I hadn't been too drunk to remember all this with certainty. But had I misjudged Franny's comprehension of it, even her attention? Now I remembered the scene differently. This time she wasn't quite present—lost in a rare level of arousal, or maybe just blind-sided by my sudden readiness for children. A stark contrast to the face I saw now, which was giving me its undivided attention. Her eyes reminded me of the first time I saw them, I still remembered my exact thought: that she couldn't possibly fulfill their promise, no person could be that present, acute, perceptive.

I looked down at the floor and then back at Franny. No, she had no idea what I'd done.

The doctor gave up on getting anything more out of us and set down his pen. *Because you're not kin, I'm really not supposed to share a prognosis with you. But based on an MRI and an EEG we performed this morning, I would be very surprised if she emerged.*

Emerged? I asked.

Emerged into a vegetative state. It's possible she may not wake up.

That's terrible, Franny said. *Awful.* Her tone was off; she had no tone. But I understood, I felt the same numbness.

The doctor said something I didn't hear, and then, taking one last look at Birdie, left us. I asked Franny what he'd said but she hadn't paid attention either.

We sat in silence watching her. Slowly her body seemed to absorb his prognosis, the rise and fall of her chest given new meaning. This was the time to do it. We now had enough privacy to talk things through, to strategize if need be. But the words wouldn't come; when I looked at Franny I became too focused on her face, I was trying and failing to imagine her disbelief, her disappointment. I'd never witnessed such an expression on her, not at that magnitude. I had to extrapolate from what I knew; quickly the image became monstrous, unlifelike, and once it had lodged itself in my head it stayed there, it choked the words as they tried to come out a second time, a third. Her face seemed to be getting bigger, but it was just that the rest of the world had narrowed—a cliché, fine, but I had tunnel vision: when I looked down I saw my pink hands, my thumb, my pants, and the floor, that was it, there were curtains of darkness on either side, and when I looked up to the bright ceiling light the curtains only closed more.

Herschel, she said. I turned toward her, my vision abruptly normal again. *I can't do it. I can't be here when Will arrives. She's already told me so much about him, and I just can't be here for that.* I nodded even though it didn't quite make sense. *The doctor said that there's nothing to do, that these things can take time. Would it be horrible if we left?*

I agreed, I nodded again. I was staring, I realized, at Birdie, her eyes. Did the doctor know he'd left them open? Did it not matter? I thought of her seeing into the room, of her hearing us. I was suddenly aware of my own body again, its mass; this was the same sensation I'd felt the few times I'd smoked marijuana. Back then it had seemed up to me whether I found this awareness disturbing, but this time it didn't feel like a choice. I was disturbed, not just by the intense recognition of my own body, but also by the fact that it somehow displaced all other feeling, it was as if my sensitivity to the world had turned inward. I was, if anything, angry; I didn't *feel* angry but I thought angry thoughts, I resented myself, for being so unemotional, for failing to react physically. Why wasn't I vomiting at such a dreadful sight, and one I myself was responsible for? *Dreadful*, I thought again, but the word was hollow, pronouncing it in my head was like a puff of voiceless air.

You nodded, she said, *but you mean it* wouldn't *be horrible, right?*

I looked at her. *Yes, that's what I meant.*

We spent another minute or so in solemn silence. *Solemn:* another meaningless word. Franny walked up to the bed and squeezed Birdie's hand, she studied the vitals monitor, its beeps only now entering my head. It seemed false, cruel even, for her blood pressure, her heart rate, to be so normal. Finally I heard the last thing the doctor had said. Something about her vitals, and then, *It'll be up to her husband to decide what to do.*

We gathered our things and called an Uber. On the way out Franny used her phone to photograph the vitals monitor, the chart behind Birdie's bed, even Birdie's face. She also took a video, slowly rotating to record a panorama of the room while I stood behind her, swiveling too so I wouldn't be in it.

Outside we waited for the car, her head buried in my shoulder, the light drizzle and distant thunder helping to drown out her sobs. I sensed that she hadn't cried the whole time she was in the room with Birdie by herself; only when she was with someone else, with me, was she overcome. This made me think of when her dad died a couple of years ago. I found her in our old guest bathroom, sitting on the edge of the shower. It was her posture, her expression—I sensed she was hiding from me. She didn't even want to make eye contact, but when she did a great wave of relief passed through her. It seemed like a revelation to her, this relief, as if she was just realizing that someone else could help bear the weight of her pain. It made me wonder about her past relationships— she'd broken off an engagement a few years before we met— and how, if they lacked openness, we could ensure that our relationship didn't. Well, ours didn't, at least from then on; I'd never dreamt of being so vulnerable with another person. Revisiting that memory now, I suddenly questioned why she'd sat where she had, facing the door—instead of on the table beside the toilet, or on the toilet itself. Had she, in some way, wanted me to find her? I visualized the room, putting myself in her shoes, and had another thought: she'd only wanted to avoid the mirror over the sink.

At home we kept the lights off, kept the darkness of the overcast sky. In silence we prepared the leftovers from last night—the escarole, ravioli, and pork—and ate them in front of the family room television. We pulled up the movie at the top of our list, *The Banishment*, or *Izgnanie* in its native Russian. Изгнание. Each of these words seemed more truthful than the last, perhaps because they made less and less sense. The film was slow, beautiful, and depressing. I became bored midway through, bored enough to forget to read a few of the subtitles. I didn't want to ask Franny to rewind, I didn't want to speak at all, and so with the feeling of having missed something small but vital, I stopped paying attention altogether.

By the one-hour mark my restlessness had become impatience, and then a feeling of laziness, an accusation: Why wasn't I using this time better? I allowed the guilt space, I often do; it gives me the motivation I need. I looked to Franny, who was absorbed in the film. I squeezed her hand twice, our way of excusing ourselves, and went up the three flights of stairs to my office, grabbing a brownie and a glass of milk on the way. When I turned on the light it felt like a new day, like I was this small world's God. I thought again of that afternoon's failure of a pitch, of Milosz's sharp shoulder blades as he erased the chalkboard. Then I recalled my brief chat with Colin, which in retrospect seemed more positive than it had initially. After all, there'd been busting of chops. There was even mild flirtation, at least the kind you can achieve with such a straight-presenting man. I sat at my desk. I wrote a nice, unadorned email to Ian, asking him to lunch at the most expensive, most pompous restaurant in the vicinity of the office. I reread it and decided on a closing flourish: *I hope an uptown creature like yourself will deign to dine below Houston. We bohemians must eat too.*

Again I researched him online, using a finer-toothed comb than when his name originally crossed my inbox. I confirmed my hunch that he was unmarried and without kids. He apparently played squash regularly and had, for less than a year, belonged to the board of the Neue Galerie, a museum of twentieth-century German and Austrian art. I was surprised to find that he owned no property, at least not in this country. Given his way of behaving, and the sort of people he associated with, I'd had him pegged for a Jackson Hole guy, maybe Palm Beach. But it appeared he only rented, and just in Manhattan. I shot off an email to our due diligence lawyer, Jonathan Resnick, for his take.

As soon as I hit send I got tired. I hadn't even had my brownie. I brushed my teeth, slid into bed, and fell asleep faster than I knew myself capable of. It felt like I had one long dream, as if such a simple scene could occupy me for eight hours: I was at the beach with Franny and our daughter, who took after me. A seagull began circling us, getting closer and closer until it decided to attack. It seemed to know exactly how to hurt us, how the human body worked, how its own could be made into a weapon. Another seagull came to assault us, and then another, and then crabs appeared at our feet, biting. Soon, other non-beach animals joined in: squirrels, pigs, cats. It wasn't long before, from a distance, you couldn't even see the humans inside the flurry. Despite the animals' intelligence and brutality they never incapacitated us, we were always fresh, full bodies for them to dismantle. And despite all the horror, the feeling that persisted, that lasted even after I woke up, was amazement at my ignorance—that all my life I had never bothered to think about how easy it would be for animals to use themselves against us if they only knew how.

———

Franny was sleeping in. This she communicated by pulling the sheet over her head when I turned on the lights. She only slept in when she really needed it; to avoid waking her I forwent my morning espresso, the news on the television. The house was so silent and dark it seemed heavy; I was aware of the building's mass. If this made me feel cocooned, somehow protected from the outside world, it also made the air inside feel slightly pressurized, as though we had our own, stifled climate. I read the *Financial Times*, without caffeine it took me longer to make my way through it, but the words sank in more. Well, no; they sank in less, they were harder to read, they showed themselves as words. *Talks on the UK's future relationship with the EU boiled over when Britain lashed out at an indication from* . . . Each time I came across one of these physical metaphors—*boiled over, lashed out*—I took it at its primary meaning, I imagined a pot overflowing, one man whipping another. For financial writers to use such language seemed either silly or violent, the two perspectives irreconcilable, the choice of which to take up to me, but as I kept on reading I began to inhabit the latter. In just a few paragraphs I came across *largely fruitless* (a barren vineyard), *talks bogged down* (gods sending storms upon the earth), *points that have dogged the negotiations for months* (ruthless, ravenous hounds), *dealing a blow* (one final, fatal strike)—as if there were, underneath this world of finance and politics, a Greek tragedy, or a Biblical parable, an unrelenting battle between good and evil with humanity stuck in the middle.

I took a slow shower. I put on one of my best suits. I called a livery car, gathered my things, and grabbed an orange from the bowl, sending a troop of flies scattering. I nearly fell down the stairs to the family room when I caught sight of Franny sitting on the couch, her face lit by her laptop.

I thought you were asleep, I said. She didn't respond, or even look up. She had on her signature frown, the near grimace that attended her most serious ruminations. *Getting an early start on work?*

Yeah, she said. *No, I mean no.* She shook herself out of it and looked up at me. *I'm researching Birdie's condition. Traumatic brain injuries. Uses of hypothermia, and* . . . She trailed off. I walked over and sat beside her. On the screen was a medical article: "Cooling the Injured Brain: How Does Moderate Hypothermia Influence the Pathophysiology of Traumatic Brain Injury." Beside her computer was a notepad with a list of names and numbers. Beside that was her phone, the image of Birdie's vitals monitor zoomed in.

Her phone would give us timing, she said, looking at me. *I mean, how long the ride took. Brain injuries are a matter of seconds. If they'd done hypothermia right when she arrived, she might already be better.*

Right, I said. *But now, given—*

I really wish the Uber had taken her somewhere else. Really I wish I'd escorted her out or had her stay over. We haven't used that Murphy bed once.

No, I said, rubbing her back. *We couldn't have known.*

She nodded, she admitted as much, but if she couldn't rectify this fact, she still needed to compensate for it. She was hoarding knowledge, practically, as if some blithe lack of it had allowed such a fluke disaster to occur.

Have some coffee, I said, squeezing her hand goodbye.

Outside I waited for the car and peeled the orange, pushing down on the crown until it gave way, my thumb burrowing between the thick skin and the dry, white tufts protecting the fruit. *I'll eat that too*, I thought, *the pith*—such a submissive word. I wondered what it would be like to eat an orange without that word or any other, without *rind* or *pulp* or *juice*, without even the name, its own color, and without any way to pronounce it good or satisfying. Would that not be transcendent? To experience without the urge to simplify, catalog, condense the present into some sort of future— A bird cawed and I looked up. It had no colors or patterns of note but I knew it wasn't a common pigeon. I thought of my dream; in contrast to the attacking gulls this bird appeared remarkably indifferent, of its own world. It settled on a branch of the oak tree in front of our place. Its head twitched a few times and then it was still. It looked young. I'd never before considered the age of birds, that they aged at all, but this one seemed to me an adolescent, newly capable but still somewhat unaware, his face—how did I know it was male?—sharply defined: the fleeting, easy beauty of youth.

The car came and I quickly peeled the rest of the fruit and put the skin in the compost bin. I'd had this driver before. *Cedric, how are you?* He nodded exuberantly but didn't speak. As I buckled my seatbelt I yawned, a yawn that seemed to never end, that nearly hurt my jaw. I rolled down my window and saw, across the street, tied to the railing of a stoop, a beagle. Her fur was white with big black and brown splotches that looked painted on. The dog belonged to the man who lived on the top floor of that building, the one across from ours, a man I didn't like not just because he seemed pretentious and aloof—I'd tried and failed to make conversation twice in our first week here, all I'd gleaned was that he was a book editor and married—but because I suspected he didn't pick up his dog's shit. I had stepped in some during my first stroll around the new neighborhood, it was the kind of shit a medium-sized dog might leave.

The dog had been panting. I wasn't really aware of this until she turned her head to look at me and stopped, she retracted her tongue into her mouth and closed it. Her brow knitted and then settled down again. I sensed sympathy. How? *Wait,* I said to Cedric; he'd put the car in drive. *I might have left something.* I pretended to search my wallet and continued looking at the dog. How did I sense sympathy? How does anyone? It was the ratios of her face, the tension of its muscles, her eyes. I squinted; they were chestnut brown. I tried to swallow but didn't have enough saliva. I sensed Cedric's attention, I'd stopped pretending with my wallet, I heard his head swivel to face the dog. No, it wasn't sympathy I saw, it was simpler than that, but deeper too. It was recognition. She recognized my guilt. Yes, guilt: that word—unlike *dreadful,* unlike *solemn*—wrapped fully around its meaning. It was such a pure, true thing, *guilt,* it was something even a dog could understand. And she did. She not only understood it, she took it from me, we shared it, between us there was this thing, this thing that was *guilt* but it was so much more. Guilt can be many things, but this thing—it was beyond language, it had to be, if even a dog could understand it. Yes, of course—that was why I'd felt nothing in the hospital, why I struggled to feel anything even now: I was trying to put something into words that couldn't be. I was trying to construct a coherent narrative about what happened and why, but there wasn't one. I wanted to laugh, I wanted the dog to see me laughing, she should know how she'd made me feel. I started to smile, I—

Are you okay, Mr. Caine?

My throat was too dry to speak. I coughed out empty words, the harsh air scraping my trachea, and then, inhaling again, filled the car with a screech.

Cedric winced, he turned to face me and repeated his question with more urgency.

I looked his way but stopped short of eye contact. *I'm okay*, I said. *And we can go, I found what I need.*

———

The activists, again. At eight in the morning. This time they only glared at me. They chanted more vigorously than their afternoon counterparts, and they were better dressed, too; maybe they had jobs.

I walked onto the trading floor, saluted Peter, and was stopped in my tracks by the sight of Simo at his desk. Simo was a Serbian researcher who I played at disliking but really was fond of, we all were; he had way too much charm for someone with his kind of brilliance. His focus was computational linguistics, in his past life he had published a well-referenced article on predictive modeling for infant vocalization. (His nickname—which he loved so much he asked for it on his business card—was G4, as in *goo goo ga ga*.) In his final interview with us, Simo had said he had one require-ment, which was that he never wanted to be in the office be-fore eleven a.m. We allowed it and, up until now, had never seen him a minute earlier.

I turned to Peter. *He was there when I got in*, he said.

I asked him to check the logs and he did, rotating his lap-top so I could see. Simo hadn't left since yesterday, he'd been here all night. I strode over to his desk, but before I could pro-nounce the second syllable of his name his hand shot in the air.

No no, he said. *No.*

I walked up behind him and looked at his screen, as if I could tell what he was doing. Deafening house music wafted up from his earbuds. How could he even hear me?

I made myself an espresso and went to my office, where I found a sticky note on my door:

DO NOT DISTURB SIMO.
— SIMO

I pulled it off, dropped it in my wastebasket, and sat at my desk. I was eager to get the day going. That odd moment in the car had stayed with me, nagged at me. In retrospect it was ridiculous, the whole thing was, my connection to the dog, the belief that what had happened with Birdie couldn't be put into words. On the drive in I had done exactly that, I'd re-peated to myself the sequence of events, over and over. We had a dinner for friends we were trying to impress. We invited Birdie with the hope of impressing them further. Birdie was so obnoxious I had the idea to accelerate her jet lag by mak-ing her a cocktail with ZzzQuil. It worked, she left, and on the way home she apparently fell, causing a traumatic brain injury. Though it was impossible to know for certain, it was likely that the ZzzQuil had contributed to her fall. I was guilty of a terrible mistake of judgment, but only in hindsight. I could just as well have acquiesced to her request for more and more booze, and if the same thing had happened, what then? She was in critical care now, what was done was done, I wished it had never happened and could only pray that she made a speedy recovery. I should have told Franny but I didn't, and if I told her now it would only cause her serious distress; it would be a secret she'd also bear the weight of keeping. Yes, she would come to my same realization, that it would only do more damage to force onto Will or Birdie's family or anyone else the painful knowledge that it all could have been avoided. My own distress was affording them ignorant bliss; all the pain they were spared was passed on to me. And it *was* pain, it *was* distress. Every minute in the car had felt like an hour, all I wanted was to be at work, because then all this extraneous thought would be washed away. And here I was. Except when I pressed my finger onto the keyboard scanner, instead of opening my desktop, the screen showed five red asterisks below my name. I tried again, and then again after wiping my finger clean. I felt my fingertip with my thumb, as if there'd be a discernible difference, as if it were my skin that was the problem and not some system error.

I called Milosz, who picked up immediately. I explained the issue and he said he'd fix it when he got into the office, he was on his way. I asked if there was an extra laptop I could borrow, though I already knew the answer: no, he'd built our entire infrastructure—from our intranet to our email servers to our data servers to our fucking catering system—expressly so that no one could just *borrow an extra laptop*. We could each access our work only from our office computer, with Milosz's and my phones and home computers being the exceptions.

But I think I know what's wrong, he said. This was one of his favorite lines, he wouldn't care much if the world was in flames as long as he knew why. *Yes, I know now. Simo needed more space on the server so I—*

Simo was here all last night.

I know.

Why is that?

I heard background noise, he was in Grand Central. Why did someone who had made more than a million dollars a year for five straight still take Metro-North? *Listen, Hersh.* He never called me that, even though I begged him to. *Simo found something very interesting yesterday. Something that might be, you know, big.*

What's big?

Our phones aren't as encrypted as they should be, as we've discussed. And anyway I want to double-check his work myself before we start larger conversations. Larger conversations, I loved it. Finally he was realizing that he had some agency, that he too could be an entrepreneur. Maybe he'd even buy himself a tailored suit.

Absolutely, I said. *Double-check his work, and when you need me I'm here.*

He hung up without a word, forgoing the usual *Goodbye, Herschel.* This made me even more optimistic, it gave me a great feeling, one strong enough to focus my attention on and finally cast out all the other loose thoughts.

—

And yet. With access to the internet but none of my email or work accounts, I couldn't help but spend much of the morning researching injury liability. It was more curiosity than worry, at this point I had a clear head about it, I just wanted to know what the law said, I often found it surprising, it was like math or computer programming if they weren't undergirded by objective truths or relations but instead by realpolitik compromises between very human preferences. In this case, it seemed liability presupposed negligence, which in turn required proof of all of four distinct elements: duty of care, breach of duty, causation, and damages. Regarding my negligence in what happened to Birdie, these elements were, in my estimation: probably not, probably not, probably, definitely. The jurisdiction and the judge's personality seemed to matter—more proof that law was hardly even a social science. I tried researching the legality of the specific act, but drink spiking was associated with far darker territory; by then I was at the restaurant and didn't need that on my mind.

I didn't want to be impolite and order a drink before Ian arrived, but if I'd known he was going to be twenty-five minutes late I would have had one to relax, tardiness being one of the only traits I cannot abide. Instead I had to play whack-a-mole with the waitstaff: *No, water is fine; Yes, I'm fine for now; Just water, thanks.* It was a new waiter each time, each quite distinct from the last but all in the same disconcerting dress—high-waisted, oversized navy blue pants, the material more cottony than cotton, the texture like overlapping blurs—which matched the art, mostly de Kooning knockoffs and the like, though right in the center there was an authentic flake of art history, an amorphous, grotesque portrait by Frank Auerbach, *Head of J.Y.M.*, apparently on loan from a museum in Madrid. It was the restaurant's focal point, the main attraction of its website, too; I'd read about it when I looked up the menu. The painting was given yards of space on every side, and a dedicated trio of light fixtures; I wondered if the *museo*'s curators would approve of such direct illumination. I sat facing it but, just a minute before he arrived, moved to the opposite seat.

He walked in, gave his name to the maître d' and was escorted to our table. As he made his way over I was taken aback. Here was a new man, downcast, his pallor put in stark relief by the warm, golden lighting. I was ready to ask him if everything was all right, if he preferred to reschedule, but as soon as he saw me his face lit up, and he reverted back to the person I'd met two days ago.

We shook hands, exchanged *Good to see yous.* As we sat down I waited for an apology for his late arrival, even a perfunctory one. Instead I got *Caine's not a Jewish name, is it?* I laughed, I didn't know what else to do. I wanted to ask how he knew I was Jewish, but couldn't. Was that the point? I tried to read him but he seemed absorbed in the décor. I followed his gaze to the painting behind me.

Auerbach, I said, *at least from the looks of it.*

Mm, he said, bringing his eyes down to me; they were alert, expectant. What? Still that first question?

You're right, of course, Caine *was* Cohen. *It was changed during the war, for the obvious reasons.* Why had I said it like that? As if it were some small inconvenience.

Yes, he said. *The war erased so much. Up my mother's side of the family you'd find prominent landowners in Austria, but it all went away during the* Anschluss.

On my own mom's side you'd find most of two generations gassed or starved. *Terrible*, I said, and glanced at the menu. *Will you be indulging this afternoon?*

If you will.

I called after the waiter and ordered two glasses of Gewürztraminer. I'd normally offset the choice with a comment about my sweet tooth, but I suddenly didn't care to.

He took some time to scan the menu. *It all looks great,* he said. *But the cacio e pepe has me at truffle.* Did I sense pride? For favoring something even pigs enjoy? He closed the menu and set it down. We made small talk about the neighborhood until the waiter came with the wine, at which point we put in our order: the cacio e pepe, and a lamb shank for me.

So, he said, picking up his wine glass. *To Colin, our public intellectual nonpareil.* In recent years Colin had begun moving into the Davos phase of his career, booking sundry speaking appearances, expounding on public policy, and democracy, and any other subject he was deemed to be expert in purely due to his net worth. We clinked glasses. *No, the man can get ahead of himself, but he's got more bona fides than he gets credit for. It's not the attention he's after, really, he's just an obsessive at heart. Last month, for example, he dedicated himself entirely to affect theory. He read all the books on it, could talk for days. Did, actually.*

And this month?

Charisma, he said, not missing a beat. He took a sip and I followed. *It's a topic we're researching together. Amazing how we take something like that for granted. It's in every story, at the core of every great man who's ever changed history, and still we don't know much about it. And I mean the real kind of charisma, by the way, not that salesman-y sort.*

I nodded, I looked into my glass. *A bit sweet, no?*

Maybe, he said. *But this is a sweet occasion, after all. Yeah, let's get down to it.* He set both palms on the table. *He's sick of the usual, the Webber crowd and all that. We both are. Every year they seem more and more behind the times, and now, finally, he's warming up to making a move—something I've been hinting at for years, by the way. But it's good timing. I think it was just at the end of your and Milosz's garden leave that he decided we should look around.*

Mine, or Milosz's? He must have known they were different, Webber had done a great job of making that public, that I was precluded from working anywhere else (while still receiving my salary) for two years to Milosz's three, the implication being that Milosz would be a greater asset to the competition, the purpose being to make me livid, which it had.

Behind the times, I said. That's putting it mildly. I wouldn't be surprised if they were felled not by obsolete strategy—and their strategies are, definitely, obsolete; I'd sooner put my savings in some fucking robo-advisor—but rather a series of crippling lawsuits.

You think they've played on the inside?

Oh, I'm sure of it. Why else should their biggest coups come from pharma? They just happen to put their chips on all the right drugs pre-approval, hmm. But no, I'm talking about more prosaic legalities. The place is brimming with sexism, homophobia, casual racism, it's basically a time machine to 1985. I ran my thumb down the wine glass, taking off a streak of condensation. *I remember a managing director musing about how to incentivize women to stay home and have children. It wasn't a joke. He and his deputy crunched some numbers, landed on a salary of sixty-five a year. This was in the presence of our whole group, including two women. It's not just sexist, it's demoralizing.*

He shook his head in disbelief but couldn't hide a small trace of amusement. I felt challenged to pull out even more abhorrent examples. I told stories involving sexism and racism as well as terrible investment strategies, even investor deception. There was no question he was more interested in these latter categories, so I leaned in that direction. As the minutes flew by I found I was describing that byzantine, crumbling empire in perhaps too much detail, but I didn't care, my NDA with them didn't cover this sort of nonsense, and even if it did, people shared these things all the time.

It wasn't until the food came that we broached the topic of Atra Arca; in fact his questions began right as the plates hit the table. I was surprised, for someone supposedly *sharp as hell* he mostly asked for info he could have found online: the size of our first fund (besides, hadn't I told Colin?); whether we were using a master-feeder structure (ditto); whether we were an LP, an LLC, or a corporation; plans for satellite offices. I could have answered each of these in just a few words, but I padded my responses, spoke about what the leading quantitative hedge funds were doing, showed that I knew the field, that I'd even acquired privileged information. At some point he looked down at my plate and, seeing I hadn't taken my first bite, put down his fork and spoon. I usually lost my appetite in the thick of work. To appease him I started, I set the tines of my fork on the meat and stuck in my knife, down to the plate. The metal sliding against the ceramic sounded like nails on a chalkboard, I tried to be more careful as I began cutting, but each time a serration severed a hank of protein I felt a disturbing vibration in my hand. It reminded me of when I'd learned the saxophone as a child, the day they had us start to play with our teeth against the mouthpiece. No one else seemed to have a problem, but every time I blew into the instrument the hard rubber would vibrate against my teeth, bringing goosebumps out of my skin. It was an odd sensation, not only for being uncomfortable to me alone, but self-inflicted, too; every second of music was a second of pain. I'd refused to do it, learning to play without using my teeth.

Is there a problem with it?

I looked at the dish. It was magnificently arranged, not clever but well done, the braise a deep, smoky red, the bone dry and sliced impeccably flat, in the middle you could see the marrow, undisturbed. How did they manage to cut it so evenly? A saw, or— I was staring at it, I hadn't answered.

No, I said. I squeezed the utensils harder but that was as much as my hands would do, I couldn't stand to have that feeling again. I lifted the fork off of the lamb and, keeping the knife still, gathered a bite of the side dish, charred eggplant and onion. I waited for the strange sensation to return. In its absence something like pleasure shot through my arms and shoulders, like when I'd first sipped the wine. I placed the forkful in my mouth, it was cooked perfectly, some cardamom, something sweet. Ian was looking at me. My skin had gotten clammy, and my own awareness of it didn't help. Could he sense what was going on? What *was* going on? What was this, this all-consuming uncertainty, I hadn't felt anything like it in years, decades, I was like a child who hadn't done his homework. I needed the moment to pass, I looked down at the meat, the braise had already dripped into the cut. I put the fork back on top of it and, using the knife, widened the incision just enough to peek inside. I set my utensils down. *Well, maybe it's a bit undercooked. Not to be picky, but you know, even with this sort of farm-raised blah blah blah you find terrible things. I'm sure they won't mind me sending it back, the last thing they want is a record of food poisoning.* I raised my hand for the waiter.

Well, maybe it was done on purpose, he said, flashing a smirk. *Some plot to stop the rich bastards that run this city. I say eat it anyway. You'll get good money, intentional torts are big business.* Intentional torts. *Oh, really.*

One semester at Harvard Law. Torts is as far as I made it.

Hello again. The waiter. He gave us a small bow. *May I help with anything?*

I think this is a bit underdone, I said. *But you know, I really love this eggplant, I think I'll just switch to the eggplant tagliatelle.*

Excellent choice, he said, and removed the plate from the table.

Ian began speaking again. I couldn't focus, I only knew he had circled back to business by the way he laid his palm on the table, his other fist casually supporting his jaw. It took the word *Milosz* to make me present again. His head was bobbing to either side. *Two days. Three at most.* He was—what? Suggesting he meet directly with Milosz? Why would he need to do that when he had the CEO right in front of him?

I'm happy to assist in any way I can, I said. *I'm an open book, more to you and Colin than any other—*

But you're not intimate with the algorithm, or the data for that matter. Herschel, you're not a numbers guy.

But neither are you, no?

I'm not a PhD, correct. And anyway, this is just to cover our asses. Legally, I mean. What you're doing, it's uncharted territory, you said it yourself.

But why the need to see—

Herschel, listen. He stared at his plate for a protracted moment, returning to the face he had when he first came into the restaurant. *This isn't a negotiation. This ask, it's not a nice-to-have. We're not investing $220 million in a brand-new quantitative* *fund without knowing that we can access, if need be, every line of code.*

Well, you can't, I said. *We just don't do business that way. And please quote that to Colin.* I needed to digest a lot of this but I didn't need another second for that. Two hundred twenty million dollars was a lot, it was foundational, but we stood to make billions, tens of billions. I'd heard this story before: I compromise, I give in, and then down the road I find that some other firm Colin and this stooge invested in just happened to make the same inroads. I inhaled, I held the air. He leaned back and folded his arms, his hands clutching his biceps.

That's quite a disappointment, he said. The blood had returned to his face, he was his sly self again, the person he was always pretending to be. *But we can still enjoy this meal as friends.*

Your pasta, sir. A new waitress, this one short and pale with cropped blond hair.

She laid the dish in front of me, the steam rising into my face. I remembered how I'd begun to sweat earlier, and was afraid, for a moment, of pushing my fork into the food. But when I did I felt only the familiar sensation of metal against pasta, that reminder to assume a light touch; without it you'd hardly feel the food at all.

⁓

I spent the walk back to the office much the same way I'd spent the one to the restaurant: researching law on Wikipedia. I hardly gave myself a second to think about anything else— and that was the point, wasn't it? There wasn't a single thing from that meal I wanted to remember, starting with the lamb. Was I having a fucking stroke? I'd checked my heart rate, I'd recited the alphabet backward. I would talk to Magda about it in our session tomorrow, if it came to that—no, I was sure by then the episode with the lamb would feel like it had never even happened. But it would be impossible to forget the rest, each and every moment after my first bite of tagliatelle had brought some fresh hell.

First I had to endure an endless stretch of silence in which we both ate our food, looked around the restaurant, and avoided eye contact. I contemplated leaving—probably he did, too—but that would have meant burning the bridge for good. In that period of solitary eating I managed to convince myself that the relationship could be salvaged, that a perfect email later in the day would erase the lunch—and, if it couldn't, that maybe his suction with Colin wasn't as strong as he'd led me to believe.

And then, after we finished, while we waited for the opportunity to call for the check, and then as we waited for the check itself, he told me a story, unprompted, his voice like a knife cutting the air between us. It involved a Turkish artist who had been commissioned by an upscale French restaurant in Midtown—*in the same vein as this place*—for a painting that would be the dining room's center of attention; it would even grace their business cards. He took six months to finish it, and then had a handler bring it to the restaurant. The work was similar to Picasso's *Guernica*, too similar: there were the fragments of limb, the bull, the flames, even the light bulb eye overhead, not to mention that the colossal dimensions were almost exactly the same. Perhaps the painter was challenging the restaurant not to accept the work—he'd shown disinterest in the project from the beginning—but they did. Well, once it was hung and featured on their business cards, website, emails, et al., it was leaked to the media that the rich crimson that filled the background was made using the blood of human trafficking victims. Was it really? Who knew, the authorities didn't get involved and certainly the restaurant wasn't going to get a forensics team on it. At first, the incident seemed to prove the old saw about bad press—who wouldn't want to see the painting in person? But it quickly became a symbol of decadence, of the violence inherent in inequality, and who would be caught eating a seven-course meal under that thing? He finished the story, just as the check hit the table, with some derogatory remark about the Turks, how the *ottoman*, the stool, was the perfect word for what it was.

The way he told it—so knowingly, so self-tasting—made me think that I was missing a world of subtext. It was too neat a story, too unbelievable. But I couldn't figure out what the hell it was about, my concentration being spent on the check—rather, on not looking at it, at that point any hope I had for rapprochement was supplanted by my renewed desire to show him I wasn't going to grovel. For multiple minutes we again sat in silence, not even looking at our phones, a game I either won or lost when he said, so suddenly I almost flinched, *Let me get this.* He took out his wallet, smiling as if nothing had happened, and then dropped a heavy, jet-black American Express card on the bill.

By the time I got to the office I'd been able to focus on my phone just enough to confirm that, yes, intentional torts were *big business*, as he'd put it. And the term was quite a misnomer, torts need not be intentional at all, such as in the case of a prank with unintended consequences. It was fine, the potential legal severity of my deed made the whole thing easier. That is: over. There was simply nothing more to do. I regretted the act with all of my heart and that would have to be enough, I was not going to prison for doing something that was the equivalent of serving her two more drinks. I just wasn't.

I shook the thought away. For the past hour I'd been doing nothing but shaking thoughts away, but now I had a proper distraction. As I stepped through the doorway I saw, across the floor, Simo at his computer and Yuri by his side, looking on with a notepad. I made it halfway there before I was intercepted by Milosz, who put his hand on my back—had he ever touched me of his own accord?—and directed me toward my office.

Your computer should work again, he said, handing me a piece of paper. *But I had to change your password to this jumble. You can reset it, just not to your old one.* He opened my door for me, watched me sit down, and then closed it behind us. *How'd the meeting go?*

It was a success, I said. *I mean, I'd prefer to work directly with Colin, but—* He wasn't listening, the question was a formality.

I'm ready to talk, he said. *I've checked the work.* Was this what he'd looked like when his wife had given birth? No, this was more; it was his own gift to the world. *It appears we may not need as much data as we thought. We're getting confidence intervals that— Okay, um. We set a price. It did, the algo, it gave us a stock and a price and a time. It gave us $1.27 at 12:34, exactly. We'd only asked it to choose sometime today. So we waited for 12:34, in the meantime we tried to figure out how it got there, what it was putting together, if there was some industry trend, or maybe a sympathy play, but there was nothing remarkable. The stock started the day* *at 1.13, the algo bought some there and along the way, and then, at 12:34, we sold at 1.26. We couldn't believe it, a point away from the prediction, this was miraculous, enough cause for celebration, but then we looked at the order book. There was a single trade for one hundred shares, at 1.27, at 12:34. Ten minutes ago, last I checked, it was back down to 1.15.*

What's the stock?

It isn't consequential.

I know. I'm curious.

OBLN. Obalon. They make a balloon that you swallow and then it inflates in your stomach. For weight loss.

What's average volume?

One hundred thousand. It's small, sure. We made about $15,000, it was the max the algo would allow. But this isn't about profit, it's about validation. Simo calculated the odds of it hitting that price at that time, he took into account volatility, he took into account everything. Now he stopped pretending to play it cool, that this wasn't the best day of his life; he was a priest who had been visited by God. *Hersh, it was one in fucking seven hundred something. He just— Well, we'll need to give him a raise. We'll need to rethink bonus structure.* We prided ourselves on our egalitarianism. Every researcher had two coefficients, based solely on seniority and education, that defined how much they'd profit from the company's success. It was more Milosz's idea than mine.

Let's just stay level for a second, I said.

No, you're right. We'll need to think through some things, legally, I mean. I don't know if the laws even cover—if this would be— We'll need lawyers. Patent attorneys absolutely, and finance attorneys, I'm not sure. This is your side of things, no? Law? Apparently not. But hiring the best people to do our work? Yes, that was my job.

We already have patent attorneys. For the rest I'll talk to Mathis, see who she suggests.

Okay, and I'll— He looked up, moved his hand in a circle; this meant he was trying to convert his thoughts into words I could understand. *We need a new security system. Not new—*he knew *new* was a red flag—*just more. More, and—like, bolts, theoretical bolts. Not, I mean— It'll be a day of work, max, and less than the last upgrade.*

The last upgrade was $53,000.

Godspeed, I told him.

Godspeed, he said. He held his fist in the air. He was beaming. He left my office as promptly as he'd brought us in.

I opened my computer and entered the thirty-two-digit password he'd assigned me. I had eighty-three emails. The third most recent was from Resnick, a reply to my inquiry about Ian. *I couldn't find much except for the attached, which is as good a sign as any to keep away from the guy. FYI this settled out of court.* The document was a court filing from three years ago, alleged securities fraud, with Ian one of two codefendants. From the brief it looked like a classic pump and dump—a scheme to artificially boost demand for a stock, these days usually involving networks of message boards and the like—until I noticed that the plaintiff wasn't the SEC, but three hedge funds. He hadn't defrauded some schmucks on Reddit, he'd taken actual traders for a ride. (The filing even referred to Ian as *an experienced quantitative analyst,* which meant that he'd either fooled the funds into thinking so or downplayed his own capabilities to me.) It made sense then, why they'd settled, and why I hadn't found the case online: the hedge funds would have been embarrassed for it to see the light of day. Yes, the lawsuit certainly suggested I should *keep away from the guy*—this wasn't the sort of hijinks Liz Warren was always yelling about; it was abjectly criminal—but it implied much more. I had underestimated him. He'd not only done what he did but, even with that record, managed to get himself into the good graces of a man like Colin.

My inbox chimed, another message from Resnick. *And yes, you were right: He doesn't own property anywhere, not even under a shell co. And no wonder: Just last month he defaulted on a loan of only $225,000 from Deutsche.* Unscrupulous, wily, and (likely) bankrupt. I knew the type, in this industry you met him every once and again: the guy with more than enough cunning to make a decent living, but too much to ever do it the right way.

Just below Resnick's initial email was one from Colin, an empty message, the subject line *Call me when you're back.* Right, *you're back* implied *back from lunch*, he'd already been filled in. It hit me then, what was happening, not with Colin or Ian, but what was unfolding yards from where I sat. I closed my eyes. It wasn't so much what Milosz had said but the way he'd said it—even if I'd watched that scene without volume I would have understood what it meant: This wasn't just the best day in Milosz's life. It was, it could be, the best day in all of ours, everyone in this office and their families, their unborn kids, their kids' kids' kids. My arms filled with goosebumps, it was almost uncomfortable, like my teeth on the mouthpiece, like the lamb. Fuck the lamb. I stood up. I walked to the window, then back to my desk and then back to the window. Across the street I saw into another office, a company I'd always suspected was a design agency based on the spare space, the spare dress, those beanie hats they wore. On the street below I saw the protestors, there were now just four of them. Back up to the office. A woman at a printer, flipping through a pamphlet of oversized pages. It seemed like a scene from the past. It was, I really felt it: What had just happened, what was happening, was a first glimpse into the future of the markets, a paradigm shift that would eventually—not instantly, but over enough time to make enough people profoundly rich— upend the very definitions of public stocks, investing, money itself. Yes, I'd started the firm with ambitions no less than this, we'd sought to build an algorithm that could, without human intervention, systematically harvest profits from the public market. I'd just never let myself believe it was possible.

I went back to my desk; it was hard to sit down but I made myself. I grabbed my phone and called Colin. He picked up on the fourth ring.

Hi, Herschel.

Why hadn't I given this more thought? What exactly was I aiming for? Or rather, what—

Herschel?

Colin, hi, I said. *Sorry, just getting my bearings here.*

But you had only one glass.

Did you install a spy cam on the man? Or is he just one big recording device? I swear, I almost knocked on his head to see if it'd clink.

He laughed, a real one. *He's more warm-blooded than you'd think. But let's, uh— Well, Herschel, I want to be clear that what he said was right. We'll need to reestablish some of the working assumptions on our deal.*

That's why I'm calling, I said.

Oh, he said. *Good.*

For one, we'll need to cap you at 199. We've decided there'll be no majority investors. Also, with some recent news we're only able to offer you a seven percent stake instead of the twelve percent we talked about, which takes into account the downgrade from 220 to 199. And finally, as I believe I conveyed to Ian, we're firm that no investor, including yourself, will have access to any IP or proprietary tech. A cap? And just seven percent? I can't say I'm not curious, just yesterday—

Things have been accelerating over here, and much faster than we could have anticipated. So I'll send over an updated draft of the contract and invite you to get your paperwork in before they accelerate further.

A cough, a reset. I could imagine his eyes swimming above his well-fed British cheeks. *Well, you've said your piece, then. I'll think, okay? I'm not pleased, but you know that. I'll think.*

He hung up.

Just like that, I could feel that our buyer's market had become the seller's. With this new energy I drafted an email to all those unpromising souls who'd come in yesterday, and everyone else I hadn't counted on making a move: Friday was the deadline. And then I wrote one to those I believed would sign, eventually; I'd done enough deals to know that, with enough heat, *eventually* could be smelted into *tomorrow*. I batched the emails and sent them all at once. I'd be fair. First come, first served. And unlike Colin they could keep the current terms. After all, we still needed to fill the fund. I stood up to go to the window again but on my way I heard a yip—there was no other word for it—from the trading floor.

I left my office and found, huddled around Simo's desk, almost everyone, nine or ten in all, including researchers, two traders, and Peter and Milosz. They were exchanging exaggerated *shhs*, and then, before I could make my presence known, they erupted, fists in the air, high fives, a hug, there could have been a football match on those screens. Peter and probably even the traders couldn't possibly have understood what was happening, but that didn't matter; they knew that whatever it was would likely make each of them millionaires. (Even Peter's relatively negligible equity could, given the new developments, amount to seven figures.) I hardly saw Milosz approach, he grabbed me by the shoulders.

CTHR, he said, shaking his head. *1.81 exactly, and at exactly 1:54. Simo had it at*—he snapped his fingers at Simo—*What was probability?*

One in two hundred forty, Simo said, still facing the computer, the only one who had kept himself together.

OBLN was one in seven hundred, Milosz said. *Together that's a probability of one in one hundred sixty-eight thousand.*

I shook my head, there was nothing else to do. The moment was too large to have any sense of, and so I hardly felt anything at all. Déjà vu—this same sensation had visited me recently, it took me a second: misaligned pupils, mouth agape, Birdie in the hospital.

Herschel, Milosz said, leading me a few feet away from the rest. *When I said we needed more security, I didn't—* We need a new system outright. Look, retrofitted—it's going to cost a lot, I mean, as much as we've made today, which is now a hundred and sixty thousand. And we need to make some changes, some internal changes, the open-office policy, something more— Oh, a firewall, a serious firewall.* Firewall. I thought back to the *Financial Times* that morning, my urge to take words literally. *Starting now.* He looked back at the rest of them. *I mean right now.*

Right, I said, and rejoined the group. *Look, this is exciting*, I told them. *More than exciting. But it's not the end of our hard work, it's the beginning. So let's enjoy a bit of a reset. All support staff and traders can take the rest of the day off.* Peter looked disappointed, the traders ditto but they hid it better. *Researchers, please meet us in the conference room in thirty. By then we'd like everyone else gone. Thanks.*

I turned around and walked back to my office. I expected Milosz to follow but he didn't, probably he was feeding every stray paper through the shredder. If this new security spree was how he wanted to celebrate, so be it. I myself preferred to pretend as much as I could that nothing had happened, indulgences were a great way to lose sight of all that needed to be done. And yet, okay—when the idea came to me, I had no choice but to entertain it. No, it was too obvious, really. But the last time Bruce and I spoke, hadn't he said to let him know *how the whole endeavor shakes out?* True-to-form prick-speak—and reason enough to call.

Rebecca picked up, she didn't recognize my voice. She was about to tell me he was *in a meeting* but I said the call was about *a disturbing performance discrepancy.*

That same hold music, hopelessly optimistic.

Bruce Burns here.

Herschel Caine here. He laughed. Before he could say *The prodigal son returns* or something equally unimaginative I said, *I'm calling you as a courtesy. I wanted to let you know, before you hear it elsewhere, that things have picked up over here. To be candid, you may soon find that one of your old reliables has pulled some cash to throw into my endeavor. And before you call legal—yes, I've read the noncompete, inside and out. As have my lawyers.*

His silence lasted a moment, a moment more, long enough that I started looking around my desk, rubbing my hand along the wrinkled leather of my shoe.

You haven't changed, Herschel. You can sell, I'll give you that, but you treat funds like they're cars. God, he loved to hear his own voice. *In finance you sell money, you trade like for like. Sometimes it can be unclear who's selling who.*

He hung up, or at least he thought he did. Through the line came the white noise of his office. I continued to listen, waiting for him to curse me, to call someone and tell them what I said, but all I heard for the next five minutes was the steady rhythm of his typing.

We used the meeting with the researchers to reiterate our privacy policies, their NDAs, and the code of conduct around the dissemination of proprietary information (never ever). Milosz also introduced new security measures, including a reinforced VPN, four-factor authentication, security cameras in every section of the office, a new no-bag policy, lockers for electronics including phones, a firewall between researchers and the rest of the team, and standardized hours of 8:30 to 6:30. (Milosz had already talked with Simo about this last point. For this sacrifice—and, more so, his work—he'd been low-key promoted to vice president. *Low-key* meant that we weren't ready to announce this to the team, and *promoted* meant we were sidestepping our merit policies to give him 1.25% of the company up front, and an additional $200,000 in salary, effectively doubling it.)

So as not to let the meeting be a downer, we ended the workday early and Milosz took the team out for the most expensive sushi lower Manhattan had to offer. I was awkward at dinners like this, or maybe I was just the only one who wasn't; I said I couldn't go, that I had to lend a hand at home. When I returned to my office I found that the excuse had been made true: Franny had spent most of the day at the hospital and texted to ask if we could have dinner together. I said I'd order Indian and scheduled a delivery for later. I emptied my inbox and caught up on the market. I gathered my things and left, clocking out at what was probably a career best (except for holidays and the like): 5:45.

It wasn't until I stepped out onto Wooster Street—the May afternoon feeling more like July, the activists looking more like tired loiterers—that it struck me: I'd ordered a completely vegetarian meal. A coincidence, surely. I thought back to when I'd scrolled down the menu. Yes, I had only asked myself, *What would Franny want?* This day was too meaningful—was it not the most significant in my life?—to waste on worrying, and over something so trivial. I felt nothing but the wind at my back, my limbs light and agile, my joints frictionless. I wanted to sprint down the street, run into next week, next year, see all at once what difference I'd make. Earlier in my career I'd dreamt of a press profile, my face in *The Wall Street Journal* or *Bloomberg*; I would have settled for *Forbes*. Now that thought seemed so small, provincial even: to be yesterday's news, to keep a stash of copies in my office—for what? To show people? I felt sympathy for that man, but not empathy, I didn't want to repossess that mentality, let it repossess me. A well-managed career meant never decreasing your ambition (one of the few worthwhile lessons Bruce had taught me).

I'd write a book one day, I decided then. Not a business book, something more philosophical. How to apply the best lessons of finance to life. After all, this spirit I felt moved by, the spirit of forging ahead, it wasn't just about making money, it did not prescribe a one-track mind. Success meant applying yourself equally to all parts of your life, treating every aspect as worthy of your time, consideration, and courage. Like the situation with the meat, a great example. I could keep on ignoring it, this vague angst, or I could confront it head-on, look it in the eyes, acknowledge what I knew, deep down, must have been its source: I was fooling myself into thinking I couldn't eat meat just because of that dog, just because she'd justified, for a moment—through some ludicrous mental gymnastics—my numbness to Birdie's injury. As if it needed to be justified. As if I could go on like this forever.

I walked over to the halal cart at the corner and ordered a lamb shawarma in a pita, with none of the fixings; I wanted to see the meat as I ate it. A cab rolled up just as I paid—more wind at my back—and I got in. Tawfiq was the driver's name, I was about to ask how his day was going when he spoke in what I guessed was Urdu; he was on the phone. As we drove through SoHo and Chinatown I watched the commuters, the delivery bikers starting their night shifts, the street grocers with nearly depleted bins of produce. I didn't normally get to witness this part of the city at this time of the day. On the Brooklyn Bridge I craned my neck to see the tourists taking selfies and panorama shots. I picked up the sandwich, felt the weight of it in my hand, and parted the foil. There was no steam but the smell traveled fast, I couldn't help but visualize the odor. What shocked me was not that the familiar scent was now fetid, but that the particles carrying the putrid aroma were now in my nose, on my face, that even if I wasn't going to eat the meat—and I wasn't, I would vomit before it hit my lips—it was now a part of me, it was inside me, I had already consumed it. I moved it away from my face, my arm as straight as possible. I was conscious of the driver, that he might wonder what I was doing, I thought to just throw it out the window but then, making eye contact with him in the rear-view mirror, reconsidered.

I'm not sure it's good, I said. *Does it smell weird to you?* He said something into the phone, checked the road and then flashed me his eyes. *Do you not eat meat?* I asked, but he didn't answer, just reached his hand back and held it open. I gave him the sandwich, he brought it to his face and then gave it back.

It smells fine to me, he said, and continued speaking in Urdu.

Again I felt its weight. Now that I wasn't going to eat it I was curious, it was intriguing in the same way any ambiguous, terrible stench was. I gave it a brief sniff and then a longer one. It seemed obvious now that it would be so repugnant, after all it was a dead animal, one that had been killed, allowed to rest, and then heated, the fire annealing its cells, making waste of the bacteria and pathogens that had been otherwise thriving. I'd had enough. I rolled down the window. The wind muted the odor, fresh oxygen cleansed my passageways. I looked back at the sandwich, remembering the feeling of the knife going through the lamb. I held my hand over the meat, I extended a finger, and before I could do anything more I tossed it out.

I spent the rest of the ride listening to Tawfiq talk into his earpiece, half expecting the chatter to coagulate into something more than noise. If at first I felt like an infant, waiting to acquire speech, by the end I realized I was more like a dog; even as I became familiar with the sound of the language—the cadences, stresses, intonations—not one jot of meaning materialized. We could have driven like that for the rest of our lives and still I'd never cross the invisible boundary between us.

When we got to the house I gave him a tip as big as the fare. As if to make up for my behavior, as if I had to apologize—no, I wouldn't even be the weirdest passenger he had today. As he drove away I felt funny, as if I were, somehow, still in the car. It was déjà vu, again: I'd been in this exact same spot before, this morning, when I'd seen the dog. All of this nonsense had started then, when I sensed that the dog could sense me, sense my guilt. Of course it was all just my conscience, compensation for my inability to face Birdie's accident and my part in it, I'd deluded myself as a punishment, to atone. There was nothing special about the dog, a fact so obvious I almost laughed. I only needed to see it again, to come face to face with it, then I'd see it as it was—a dog. And then I'd understand how much of this was all in my head, could be done away with, but properly: through careful introspection, coming to terms. I'd wake up early tomorrow, be on the lookout; its owner, Ben, walked it every morning. I looked up to my office window, and then to all of the other windows of our house. Was Franny home? It didn't seem like it, but she would be soon. I imagined us in the dining room, eating, her telling me about her day. No, tomorrow morning wasn't good enough, between now and then was tonight, and I couldn't deal with more of this, another moment like the lamb, not in the presence of Franny, she knew me as well as I knew myself, she'd pull the thread as I had, see what a tremendous ball it was part of.

I looked from the windows of our place to those of the top floor of the building across the street. I walked over, opened the black metal gate and hopped up the stoop. I buzzed number 3: *Ben & Hadley John.* I waited a moment, looked back at our place. The intercom: *Leave packages in the foyer, thanks.* The door unlocked. I waited, buzzed again. When the intercom clicked I said, *Hi there, is this Ben?*

Yes?

Hi, it's Herschel, from across the street. I hope you don't mind the impromptu visit, but I wanted to talk about something, if you're free, of course. It's about a book idea, actually. Silence, a long one, well past polite. *Sure, you can come up.* The door buzzed again.

The stairwell was musty, dark, carpeted. He met me at his door, his brow furrowed until I was a few feet away, and then his face melted into genuine friendliness. *Herschel, good to see you.*

Likewise.

He stepped aside and I came into the apartment, where I saw no dog, not even a trace of one. There were rugs everywhere, books on every wall, dark wood furniture and a couple of mid-century modern statement pieces. It was exactly how a book editor might live, but there was another gestalt at work that I couldn't quite put my finger on. Then I saw a Chagall print, and then another. *The Essential Leonard Cohen* facing outward on a shelf. A framed illustration of an everything bagel. Yes, it seemed to be a Jewish household. He wasn't, I was sure, his nose and—he just wasn't. His wife, maybe, that would explain the décor, but now I spotted one more object of that order: his hair. Yes, he had a Jew-fro. And the facial expressions too, the way of being. But perhaps I shouldn't have been so sure. I recalled our past encounters, yes, he wasn't just neurotic but the exact right valence: aloof, vigilant but distracted, quick to laugh, to demur.

You've disproven a theory of mine, I said.

Oh?

It's that Brooklyn Jews don't own dogs.

Oh, I'm not— He laughed. *We're not.* Yes, my comment had given him some small pleasure. And now that I knew for sure,

I saw the sliver of daylight between him and my people; his wasn't disposition but affectation—permanent by now, sure, but it was fundamentally contrived. It wasn't the only thing that now seemed like a performance, it was like his whole personality was; he presented himself as some serious man, a man attuned to meaning, as if he'd tapped into a deeper stratum of life. He was the type to look down on a businessman, as if the world didn't show itself to me the way it did him. I'd read Whitman, Austen. I took an entire class on Barthes in college. Sure, it was good with a few glasses of wine, but in the morning it didn't mean anything.

He invited me to sit down and I did, on a couch, across from him. I was about to mention the dog, a comment meant to make him call it into the room, or tell me its whereabouts if it wasn't here, but then he said, *Remind me what you do. For work, I mean.*

Right. So, I run a hedge fund built around algorithmic trading.

I've read about that. He seemed to be putting two and two together, or failing to. *Have you been in the neighborhood long?* Ah, so he didn't think a verified Finance Guy could appreciate the modest charm of Cobble Hill.

Since February. So, no. I laughed. I readjusted in my seat, taking the opportunity to again look for the dog. *Co-op, I assume?*
We rent.

Right, much easier that way. The second you buy you find a million little things wrong.

He gave a slight smile. *So what's this book idea?*

Of course. So, it's—it's really about how to apply the best lessons of finance to life. His face fell; the pitch was dead on arrival. *Treating yourself as a business, one run by the finest—*

Ah, I should have made it more clear, I really only do fiction.

These days, anyway. He glanced around, surely looking for the words to kick me out.

And I should have gone with my gut. I just thought self-help sold well. No, I've got something much better. It's not fiction, exactly. Stranger than. What my firm aims to do, it's— Well, if we're successful—and trust me, it's just a matter of time before we or one of our competitors are—there will be no such thing as a stock market. Bingo. You see, people buy and s— My consonant continued, starting before and ending after the interrupting noise: a ragged tear that ripped the air and made my steady *s* seem as artificial as a computer sound. I swallowed, I felt the air against my neck, my wrists.

Lucy? Ben shouted, his expression both grimace and frown. The noise again, now so obviously a bark, and then the scampering of feet and the chime of a collar. She jumped on his lap, he ran his hands up and down her neck, saying *Okay okay okay.* He was trying to take her interruption in stride but he seemed annoyed; probably the dog was his wife's idea. He looked at me, felt my glare, performed enjoyment. The dog had gotten what she wanted, she barked again and then hopped off him. She made a half-turn, facing no one, and then snapped her head in my direction. She cantered over and lifted her front legs, resting her paws on the couch, right next to my thighs. I flipped my hands palms up and she answered by placing her paws on top. The motion was inelegant, like she'd forgotten about gravity, to stop herself from slipping off she had to dig her paws into my hands. It was pleasantly strange, her claws were made of such lifeless material—the pads underneath, too, like a baseball scuffed by pavement—and yet it was through these dead cells that she felt the world. I peered into her eyes, my body tight. I expected the same look as before, the recognition of my guilt, but the transmission of emotion had reversed. Now she was open to me, the expression on her face naked, like a human in a play or a bad movie. I was embarrassed by her sincerity, and then in awe, nearly jealous of her guilelessness. I saw sadness, and loneliness, but I didn't, really; those two words needed to be added to the list, after *solemn* and *dreadful*, more examples of the hubris of language. Words and logic could not help me describe to myself the kind of pain she felt in this world, a world mostly confined to an apartment filled with things that meant nothing to her, supervised by a man and woman who lived a life she couldn't make sense of and never would, and when her day finally brought her into contact with a like mind, in a park or on the street, and she erupted in emotion—in all emotions at once, after all she'd finally met another being who could recognize the full spectrum of what she felt—she was scolded, her collar pulled, the intensity of her passion matched by the discipline imposed to smother it. But stop. I was still clutching language, clinging to it as I would to a ladder over a too-cold pool. If I was afraid the water would be painful, still I knew it wouldn't hurt me, really, and when would I ever have the chance to feel something like this again? I let go, and the second I was immersed I knew it would be just as cold getting out as it was getting in. I was already acclimated, the world had shrunk, it had become muffled, pale, all the colors were still there but they were severely diminished versions of themselves. Still underwater, I lifted my hands from under hers, ran them up her arms to her shoulders and back, to her neck, I ran my fingers through her hair, feeling her skin and the pounding life beneath. It took a lot to force me up to air: my name, now being practically shouted, *Herschel. Herschel!* I looked up to see

Ben across the room, his hands on the seat of his chair, ready to push himself off if necessary. Colors refilled; sounds were crisp again, no longer that oceanic rumble.

What are you doing?

I couldn't help but let his words infect me, force me to think through language, too. What *was* I doing? I was holding his dog. I was crying. I wiped the wetness from my cheeks, I could feel my face tighten in consternation. He gave a brief laugh, so contrived, so obviously meant to release the moment from its gravity, that it disgusted me. He snapped his fingers twice, ordering the dog to return to him, and dutifully it did.

It's been a day, I said. For a fleeting moment I was aware that I was debasing myself, matching his deception—and then I didn't care. *I'm sorry, I've just been under a lot of pressure at work. I guess it was bound to come out somehow.*

He nodded, and then again, more reassured, happy that we'd found an explanation.

No, he said, *I get it. I mean I think I do. I imagine that kind of workplace doesn't allow for much show of emotion.*

It doesn't, I said, looking at the floor, the whimsical patterns in the Tabriz-style rug. Back at our place we had the real thing: $12,000, another $1,000 to ship it back. *Though I don't imagine you bawl your eyes out in front of colleagues.*

Not every day, he said. I laughed, but he wasn't kidding. *Really, I'm often moved by my work. When I find a manuscript that I love— Well, actually, it's not when I'm reading it myself, but communicating my love of it to my peers.* He nodded to himself. *It's interesting.*

Indeed, I said, glancing at him before scouring the rug again. Finally, he snapped his fingers and pointed to the door.

The dog barked, bowed its head, and with its collar jingling scuttled out. I leaned back on the couch and resumed eye contact.

So, he said, *there will be no such thing as a stock market.*

That's my take, at least. But actually, I think I ought to call it a day thinking about work. So let's pick this up some other time.

He sucked in his lips, nodded, and stood. I got up, too. As we walked to the door I watched his face, worried what it would show, but he seemed, if anything, amused.

I trotted down the stairs and out to the street, which had already darkened and dropped a few degrees. Franny had arrived home while I was at Ben's, or had only now turned on the lights. The warm glow of the living room and kitchen made it seem like a home; if I were a stranger walking by I might feel envious of those inside. The wind blew in from the piers, making me aware of the wetness still around my eyes. I wiped them dry and then again, the cotton of my sleeves too abrasive for that thin skin. I breathed in, and out. If I could still access that moment, just a few minutes ago, it was only as an echo. I was happy it was over, I felt at home in my body again. I imagined being in the house with Franny, between the thick walls of our relationship, her gaze reaffirming exactly who I was.

I crossed the street and stopped at our steps. I was surprised to find that I was looking forward to hearing about her time at the hospital, as if I was about to be updated on some national issue. It gave me pause, this new peace, it was detached enough from reality that I feared she would notice the space between, stick her hand in, tear it open. I needed to get my head right, think critically. Yes, and this started with catching a blind spot I'd failed to see before: the color of the drink

I'd served Birdie. It had been a deep crimson unlike anything we had on our liquor cart. What if Franny asked? Thoughts like these came to her all the time, it was like her brain was constantly being dredged, minutiae surfacing for no reason at all. I turned and started down the street, east, to the liquor store.

Yes, she had a genius for loose ends—not that she was scatterbrained; no, I believed it was the very order of her mind that made uncategorized thoughts so noticeable. I was the opposite, it seemed all of my thoughts lived in one big space with only gossamer organizing principles between them. This I hadn't realized until I'd met her, known her long enough to grade my mind against hers. We did this often, set ourselves side by side, by this point it was practically a reflex. In fact, even before I first saw her facel, we were, in some way, competing. It was a Sunday morning. The eastern leg of the Prospect Park loop. She appeared at my left, a vague figure, her pace quicker than mine, but I was at a jog. I increased my speed until it was just above hers; she was obviously keeping up with me. I slowly accelerated, so she wouldn't notice, and when she finally did, when she gave up and peeled off to the grass, I stopped and turned around. Grudgingly she met my eyes; she was a poor loser, this I'd learn over and over. But the attraction was obvious, we talked for a bit, she told me her number, without giving me the chance to write it down, and then sprinted ahead. I chanted it to myself for the thirty minutes it took to get home. When I texted her later that night, she responded with a shamelessly cheesy riddle: *Tuesday at 7 works. Meet in the middle of Tennis Court.* This took me some time to decipher, as there was a large tennis facility adjacent to the park, but she didn't seem the type for errant capitalization.

Sure enough there was a *Tennis Ct*, a short road south of the park. It was a bit precious, out of a fairy tale, nothing I was used to—she either, I'd learn. But it made sense in retrospect, she had a side to her that was so childish, so unguarded, she was the kind of person to search Google for *bagels near moi*. And this trait was put into sharp relief by the rest of her: she was brutally honest, profoundly self-sufficient, and unyielding in her professional life. She was well aware of the distance she set others at; she owed it, she said, to her upbringing, which she described on our first date as *joyless*. When I told her she had an interesting laugh she just nodded, she knew. She believed it was because she had rarely heard anyone in her family laugh, and so she'd had to invent her own. This laugh she deployed mostly in the face of life's biggest tragedies; or maybe it was just that her laugh expressed exactly this, that life was tragic.

I walked into Ruben's Liquors, nodded at the cashier, and, making my way to the back, spotted the exact color I needed: red apple schnapps. At the counter I asked for a bottle of Laphroaig 16, too—what we drank at the end of our first date.

We were ecstatic together, bewildered by one another. In the beginning it felt like it was us two against the world, a feeling we were guilty of indulging. In the first nine months we went on three trips to six different foreign cities (this was at the beginning of my garden leave), and in each we faked a proposal in the middle of the city square: in Plaza Hidalgo, Trafalgar Square, Östermalmstorg, Campo Santa Margherita, Piazza Navona—even in the crammed grand Bazaar of Tabriz. We never told anyone we did this, it was obnoxious, and besides, we were, in a way, superstitious. It seemed to us that out of the couples we knew, the ones proudest of their relationship in the

beginning—those who were the most conspicuously happy—
were the ones falling apart. The couples going through the
slow drudge of divorce (or headed in that direction, anyway)
were the ones who never appeared to disagree, who were always polite to each other. In retrospect it was obvious: po-
liteness implies distance. Franny and I disagreed frequently,
openly, perpetually we played each other's devil's advocate.
Likewise, we often discussed the attractiveness of strangers, I
felt free to check out women, and she men—often she'd point
them out to me. In some unspoken way we were ashamed of
this even though we knew we shouldn't be; when with friends
I wouldn't dare let my eyes wander. And it seemed to be the
couples I feared would be the most judgmental who were now
fundamentally unhappy. It was no small irony that their problem appeared to be, at its core, a crisis of morality. Sometimes
it seemed as if they treated virtue the way previous generations had treated wealth: not just as a precondition for social
acceptance but as something with only one number attached
to it. They fetishized morality, practically, they forgot the very
thing it was, that it was not about scale but priorities, that its
power came from compromise, that two people might both
strive to be *good* while having irreconcilable definitions of the
term. It was as if, after having spent years not coming to terms
with who their spouses actually were, these couples were suddenly realizing there was a foundational discrepancy between
them. Years ago, when most of my friends were more or less
single, they looked for partners with certain traits—charms,
talents, kindred deficits or proclivities; and maybe morality
was on the list, too, but it was at most a minor box that could
be checked off with just a few evident acts of probity: donat-
ing, volunteering, palpable displays of empathy. They now

hated each other, these couples, hated even the other's laugh; it seemed that once someone stopped being *good* in your eyes, it was only a matter of time before they'd earn your disgust.

I saw Franny now, through the window. She was lifting our dinner from a large paper bag. Her movements appeared languid, but perhaps I was only projecting, given the day she'd had. Either way, I felt ready to hear about it, I was bracing myself: the proper emotional state for what was to come.

I opened the door and walked up to the kitchen. When Franny saw me she stopped what she was doing and came over, slowly, her head and limbs limp. Her arms wrapped under mine and around my back, she squeezed me harder than usual; through the pressure of her clasp I felt my own muscle, fat, ribs. We lasted like this for a minute or more, I let her be the one to end it and when she released me I saw her eyes were wet. It was unlike her, I thought it was proof of her difficult day, but then she said, *I'm so happy we're trying.* That word, *trying,* repeated in my head, each time attached to a new meaning. Inside of me bloomed an unexpected joy, but it seemed unearned, premature, we were so far away, after all we were only trying. The feeling was familiar; I'd felt it earlier, at work. Sure, if it wasn't full-on kismet it at least felt right that the firm was in a similar stage of inception. Yes, the algorithm doing its job was wonderful, a miracle even, but that was just the first step of Atra Arca as a business. As I'd already learned, and brutally, getting the capital we needed while protecting our intellectual property was not—

What are you thinking about? she asked.

A lot, I said. *New beginnings.* I thought to tell her about the breakthrough at work but wanted to wait until I'd heard about the hospital.

She looked down to the bag in my hand. *Something good?*
Not really, I said, which I thought, incorrectly, would de-
crease her interest in it. She watched as I walked over to the
liquor cart and, with my back to her, crouched in front of it.
I placed the red apple schnapps behind an oversized Svedka
bottle, and the Laphroaig in front.

What do you think of the door? she asked. I didn't understand. I stood and she nodded down to the foyer: in place of
the painted gray front door was a dark walnut slab. *I'm sick of
feeling like we live in someone else's home. It's one of the few things
you don't need a permit for.*

I'm sorry, I said. *I hadn't even noticed.* I walked down the
stairs, ran my hand over the smooth finish, admired the pattern in the grain. My eyes went to the distortions where
there'd been knots, the nested ovals like rings around planets.
I imagined being the first to discover that this was what was
in trees, that our universe hid such beauty, and the power I'd
feel from that. I thought of being on Wooster after I left work,
wanting to sprint down the street.

I felt her stare. Even from a distance she could tell my mind
had wandered. I couldn't help it, I hopped up the stairs and
let it spill out of me, I told her what happened as I'd lived it,
starting from when I got back from lunch and ending when
I left the office. She was excited, proud, curious—all of the
things she should have been, except their intensity continually
lagged behind what I myself felt, what I was hoping for from
her. We both felt this gap, just as we both knew its cause: the
guilt of having this conversation instead of the other one. She
asked the right questions, I expounded with the requisite en-
thusiasm, we shook our heads in wonder. And then, to allow
for a proper reset, we didn't speak at all. I set the table, she

apportioned the meal, I opened a bottle of Malbec. After we'd each tried the food, taken a few sips of wine, and felt fully in the room, at the table, she told me about her day.

She didn't know where to begin, she started and stopped multiple times and then left to get her notepad from the other room. Even before she went to the hospital she'd tried calling over two dozen doctors, nurses, and administrators, at Methodist and elsewhere, first to find out precisely what had transpired when Birdie arrived, then to determine if it was medically safe to move her to another hospital (it wasn't), and finally to see if she herself could be designated as Birdie's health care surrogate (that would be up to Will, though transnational laws complicated things). She now had a grasp on traumatic brain injuries, phases of consciousness, diagnostic imaging, standard neurological exams, and the overwhelmingly wide range of prognoses. (*No two brain injuries are the same*, she said. *I must have read that or heard it fifty times today.*) She filled me in with the expediency of someone who only needed to deliver herself of her burden, her words came too fast to carry tone, sentiment, emotion; that seemed, in some way, to be the point. It was only when she'd reiterated everything she'd learned, or at least everything she could remember to say, that she returned to herself, the same woman who'd sat next to me in the hospital, just as dumbstruck as I. And then, with a slow, weary voice, she spoke to me not as a case manager but as someone who'd just visited a friend afflicted by tragedy.

The biggest change since yesterday was probably the presence of Will. He hadn't slept since he'd heard the news; mostly he stared blankly at Birdie while Franny tried to find encouraging things to say or else just talked about her own life, asked about his. They were strangers united by something that affected them at a severely disproportionate scale, and Franny confided to me that she felt nervous about outdoing him in grief, about even showing emotion if he wasn't.

The only good news was that Birdie might have temporarily *emerged* from her coma into a vegetative state; this was exactly what yesterday's doctor had said wouldn't happen. Franny hung on to this error, as if it might mean that his entire summary of her condition could not be trusted. But today's doctor was actually much worse, he seemed to have an affinity for disabusing Franny of her optimism. She preferred to listen to the nurses, who repeated that her condition was *stable*. Being the only positive word that could describe Birdie's state, it bore the weight of all their encouragement to her, and, in turn, of her encouragement to Will, and to Birdie, whom she often spoke to, even if—as today's doctor repeatedly reminded her in his blunt tone—Birdie couldn't understand her. This was easy to forget, or choose not to believe, because for a few minutes Birdie spoke. Maybe it wasn't *speaking*, but that was the word Franny used with Will, with me, too. The noises that Birdie produced, which didn't seem to be in response to external stimuli, were too unusual to explain in words. Franny tried. *Primal moans*, and *Down syndrome-esque*, and *brassy brays*. After every attempt I nodded as if I got it, not just because I was desperate for her to stop, but because I feared exactly what happened next. She prefaced it by saying she didn't want to do it, only that she wanted me to understand. And then she did the impression.

My anticipatory dread had been inadequate. The sound filled my head, I was aware of the depth of my skull just as her earlier hug had made me feel the dimensions of my torso.

It was more than noise, I saw it in me as smoke, it left a trace of moisture that occasionally collected into a drop and fell, causing me to hear again an echo of the original imitation. Each new time I experienced the sound, it seemed more and more like a caricature, something grotesquely humorous, it was cruel of her to do, disrespectful even. I was being unfair, but still I now wanted to get the meal over with as soon as I could, I couldn't stand hearing those echoes in her presence, couldn't stand to blame her any more for putting them into my head. I ate as fast as I could without being obvious about it, and when I'd finished my plate I excused myself, saying I needed to go upstairs and catch up on work. To make up for it I told her I would clean up, and when she went to the bedroom to call her mom I came back down and washed the dinner dishes along with all of those in the sink; we had a dishwasher but it felt good to do it myself, to feel the grease come off, at least the running water helped muffle the echoes, which had become less frequent but more—what? They had become something else, louder and more pixelated, a noise I could no longer imagine coming from Franny's throat. As we went about our evening I found that their infrequency was its own curse, I could no longer anticipate them, feel the condensation gathering on the ceiling of my mind. After Franny went to bed, early even for her, I tried reading in the living room. The book was about the history of debt, it was repetitive and left-leaning, I hardly read two full paragraphs before I surrendered. The echo sounded again as I closed the book, and then again as I put it out on our stoop for the taking. It happened as I opened the fridge, and as I checked the thermostat, and it would happen again and again, follow me to bed and into my dreams, if it let me dream, if I could fall asleep. I turned on

music, *The Four Seasons*, Max Richter's recomposition. I knew
every movement, it was stabilizing, already I sensed that the
echoes would stop. I needed it louder just to be sure, but I
didn't want to disturb Franny, so I put on my noise-canceling
headphones and set the volume so high I couldn't even hear
the liquor bottles jangle as I fished out the red apple schnapps.
I loved *The Four Seasons*, it made me feel like a boy, especially
the first movement of "Spring," which was genius in art, it
was truth, this was what spring would sound like forever:
rebirth, renewal, reawakening—concepts that were around
long before we were, you could play *The Four Seasons* to a pig
or an elephant and they would have to feel, somewhere, what
it was all about, what Vivaldi and Richter had captured, trun-
cated, transmuted to fit our conception of beauty. No, maybe
it would only repulse them, serve as just another example of
our need to abstract everything away from what it actually
is. I emptied out a quarter of the schnapps into the sink, and
then poured myself a glass. As I took my first sip my finger
brushed against my eye and I realized I'd cried. Past tense. So
it had been brief, surely just the rapture of the music. I sat
down and listened more, but by the end of the third movement of "Spring" I felt nothing, it was maudlin and contrived,
the soundtrack of some romantic melodrama. The moment I
thought this thought, *I feel nothing*, the echoes returned, louder
and longer and more warped, one elongated vowel that hardened into a consonant. I stood up. I finished my glass. This
was the power of my imagination, I reminded myself, this was
only a punishment inflicted by one part of me on the rest. But
if I was acting this irrationally, volunteering myself for some
bogus moral retribution—well, what else hadn't I thought
through? Wasn't it also possible, for example, that I'd failed

to properly investigate the supposed offense? Was I taking my own involvement for granted? NyQuil put me fast to sleep, sure, once I was already in bed, usually late at night. But what was the effect when you were trying to stay awake? When you were outside with the cool night air on your face? Birdie had started with a glass of wine, just as I had tonight. Then she'd had that black currant cocktail with barely a splash of vodka, the alcohol content far less than that of my glass of schnapps. Then she'd had the ZzzQuil, with another splash of vodka. I went to the liquor cart and picked up the Laphroaig, I filled my glass a quarter of the way and shot it. I listened for Franny, there was only silence. I went up the stairs to the bathroom, retrieved the open bottle of ZzzQuil, and came back down and into the kitchen, where I emptied it into my glass, filling it almost to the top. This would make up for the difference in weight between Birdie and me, if there was one, and my presumed short-term tolerance, given I'd had ZzzQuil two nights ago and NyQuil three nights before that.

I sat down and looked at my phone. 9:52. I'd give myself half an hour, that was about how long Birdie had stayed after drinking the ZzzQuil cocktail. I'd forgotten about the music; I was now on the second movement of "Summer." I listened impatiently, taking the echoes in stride. I tried to hear them as part of the composition, evaluating the new work as a whole. By the end of "Winter" it was 10:16, which was good enough. I grabbed the empty ZzzQuil bottle, put on my jacket and shoes, and stepped outside. The air was like it was two nights ago, same temperature, same humidity. There was even the residue of a light drizzle. How had I forgotten about that? It was so important. I walked down the street in the same direction she had. I threw the ZzzQuil bottle into the trash can of an apartment halfway down the block. I felt a bit woozy, tired—like I'd had a few drinks and a lot of ZzzQuil. At the end of the block I stopped, stood still, and then began walking slowly. I watched my feet, deciding which exact spot on the pavement I wanted to plant each step on. I walked forward and in reverse; I was, for the most part, precise. The investigation was complete, it should have been at least, but then I remembered there was something else I could try—an idea I'd dismissed when it first came to me as I left the house. I walked toward the street and then, without looking at my feet, stepped off of the curb. The movement felt natural enough, but when I brought my other foot down it surprised me, it touched the ground a moment sooner than I expected. No, I hadn't slipped, I hadn't misjudged where it would land, but before I could put those facts to work the echo came, and not as some monstrous version of itself but as Franny had initially done it; I remembered her face, too, which wasn't meant to mimic Birdie's but, without her even trying, showed me how she herself had looked when she heard the noises. I felt I was inside her, Franny, looking at Will looking at Birdie, those whines filling the room, how empty they were, it wasn't even communication, it was one-way, the emanations of a mind that could no longer latch on to the world.

I was sprinting now, the wind against my face negating what I'd drunk, it even seemed to turn it in my favor, like I had a new reserve of energy, I could tell how fast I was going but it felt sustainable, as if I could go like this forever. I thought of earlier, my urge to run down Wooster and into the future, and how different this was, I was running only to stay present, the faster I went the more I felt in place, in my own body. The echoes had stopped, I heard only the wind whipping in my ears, the sounds of cars. I hit Court Street, a commercial strip, there was hardly anyone out but I wanted to be completely alone, I turned onto Wyckoff and picked my pace back up, I ran past the projects and down more blocks of brownstones. Soon I felt my body start to resist, not some sudden warning but a continuous reminder, a gentle plea. My lungs were fine, my legs were fine, my arms and core were barely straining, my body only asked how much longer. I wondered if I could actually hurt myself, if it was possible to kill yourself from the inside, to exert yourself past some limit, if the body had a backup plan besides the doling out of more and more pain. We could slit our wrists, take ourselves to the top of a building and jump off, pull a belt around our neck and kick the stool, but in the absence of sharp objects, multistory structures, and cords, what was to be done? My impulse wasn't to kill myself, it was to kill my body, take myself elsewhere, a thought that wouldn't have come to me even yesterday but I now knew it was possible, you could feel not in your own body, it was what I felt at Ben's, with Lucy, her paws on my hands, her sadness in my head. I needed that now, right now, that exact feeling, I slowed my pace to think. I could be there in five minutes, I'd say I wanted to talk about the book, that I'd just had an epiphany. But it was too late, of course it was; he'd suggest I come to his office tomorrow, or that we talk on the phone. That was fine, it would have to be. I thought of seeing Lucy this morning, tied to the stoop railing, and moments before, the bird on the branch, the adolescent. I knew then intuitively that the bird could have given me what Lucy had, if only I could have looked into its eyes.

I was running again, as quickly as before, and in another few minutes I came to Third Avenue. A bodega on the corner lit the street, its sign refracted in the windows of parked cars. I walked over and went inside, the door chiming above me. There were only four aisles, I went down each one and then each one again, I was about to leave but thought to ask the cashier: *Do you have a cat here?*

No, we don't have a cat, he said. His tone was antagonistic, he seemed to want to hurt me emotionally. But it was thin, a performance, he'd only wanted to say, *I'm not going to be friendly with you.* It made me sad that he kept himself at a distance, but I was happy to feel the sadness, it was a way to connect to him whether he liked it or not.

I appreciate your help, I said, making myself vulnerable, hoping he too would show himself. *And I like your beard.*

Yo, get the fuck out, he said. He leaned forward over the counter so that he could shout to the other clerk, a man stocking shelves: *Danny, get this fucking weirdo out.*

Danny turned, assessing the situation. I couldn't handle more aggression, I hurried out onto the street, where I looked back into the store and then, as another echo came, continued running east.

At Fourth Avenue I tried another bodega, but there was no cat and I didn't ask. At Fifth Avenue again the same result. By the time I got to Flatbush I didn't want to try again, I knew that even if I found a cat my behavior with it would not be tolerated. I fully understood I was in a different state of mind, one that would be categorized as that of a *fucking weirdo*, but knowing this didn't make me feel what I felt any less; still the echoes came, more frequently, unpredictably, louder.

Flatbush was more crowded than I would have guessed. Even though I didn't want to interact with more people, I thought that their presence might increase my chances of finding an animal. But there weren't any, in the nearly two miles I'd covered there wasn't a single dog or cat, how could there be miles of space without animals? It was night, they were all in apartments, in cages or designated spaces, alone, bearing witness to their owners' freedoms, freedoms spent mostly staring at screens that might have seemed magical or miraculous if it hadn't been for their owners' apparent disinterest, their expressions of laziness, apathy, inertia.

Another echo. It wasn't loud but it came from nowhere, it pulled a yelp out of me; a group waiting in front of a bar looked my way, laughed. And then another echo, and another. I was now sprinting again, looking at telephone wires for birds, at piles of garbage for rats, but I knew better, I needed to look an animal in the eyes, yes, and it was only when I said that to myself that the answer became obvious.

I ran straight through Grand Army Plaza, past the head of Prospect Park, and continued down Flatbush. The sprinting was becoming too much, as if the ZzzQuil was finally working as it should, but I was almost there, and in just a few minutes I arrived. It didn't seem right, it was too nondescript, just a banner on a pole and a small sign above a plain gate: PROSPECT PARK ZOO, A WILDLIFE CONSERVATION SOCIETY PARK. Plants in terra-cotta pots guarded the entrance; they made the gate seem even less effective. I walked up to it, looked around, and lifted my foot onto the horizontal bar midway through. I pulled myself up so I could grab the top bar, and then, pushing my foot against the crown of one of the shrubs, reached the sign above the gate. I hoisted myself on top of it, caught my breath, and then jumped down, crumbling to the ground. I stood, waiting for my body to notify me of some damaged limb, a twisted ligament, but I heard only a resentful silence.

Looking out of the gate I briefly felt like I was in a cage, but as I stepped back, giving myself more space, it seemed that it was the rest of the world that was enclosed. I turned around to find a large pool with a cluster of rocks in the middle: the sea lions. I went over to it and, leaning over the railing, saw only black, tranquil water. They must have been hiding somewhere, asleep or left to their own devices. This was the only time of the day their lives weren't entertainment, when they didn't have to perform for us, trade their presence for food; such is our power that we can impose our workday on other species. I walked around the pool once and then went down a path that led to the DISCOVERY TRAIL. Guarding it were just two linked gates I could step over. I wandered around, there were no lights and I could hardly see, if there were animals in these netted enclosures they were out of view. I'd come all this way, I didn't know if I could run anymore—I was wearing my brogues, already I felt the blisters forming. I was suddenly afraid of what might happen, being so alone, I was afraid of myself, there was no one here to call for if it came to that, if I wanted to admit that what was happening to me was beyond my control, if I needed medical intervention. I felt watched, someone else's presence, I pivoted to look behind me but stopped halfway—something had moved. I turned back. Its tail jerked, once. It was staring at me. I lifted a foot to see if the creature would flinch. It didn't. Slowly I walked up to it, past it, to a placard. STYAN'S RED PANDA. It didn't look like a panda. It had the face and tail of a raccoon, it was that size, too, but its legs were the black stumps of a much larger animal, and the fur was copper, the color of a penny, except for the ears and patches around the eyes and nose, which were pure white. I looked back at the sign. Why was my instinct to read a description of him? Why did I even care what name he'd been given?

I walked up to the animal. He lurched to his left but then turned back. I stopped, my eyes adjusted, I saw every inch of his face. He was nothing like Lucy, no, there was hardly any sadness here, he didn't even have a grasp on his own life, what was wrong with it, what humans were using him for. This made me even sadder than Lucy had. I hardly even felt like crying before the tears came. They sounded natural, my sobs, it was like hearing my own voice. It *was* a voice, a way to communicate, surely he could sense the tears, my sadness, that I was sad for him. I thought of my own life, what I didn't know about it, what was too obvious for me even to realize, and then I thought of our algorithm, how it would, eventually, see us the way we saw animals: our movements predetermined, our freedom a nice lie. The thought was oddly calming; the more I felt and believed in the algorithm's omniscience the closer I felt to Lucy, to the animal in front of me.

Suddenly he seemed naked, that one simple difference between us now glaring. I saw his bare legs, his stomach. I felt the cotton on my thighs, the polyester on my chest. I looked around, and then, as slowly as I could, I took off my jacket and shirt, my pants and briefs. I placed the clothes in a neat pile behind me, and then turned around. There I stood in front of him as he'd never seen a human before. I felt vulnerable, honest, more myself, even, and yet, when I looked down I was struck by a pang of shame: my penis was circumcised; it looked like a penis that had had something done to it. For the first time in my life I was ashamed of it, ashamed that we did such a thing. *Shame.* I'd never considered how the word contradicted itself: it was both the feeling of having done something shameful and the trait that helped us avoid the shameful act. I looked back at him, searching his face for judgment. No, he couldn't sense my shame, he wouldn't even know what it was. If anything he looked worried, as if my abruptly bizarre appearance might portend danger. This was calming, too, calming like the thought of the algorithm. I was happy to be a predator, I sat in the feeling, it meant I was no longer a spectator, some untouchable god. He flinched to the side, paused, and then ran away.

I stood there, watching the dark patch of air he disappeared into. I knew he wouldn't return but I wanted to hold on to the feeling he'd given me. When finally it left, when I felt alone again, when I felt naked, I put my clothes back on and made my way home.

I dreamt nothing, nothing I could recall. I awoke feeling well rested, I had a clear head. In fact I felt unusually myself, as if I hadn't felt like myself in years; I had none of the low-level anxiety I always had to bat away upon waking. I lifted myself up and planted my feet on the floor, the blisters on the sides of my toes proof that last night hadn't been a dream. Even though Franny was still asleep I turned off the white noise machine—it was for me, anyway; I was the one who always woke from the chirping. I heard them now, those noises I'd cursed every sleepless morning. *Trill, warble, quaver, tweet*, if I was aware of the words I had no idea what they meant, I'd never cared to differentiate them before, I'd never even heard them as language.

I grabbed my robe and walked to the bathroom. Standing in front of the mirror I put my fingers in my ears, listening for the echo, but I knew it wouldn't come. I couldn't even really remember what it sounded like. I closed the door, turned on the vent fan, and tried making the noise myself. What I produced could have passed for a tribal chant. When I closed my mouth my jaw ached. My dentist had warned me about clenching while I slept, every dentist since I was twenty had. I pushed my tongue forward and to the right—a pang of pain, but not from my jaw. I closed my mouth, recirculated the saliva, and reopened it. I pulled down my lip and saw, at the bottom of a bicuspid, right at the gumline, a chunk of tooth missing, as if it had been chiseled away. *Abfraction*, that was the term my dentist had used. *What I'd be worried about are abfractions.* The word sounded too industrial, too modern to refer to something that must have been with us for as long as we've had teeth. The thought of making an appointment made me clammy. My teeth had always been something—one of the only things—I felt deep and irrational shame about. Starting in college I had habitually, without much effort, regurgitated my food shortly after swallowing it, only to chew it more and swallow again. It was hard to explain how exactly it happened, I just tightened some passageway and brought it back up. It was a recognized disorder called rumination syndrome, but it didn't feel like a syndrome, if everyone did it I would think it was as normal as sneezing. It is quite rare, obviously, and especially for someone like me; it's usually only infants and the mentally ill who ruminate. The food is undigested, it hasn't passed from the esophagus to the stomach, so it tastes just the way it did when it first went down. This should preclude the acidic erosion of teeth normally associated with bulimia, but still I frequently wondered—and hated to think about—what effect it might have. (Occasionally, I was able to quit—in fact I hadn't done it for the past week or so—but it always came back.) It was such a sensitive issue for me that I hadn't even told Franny about it until three months before. She'd reacted well, better than my ex. It wasn't until I made a joke of it, mentioning that only animals who ruminate are kosher—goats, sheep, cows—and so I too could be eaten, that she'd seemed a little disturbed.

I went back to the bedroom. She was waiting for me, her underwear on the floor, her hair already tied back. On the smart thermostat console hung a T-shirt; she didn't trust that it couldn't hear us, let alone see us. Morning sex had always been my preference, not hers—was she ovulating now? I took off my robe and went to the bed. As soon as I kissed her she grabbed me, nearly forced me inside of her. Entering her felt more, what? Sensual? Bodily? It was the absence of a condom, of course—but had I felt this way on Monday night? I found myself less attuned to how she was feeling, I anticipated my own climax more than hers. That sex now had an objective, something at which we could succeed or fail, made me horny, astonishingly so. I pulled out of her, put my nose to her stomach and pushed it down through her hair. As soon as I started licking her I only wanted to be inside her again, but when I pulled away I wanted to be back, closer to her scent. It wasn't enough to breathe her in all at once, it was gratifying only when I wasn't paying attention, when I let it come in with the air I breathed. Again and again I considered reentering her, she asked me to, her fingers grasping at my shoulders, but I couldn't, instead I placed my fingers on either side of her, making her wider, making it easier—

Whoa, she said, sliding up the bed, away from me. *What are you doing?*

Going down on you, I said. *Eating you out*. I made the rock-and-roll gesture. *Not literally*. She laughed but it faded fast. As she searched my face I became aware of my own expression. *Did I do something wrong?*

No, she said. *I mean*—she glanced at my hand, now lying on her thigh—*let's just stick to the script*.

I laughed, but it didn't sound like me. I ignored the feeling, ignored everything and climbed up the bed. I reentered her, I was hard but no longer horny, at least not the way I'd been before.

We went through the motions, after a few minutes she came, and I did too. She smiled at me, got out of bed and, while getting changed, made her daily call to the Department of Buildings. *Hi*, she said, *this is— Yes, Francesca Olsen. Yes. Correct. Yes*. On these calls she spoke as she never did, enunciating every syllable, like a diligent pupil asking for a hall pass.

I listened to her walk down the stairs and then replayed what had just happened. Except I couldn't, really. No, and this had now become a familiar feeling: a frost that lay right across my memories. Like last night, at the zoo. When I thought of it I saw myself in the third person, blurry, the colors drained from the image. It was easier to relive it through words. *I'd gone to the zoo to see an animal, any animal, hoping the connection I felt with it would relieve me of the echoes. I found that red panda, its ignorance made me sad. I took off my clothes and scared it, which felt good, to feel our relationship was that of animals*. Yes, it was a strange experience. I felt the air leave my nose, I breathed it back in. No: it wasn't strange at all. In fact it was the most natural thing. I'd said *It was a strange experience* to myself but I hadn't thought that, really, it was just what I felt I should think, what I expected of myself. It reminded me of being in temple as a kid, saying the Shema. I could say *The Lord is our God, the Lord is One*, even though I had no belief in or conception of the words I was saying.

I got up. I went to take a shower. The water pressure was thin, I made a mental note to call the plumber. I put on pants and a shirt, I shaved and combed my hair. Downstairs on the kitchen table was a dismantled *New York Times*, a crisp *FT*. I opened the latter, the feature story was about Ethereum. Why did they continually debase themselves with this crypto analysis? Their readership thought even omakase was risky. Just beyond the paper I noticed, still out of focus, an unfamiliar cluster of color: a bouquet. A dusty black rose drooped in my direction, its color camouflaging a fly skittering across its petals. The fly moved as if in stop motion, its life just a series of images. The flowers weren't Franny's style, too recherché—had Birdie brought them? I didn't want to ask. It was certainly possible; they were wilting. I looked away and then back. I couldn't stop staring, the beauty and apparent rarity of the selection seemed cruel, the flowers were exotic not just to me but to each other, never in nature would they have sprouted from the same soil, and now in such strange company they each grasped for life, feeding off the same urn of cloudy tap water.

Franny brought me a latte and the fly flew away. By the flower she had drawn in the coffee's foam I knew it was Thursday. This same day each week she plunged herself into work, was productive from when she woke up to when she fell asleep, a mindset she'd invented in college. I liked to tease her that after her chairs were in every dining room in America she'd write her entrepreneurial self-help book. But actually she'd already started, it was titled *The Opposite of Cheat*

Day. When we moved in together I learned that this ethos extended past her work life—to lattes, for example. And now, apparently, procreation. I took a sip and told her it was lovely. I set the cup down and picked up the paper. There was a photo of the new Goldman chief. God, the way he smiled, the way all these guys did. There was a feeling in my stomach, or higher. A warm wave traveled up my neck, my hunger abandoned me. I lowered the paper and looked at the coffee, the foam flower, the small white bubbles hardened in the froth. I stood up, kept myself still for a moment, and then ran to the sink, the news still in my hand. With my palm on the faucet I unloaded what little remained in my stomach, it was really just acid. Even in the mucousy gunk I could make out the froth—the offending substance, I knew, because when I saw it I started to gag. I lifted the faucet handle but then brought it down, I wanted another look at the stuff: it was proof. I hadn't even thought, *This is milk, this comes from a cow*; it was beyond logic or intent. But then, what about last night's meal? Franny had had saag paneer and I'd tried some. This didn't undo any of what I felt, it only made it worse. I thought of my stomach acids breaking down the curds, the animal protein absorbed into my body, the animal fat burned for energy.

Are you okay?

Yeah, I'm fine.

God, was it the picture?

What?

She picked up her phone to show me but then decided against it. *It's— Well, I couldn't sleep last night. I was just— I kept thinking about her, what happened. I mean, what actually happened, just down the block. It must have been four a.m. or so, I went and found it, the spot, there was still blood on the curb. I took a photo, just in case.*

You found the spot? In the middle of the night you were able to find it?

Well, yeah, she said, peering down. Her face tightened for a moment and then she looked back at me. *I went on her phone yesterday, when I visited her. I wanted to see how long it was before she got to the hospital. And it showed where exactly she'd been picked up.* This made sense, and yet, having started the confession she couldn't help but finish it. *It was just lying there, along with the rest of her stuff. It was locked, actually. I brought it over to her, I pressed her thumb against the sensor. That's how I did it.*

Jeez. She looked down. *I mean, that's okay.*

So it wasn't the photo, she said, changing the subject.

No, I said. I turned to the sink and, seeing the vomit, washed it away.

Well, I'd guess it was the Indian but I think I know better. I turned around. She nodded toward the liquor cart. *Not like you to leave a mess. Apple schnapps, really?*

I smiled. *No reason to turn your nose up. Give it a try.*

A bit early for me. But if you take a seat I've got you a better hangover cure.

To my left was the cast iron. I leaned toward it and saw four eggs, sunny-side up.

No, I said. *Thank you, but I can't eat anything.* She looked disappointed. This was meant to make me change my mind. If she disdained her upbringing, still she never shook her rural roots; to miss a morning meal was practically impious. *I'll sit with you, though. And I'll be as quiet as I would be eating.*

She went to make herself a plate and I sat back at the table.

But when she joined me she had a plate for us both. One of my yolks had broken, it ran onto the piece of toast below. I knew that eggs weren't stillborns, but still the word surfaced, twisted, showed itself both poetic and sterile: *born, still; born still.* The sight of it sapped me of any hunger I'd reclaimed, I didn't even want to look down.

Please eat, Herschel. You're going to have a big day, I know it. Deadlines make dominoes. Dead lines. *That's what you say, right?*

Ah, but it's best to stay hungry.

Now she was annoyed; irony wasn't the move. She cut an egg in half, cut off a piece of toast, and speared them together. She lifted it and opened her mouth. I saw her molars, her pink tongue, her pink palate, it was briefly erotic until she closed her mouth and I imagined the taste, the flavors of another being. I lifted the paper in front of my face. The peace lasted a moment until I realized I could hear her chewing. She did it slowly and with her mouth closed—she always had impeccable manners—but still there was noise, the muted transfer of liquid, the pharynx and larynx working in concert to usher the bolus down into her body.

I'm thinking of going vegan.

Finally, the chewing stopped.

Really? Why?

Did everything need a reason? The environment, animal cruelty, my own health—she would have been satisfied with any of these but none was right.

It's hard to say, I said. *It's just a feeling I have.*

I lowered the paper.

Confused. Her entire face could be summed up in a word. But emotions aren't so simple unless we want them to be. She was trying to be confused, she was defensive, as if my wanting to be vegan without a concrete reason was an attack of some sort. She did a kind of head tilt and looked at her food through the side of her eyes, as if her eggs could help her figure me out. As she prepared herself another bite the eroticism returned, this time for long enough that I realized it wasn't lust at all but a distant cousin, another remorseless passion, a different craving. In some small but definite way I had hate for her.

She was now taking a bite every few seconds, not waiting to swallow before filling her mouth again. It wasn't like her, I figured she just wanted to end the meal, avoid the conversation about me being vegan, but when I told her I liked having breakfast together, that we should do it more often, she looked up at me with kind eyes.

Honey, I do too, she said. *I'm sorry, I should have checked the time. I promise I'll be out in ten.*

Out in ten. I looked at the microwave clock: 8:17. Thursday, therapy, right. *Okay, great*, I said. *I'm just going to go clear my head.* I brought my plate to the sink, pushing the food off into the disposal. I ran it and then made myself an espresso. I took the coffee along with an orange up to my office, where I sat at my computer and listened to her shuffling around, getting her day in order against the clock. I loved her, I did. If the debris of hate was still in me it was just like the paneer: already incorporated into my body, but soon enough it would be recycled, discarded.

I tried checking my email but the page wouldn't load. I went to call Milosz but saw I had a text from him, something about needing to reconnect the intranet. To pass the time I paced around the room, I looked out onto the street, the courtyard. I saw Clara there, reading a paperback and drinking coffee, her outfit more stylish than the hour required. There was something about the way she was sitting, or twirling her hand—both struck me as a bit self-aware—that annoyed me. It was the artifice of it, and the fact she was alone, that even without an audience she seemed to need to perform.

The front door closed at 8:28. I typed in the address of Magda's telemedicine portal. That same banner: SIMPLE. FREE. SECURE. I would have traded the first two for more of the third. I entered in the name I used, *Cohen*, and waited. When her face showed on my screen—always it looked the same; her hair, too—I realized I had started peeling the orange. I didn't know what the etiquette was, I asked if it was okay and she said, *Of course*, but still I set the orange down once it was naked. I started talking about work, I said I couldn't go into too much detail. She nodded graciously and said, *Of course*, and then asked me to describe how I was feeling. I told her about leaving the office yesterday, wanting to run down the street, that I couldn't wait for our recent developments to unfold, that I'd never before felt there could be such a thing as infinite potential. She laughed. I liked when she laughed, it made me feel like I was succeeding, her laughter was never belittling, always joyous. But then she said it was important to stay in the moment, no matter how excited we are for tomorrow, and I said, *Of course*. We went through a few of our normal topics, starting with what we now referred to as *the finding of Lisa*. Sometimes therapy seemed like a song, there were basically four or five dominant chords and each could color a given digression or verse, but in the song between Magda and me the one chord that every musical phrase had to be played in was Lisa. She had been my babysitter, a college dropout with platinum blond hair who, at least in memory, was the most engaging person I'd ever known. She committed suicide in my bedroom while I went to get a soda at the 7-Eleven. Yes, I was the one to discover the body, but that scene wasn't what Magda and I usually focused on. Lisa probably sexually abused me, a term I didn't think was accurate but felt compelled to use with Magda. (Although Magda generally allowed for evasion—hence that oblique handle, *the finding of Lisa*—she refused to call Lisa's transgression anything but sexual abuse.) Lisa never touched me, only had me, at age eleven, undress and watch her masturbate. It happened four times, no more. What I had regretted most, up until I started with Magda, was the narrative shape Lisa always threatened to give my life, that anything special or meaningful might always be traced back to her. I preferred to see those events in isolation, to see the version of me who experienced them as having very little to do with who I was today. I understood that this wasn't the *healthy* way to get past trauma, but it suited me just fine. I considered it a skill, even, this ability to cleave cause and effect, to chop up the emotional ingredients of my life and use them as I wished. At her best, Magda made me appreciate that this was my prerogative—that narratives were contrived, a manipulation of history, and thus we each had the freedom to plot our own. At her worst, she seemed to tie every loose mood or recurring deficit to this thing that might well be entirely distinct.

With Lisa in mind we discussed a recent visit to my father, who has inoperable lung cancer; although he is likely to survive the next year, he may not make it another three. Under Magda's guidance I drew a connection between the unfair, seemingly arbitrary failing of his physical health and Lisa's mental deterioration. We then moved on to my recent discussions with Franny about circumcision, whether our children, should they be boys, would be initiated. Franny saw my preference as a *reflexive genuflection to Judaism*; these were the same words she used to describe my automatic support of Israel. On both accounts she may have been right—of course she was—but I felt that she was overlooking her own knee-jerk aversion to all things religious. This was the first fundamental, intractable argument we'd ever had, and it nagged at me in a way that was both abstract and agonizing. At the end of the day, I just wanted my boy's penis to look like mine. By this point in the session Magda and I had begun to find our groove, where radical honesty no longer seemed radical. I spoke about the shortcomings of my parents, my concept of money and ambition, my feelings of inferiority at work, and Franny's and my decision to start trying to conceive. We had a ways to go on this last topic, I really wanted to dig in but saw we only had ten minutes left. If my instinct was to not bring up what was happening, it was a self-defeating one, the point of therapy being to mine the very things you are consciously hiding.

I started with my new perception of words, my experience reading the *Financial Times*. And then I mentioned the other glitches of speech: *firewall* and *I'm so happy we're trying* and *stillborn* and *deadline* and everything else.

She nodded thoughtfully, she seemed to catch herself in boredom and said, *That's very interesting. It's exciting when everyday occurrences appear to us differently.*

Right, I said, nodding. *On that note, I had an odd experience yesterday. A few experiences, actually.* I picked up the naked orange and jammed my thumb into the orifice at the top, splitting the segments. *Yesterday morning on my way to work I saw my neighbor's dog on the street. Looking at her I began to feel something strange, a sort of intense connection, a kinship, even. I couldn't shake the feeling, it made me feel kind of crazy, actually. Well, I felt that if I saw her again I would realize that it was all in my head, and so when I got home I made up an excuse to visit my neighbor in his apartment, just so I could see her, the dog. And when I did, when I was in his apartment, I really felt how sad she was. It made me quite sad, actually. I cried.*

She was nodding at a rhythm slower than I'd seen before. Her head settled at the lowest point, her pupils at the tops of her eyes.

You cried? Even she had hardly seen me cry. She took hold of herself, twisted her disbelief into encouraging curiosity. *Herschel, tell me about what you were feeling when you cried.*

It was simple, really. I was just sad for the dog. I—I— No. That's it. I felt I should say more, make it all make more sense to her, but I knew that every inch in that direction would be an inch away from the truth. What had happened was ineffable; that was the point.

She wore the same face I'd seen on Franny an hour ago. Confusion, unalloyed—that is, performed.

You look skeptical, I said. *Do you not think dogs feel sadness, or do you not think I'm capable of having empathy for a dog?*

Well. Neither. It's been well documented that animals have emotions similar to ours. And I myself know your empathic capacity. But, to be honest, Herschel, I do question the sudden change in behavior. It makes me wonder why you didn't experience such a strong connection to dogs before yesterday, and what might have happened to make you so susceptible.

Yeah, I said. *It's been a long week. There's a lot going on at work. And, you know, we've just decided to start a family.* I stopped speaking but she continued to stare. *Hmm. Actually, a friend of mine, or really an acquaintance, she was in a terrible accident involving brain damage. Although I had no way to anticipate it, of course, and of course I had no intent of it happening, I'm worried that I am, in a way, blameworthy.*

She nodded solemnly. That was it. Had she heard me? Did she think I was exaggerating my involvement? I retrieved my words, listened to them again.

I do feel responsible, actually.

I can sense that, Herschel. And that's such a good, strong word. Responsible. *Responsibility can take so many forms. So maybe you feel responsible for this dog's sadness, but maybe it's really some other responsibility you're carrying with you, and applying to the experience with the dog. A responsibility coming from the future, perhaps?*

Hmm. I'm not sure. The incident with the dog sort of feels detached from the rest of my life. She looked skeptical again. She needed a cause, a source—as if everything could be explained away, as if life was held together by such airtight logic. What was I paying her for? *Can I ask what you'd say if I told you that I'd found God? What if I was on my way to work and had an epiphany, and now I wanted to go to temple and keep kosher and all of that? Would you try to figure out why, exactly, that had happened?*

Yes. Absolutely. Ah, but of course she would; in fact she'd love to. When we'd first started, about a year ago, she'd constantly brought the conversation back to my Jewishness, from my distant relatives killed in the Holocaust—she was projecting, obviously, given that her parents' generation had so effectively purged their nation's Jewry—to the shame I felt for not being as religious as my parents had hoped. This last one had been a potent subject: I had, until we talked it through, pretended to be kosher in their presence; I'd even gone so far as to tell them Franny was considering converting. But after Magda and I put the issue to bed I'd gently asked that we focus on other things—and then, when she replied that *to forget history would be to forget the ground we stand on*, I'd asked less gently.

Right, I said. *Okay*. I was annoyed but didn't want to say so. Instead I made it obvious by looking at the time in the corner of my screen.

She sighed and sat back in her seat. *It's a miracle, Herschel. It's a revelation to you, obviously. But it's my job to help you explore what's behind it, so that you can understand it and even experience it at a higher level.* I nodded without making eye contact. I regretted being so immature with the clock. *You know, often when someone is about to experience a change as big as the birth of a child, they start to feel differently about the world. And when your child comes, believe me, the world will never be the same.*

We continued down that path. We discussed my hopes for a family, my fears. And when it was over, when she concluded our session with her usual courtly nod, I felt nothing.

I stared at the screen long enough that I grew accustomed to the graphics and could see my face in the reflection. I stood up, I felt light, not just from not eating but altogether, it was easy to move my body through the room. I wouldn't talk to her about it again, her very mode of thinking—her profession— was irreconcilable with what this was. The thought made me happy, elated actually, like I'd been released from some burden. It was exactly how I'd felt when I ended my relationship with my ex, uttered the words that would be the last of a long, drawn-out breakup. But as I began ambling around the room, my habit after therapy, I felt, well, also the way I had after I broke up with Kay: alone, on my own, like there was nothing to hold me accountable.

I turned on my phone. A text from Franny: *At the hospital. No progress.* I started to draft a reply—*I'm sorry, I wish*—but deleted it. I called a car, brushed my teeth, and put on socks. I went downstairs, leafed through the *Financial Times*, and then packed it away for the road. My shoes were in the foyer, still out from last night. They'd taken a beating, the leather bearing new, unexpected creases. The leather. I went into the walk-in closet and scanned every pair, if any were made of synthetic material I wouldn't know. My running shoes were, though; they would have to do for now. There was a store just up Wooster.

Outside, just as I locked the door, I felt the pressure on my hips. I took off my belt and set it on our steps, right beside the history of debt book. Philip was on his stoop next door, his hands on his waist, staring up at his place. He waved. *We had a great time on Monday, really.* It seemed such a stock phrase, a conversational set piece.

Well, it was good company, I said. I almost flinched, my words were even more contrived. Had I gone so far as to mimic his tone? *And we'll do it again soon.*

I saluted him and went down to the street. The car wasn't here yet. I turned back around. From this angle I couldn't help but question whether the oak tree in front of our house did, in fact, breach the property line. When we bought the place we'd filed an application to cut it down—ostensibly out of concern that the roots were a risk to the building's structural integrity, though really I hoped it would reduce the morning chirping—but Philip and Clara had protested on the grounds that the tree was theirs and ours both. Their objection had come through the Department of Buildings, which I thought was odd, cowardly perhaps, and for a week or two I had resented them—until we met in person and their charm washed away any lingering ill will.

Philip? He lifted his chin. *If you don't mind me asking, why did you become a vegetarian?*

The question had, somehow, polluted his smile. *You know, I just saw one too many of those films. You witness how they prepare the animals, what their life is like, and you just lose your hunger for it. And it's not just factory farms. It's the organic stuff, too.*

I nodded thoughtfully. *Sounds interesting. Can you send me some? The videos I mean.*

Sure, he said; still something sour there.

I waved and looked down the street, the SUV was approaching. It wasn't Cedric this time, but someone new. When I got in he said, *It's a pleasure to drive you, sir.* I knew he was just doing his job, being cordial, but still the words sounded ugly to me, a lie I was complicit in. I glanced over at Ben's stoop; Lucy wasn't there. I thought to look up at their apartment—had she heard the car?—but restrained myself. Already I was letting my work self take over, I needed to, needed to pare down distractions and wring the most out of the day, which promised to be a big one. It was true: deadlines make dominoes.

⌒

The new shoes were comfortable, or would be once I'd spent a few days in them.

I walked into the office, nodded to Peter, and was immediately accosted by Milosz, who paced over from Simo's desk.

Herschel, he said, *where've you been?* I was no longer *Hersh*. And he was no longer in awe of the world, or even happy.

Is everything okay? How are the trials?

The new buys? They're spot-on, exact, by now we can confidently iterate. But we're wasting time, I need your signature on new data orders, I needed it two hours ago. I thought we agreed on eight thirty?

He was artless, he'd never been anything but. I had always thought of this as some defect, his inability to cater to others, but now it showed itself as an honesty I myself could rarely achieve.

It's Thursday, I said. *I had therapy.*

Therapy, he repeated. As if I'd said *handball*. I nodded. *Okay*, he said. *I think we need to rethink some things. I already have, I mean.* I saw past his shoulder to the windowsill, which no longer featured our very expensive plants. *It would be too easy to hide a camera there, a listening device, anything. And from now on there are no electronics allowed past that line.* He pointed to a strip of blue electrical tape two feet behind me. *So, your phone.* He put out his hand. This gave me a brief, unexpected glimpse into him as a father, something I always struggled to imagine. Actually, it often felt like he kept that part of his life completely insulated from the part I inhabited. A few months ago he'd set a photo of his wife and kids on his desk. I was mesmerized by it, by his smile, which was more tender than I'd known him capable of. He seemed unsettled by my interest in it, and the next day the picture was gone.

Milosz.

We agreed on this. You yourself announced it to the team. I took out my phone, turned it off, and gave it to him. In return he reached into his pocket and handed me a large set of keys. *The one marked with your*—he stopped, noticing Peter next to us, and led me away. *The one with your height in inches accesses the server room. The rest do nothing.* He pulled out the right key, as if I couldn't calculate it myself: number 70. He walked past me, nodding for me to follow.

As we walked across the trading floor I noticed that Simo was now closely flanked by four other researchers, their computers pushed screen-to-screen. On the floor, enclosing them, was a three-sided box made of that same blue electrical tape. Their backs were parallel, their spines at nearly the same angle, they looked like they were servicing something more hands-on, a car, or maybe it was the opposite, that they themselves were being serviced, cows to be milked.

We came to the server room. On the door, in addition to the new keylock and the old padlock—I had that combination memorized better than my Social Security number—I saw another combination lock. *It's the eight digits of your birthday in the order of last digit, first digit, second-to-last digit, second digit, et cetera. But please, do not go into this room unless I'm present. There are wires everywhere, it needs to be organized, I've already ordered bins.* He looked at me, waiting for my nod, and when he got it he turned to walk away. *The data orders and VPN invoices are waiting on your desk.*

When I could no longer hear his footsteps I exhaled; I hadn't even noticed I was holding my breath. I rested my hands on the industrial metal cage that made up the outside wall and door; even that felt like a small defiance. The room emanated a subtle warmth, like breath almost assimilated into air, but this heat was different, it was dry. All over the room red and yellow-green dots blinked and disappeared into black metal or matte plastic. I listened to the hum, which was oddly diffuse, the chorus coming from every section: the soft whir of fans fighting the heat. I concentrated on a few of the blinking dots, capturing their rhythm; most kept a steady pulse but some were random. I focused on one in particular, trying to discern a pattern in the sporadic flickers, but I couldn't, not even after a minute. It was frustrating, I knew there was one; despite the complexity of the algorithm that controlled it, despite the sheer number of calculations these machines performed each second, there was no essence, there was nothing that couldn't be explained, eventually. The algorithm's victory was only quantitative, like ours over animals; a dog can understand human language—it understands its name—but at such a small scale. That was who we were to the algorithm: dogs. We understood it bit by bit but were lost in its orders of magnitude.

I felt hungry, suddenly. Ravenous. It was almost eleven and I'd only had an orange and an espresso. I went to the kitchen and grabbed two eggplant sandwiches from the refrigerator. I stood there for a moment. Something was bothering me, had been since I'd first got in. It was like it was right in front of me, I looked around and then closed my eyes: The noises. The alerts. They were gone. Of course—another of Milosz's precautions.

I took the food back to my office and sat at my desk. I unwrapped the cellophane and ate one of the sandwiches in just a few bites. I signed in to my computer and checked the market. The S&P was up 0.71%, the Dow 0.63%, the NASDAQ 0.66%. This was no longer relevant to my work but it was an old habit, a score I checked like the Knicks'. And like a basketball game, the day's trading was just one point in a much larger arc. For the past year the narrative had seemed to be, at least among the "experts," that of Icarus: a downturn was imminent, and it was hubris to think otherwise. This doomsday story seemed to exist only to placate those who had missed out on the recent upswing; year to date the S&P was already up 12%. It wasn't just that the prediction was specious, it blinded analysts to something much more interesting: the detachment of price from value. Interest rates were impossibly low, people were practically forced to invest, as long as they had savings and weren't ready to buy a home, or already had one and didn't care to buy another. And so, with all this money permanently parked in the market, prices were squeezed upward, and upward, and upward, far, far beyond the true worth of the companies they supposedly represented. It was a violation of the basic tenets of the stock exchange, but that didn't mean the trend wouldn't continue. No, the opposite: the more inflated prices became, the more everyday investors expected them to inflate more, the public market—any market, really—being one big, airtight self-fulfilling prophecy. This was all just another reason our conception of finance was ready to be torn to shreds.

Not that I don't love the market. There's truth in those sharp, jagged lines. The market's past is never changed or rewritten. Stocks move in unpredictable fits and spurts of success and failure, and just when they start to make sense they defy logic, just as reality defies logic. A price moving through time is a sound not like a song, not like the call of a bird; it's a single note but a cacophonous one, it's a million people speaking at once. No, it isn't such a coincidence that some of the original thinkers in quant trading started in speech recognition. Quant analysis is a science co-opted, the discipline haunted by its original subject. Stare at stock charts long enough, imagine where they'll be in three months, one year, five years, fifty, and yet another property of speech emerges: its brevity. Sound preordains silence. If every voice behind a stock stopped, if we all looked away at the same time, the price would drop to the ground, dead. Companies are mortal, they are. Like us they guarantee so much action but with a guaranteed end, and there is peace in that.

Continuing my sign-in ritual I checked my bank accounts—$2.8 million, all combined. It was a lot of money, I never thought I'd make that much, at least not when I first entered the working world. But it never stopped seeming insubstantial, or tenuous, it was just a number, I could spend an hour on my computer and get rid of it all. I opened my email, reaching for a notepad and pen before I read a single word. One by one I would tally the new commitments, I would circle the total and deliver the good news to Milosz. But my eyes jumped to the words *Eubanks, Colin* first. I clicked on his message. *It's a lot of pounds, need to think more.* Pounds; pounds of flesh. I went through the rest of the emails. About half of our potential investors hadn't responded to my deadline message; most of the rest had bowed out with good wishes (*We'll be watching from the sidelines.* Fuck you.), a handful had punted like Colin, and two of them had committed. One for 3.3, the other for 2. I wrote 5.3 and circled it. Not a number to take to Milosz. No, a deadline and a tone conveying my confidence were, apparently, not enough. People needed more: results.

I wolfed down the other eggplant sandwich and went out to the trading floor. There I found Milosz, just inside the blue box, watching over Simo and his gang. I stood by his side, squinting at the computers. Simo's was the most active, boxes appeared and vanished so quickly they hardly could have registered. He was now leaning back in his chair, rolling an unbitten apple between his hands. He was often this way while in the thick of concentration—childlike, almost. Maybe it was only that he was enjoying a state unavailable to most other adults. People like him—those whose work consisted of being curious, who could simply sit and think and know that their thoughts mattered—seemed to be afforded a certain wellness that could not be gained any other way. Not that having such a privileged vocation (and mind) guaranteed access to that peace; Milosz too had made a life out of thinking, but that may have been the bane of his existence. In his hands potential was a burden, something that had to be made good on, but which he never could, fully.

Milosz, I said, startling him. *You mentioned the new buys were* spot-on. *What exactly does that mean?*

All I got was a nod, his stare steady on the screens.

I think we should start putting real money into this.

Now he looked at me, his gray eyes wide open. *We have. We've put in what we can. Since yesterday morning we've made $270,000.* It was as if he'd said lunch had been successfully delivered.

That's great, I said.

He nodded and turned back.

I scanned the screens, searching for some conspicuous number or indication. It would be very like them to have the most crucial metrics look no different than the rest; it all seemed to be in ten-point type. I moved to the side so I could follow their eyes, as if they were interested in the same things I was—alpha, beta, standard deviation, value at risk, kurtosis. No, and anyway they seemed to be taking it in all at once, like pigs at a trough, greedy for any bit of information they could extract something from. *Greedy.* As if what they were doing was wrong. It's such a dirty word, *greed*, and for something so natural. We don't blame pigs for acting greedy but for us it's a sin. And pigs are hardly as tempted as we are; how would they act if in front of them weren't just their calories for the day but something they could take and keep and use to buy enough feed to last them their whole lives, and those of their kin, and buy shelter, too, buy protection from other pigs, and still have so much left over they could pay to be entertained, they could forge new modes of leisure, they could buy themselves happiness, well-being, and self-esteem. No, the word alone, *greed*, could not be trusted—it came with a morality that was false from the start.

Keep me informed, I said. *Please.*

I walked to the kitchen and got a can of seltzer. On my way back to my office I noticed that Yuri was finally wearing shoes: a beat-up pair of Adidas, but still.

I sat down at my desk, opened a text file, and spent a good thirty minutes finding the best language to describe what we'd just accomplished. It had to be sent as soon as possible; instead of running it by Milosz I wrote it with his feedback playing in my head. (Was it a coincidence that two of the words his Polish accent distorted most were *nothing* and *proprietary*?) When I was done editing I sent it to every potential investor who hadn't outright rejected us, and then went back to my inbox. There I found, along with another rejection, a message from the address Head_of_JYM@yahoo.com. There was no subject line. I opened it.

Please keep in mind that my endgame is to work together, really.

There was an image attached. I hovered over it, I savored not knowing, and clicked. The picture was so familiar it took me a few seconds to understand the severity of its arrival in my inbox. It was me, straight-on, in my home office, head tilted to the side, a slight smile on my face. In a square in the corner was Magda.

I stood up and sat down. I stood back up. It was from today, I was wearing that shirt and— I just knew it was from today. I focused on the annoying email address, the obnoxious tone of the message—it made me think of men who think they can pull off a fedora—so I wouldn't have to reckon with everything else. I closed the image and opened it again. Still I needed to delay thought, so I Googled *Head of J.Y.M.* Apparently Auerbach had painted many works by that name, each with the same essence: a face cut into pieces, or maybe collapsed inward, the thick lines that might normally form its perimeter broken into slabs that intruded on the subject's eyes, ears, mouth. Each work was immediately disturbing—the subject looked as though they had been hacked at, disfigured by the artist—but what lingered was a more muted terror. It was the lack of a barrier between the subject and the rest of the world, the sense that they might start to leak out of themselves, lose their shape, slowly fade into the background. I closed the browser and saw the image of my own, unmutilated face.

The session this morning: Simo's breakthrough but not in detail; my excitement over our progress, how I wanted to run down the street; Lisa, how she acted the last time I saw her alive; my father's recent reticence; Franny's and my arguments about circumcision; my mother's guilt and the projection of it onto the rest of the family; how I compared my worth to the firm with Milosz's; Franny's and my decision to try to conceive; language glitches and my connection to Lucy, which Magda had decided, or at least implied, was caused by the specter of parenthood. I felt the clothes on my skin, my white shirt, I imagined my sweat yellowing it. I was calm, at least I'd convinced myself I was, until I thought of all the words I'd said in that hour—words I could no longer access, but he could, probably he'd recorded the session. My fists pushed up against the underside of the desk, I gnashed my teeth, I imagined another abfraction. If I felt naked or exposed, defiled even, I also sensed that I shouldn't, that I was being too sensitive. I knew this wasn't about me, my life, my most personal information. Yes, this was obviously a better way to think about it, a way to keep my head, to deal with this strategically and summarily. It was, after all, nothing but a scare tactic, one that was meant to say: *Look, I can hack. Now give me what I want before I take it myself.* As if phishing his way into some unencrypted WordPress site was anywhere near as difficult as laying a finger on the firm's internal systems.

I picked up my phone and called Colin. I hung up, I needed to get level. I walked around my office. I opened my door and called for Milosz. While I waited for him I looked at more Auerbach, but really I was thinking about Ian reacting to the story of Lucy. Seeing it through his perspective I had the urge to laugh, I felt giddy, it was amazing that Magda had held it together; she was, after all, a professional. Milosz walked in and I waved him over, turning my screen so he could see.

From this morning, I said. *This was taken from my therapy session.* I told him about Ian, about our lunch, what the references meant. I promised him over and over that I hadn't given Magda any specifics about our progress, that she wouldn't even know the word *alpha.* I knew he was convinced only when the vertical line between his eyebrows finally disappeared, and then he seemed suddenly content, amused even.

He repeated, with evident glee, the obvious: it was Magda who had been hacked. Yes, this whole thing only underscored how imperative security was, that his paranoia was justified.

This is just the beginning, he said, shaking his head at my screen. *Can you imagine what they'll try once our returns are out there?*

I can't.

Well, he said, *you could try using a different teletherapy provider, but I'd—*

I'll stop completely, I said.

He nodded, still staring at the screenshot.

I clicked away and looked up at him. *Thanks,* I said.

I watched him leave and then walked over to close the door. I sat back at my desk, put my feet up, cracked my knuckles. I grabbed my phone and dialed Colin.

Colin Eubanks's office.

A secretary? I thought this was his cell.

Is Colin there?

Who's speaking?

Herschel Caine.

Mr. Eubanks is currently in a meeting.

This is very, very, very important.

I'll be sure to tell him you called. Anything else?

I hung up. I found Ian's number. I played a hypothetical conversation in my head. I refreshed my memory of who exactly he was, the kind of reptilian, arrogant, tedious— It didn't matter, just as it didn't matter that he knew I'd been sexually abused as a child, or even that I'd cried for a dog's pain. He still didn't have what he wanted; I did. I had all the power.

I dialed.

Herschel?

Already I relaxed. It was wobbly, that word, he could hardly say my name.

It's illegal, Ian. It's a federal crime.

What is?

Didn't Harvard teach blackmail before torts?

Ah, nice callback. You have a good memory. Mine's not so great, but I do recall all the privileged info you shared about Webber. You know, it's also illegal to—

To break my NDA? Who the fuck cares. I paused. If he'd recorded the therapy session, why wouldn't he record this, too? *I said nothing you can't find in public filings.*

You did, you said—

I said nothing.

I waited five seconds, ten. All he had was some personal dirt, some loose comments I'd said at a lunch, if he thought that was worth— I heard paper rustling, a cough.

Here we are, he said. *Tell me if these ring a bell. OBLN at 1.27. CTHR at 1.81. STAF at—* I took out a notepad. I put myself on mute so he wouldn't hear me, and wrote down the stocks. *And SPCB at .94.*

Good luck, I said, and hung up.

I grabbed a new notepad and left my office. Milosz was at the blackboard with Yuri, gesturing with a piece of chalk. He saw me, finished his thought, and joined me by the espresso machine. I asked for our recent successes, I promised it wasn't for investors. He gave me a look I had no idea what to do with, either he wasn't used to nonverbal communication or I wasn't used to him deploying it. And then he named them, I wrote them down even though I didn't need to; it was the exact same list Ian had read out in the exact same order. I thanked him.

Again he was staring at me. What would happen if I told him? No. No, no. He would go mad, he was already losing it, he'd move the business to a remote base in Nevada. I looked at Simo and co, the blue tape surrounding them. How long before there was a literal wall between them and everyone else? And how long before I was considered *everyone else*? Sure, I would have to tell Milosz eventually, I would. But only if I couldn't fix it myself.

There were ten ducks, or twelve, more. Each time I tallied them I sensed I was counting the same one twice. They didn't like to be looked at, not by me, not by their own kind. And yet I could tell by their movements that each knew exactly where the others were. They were mallards, most of them male, their heads that opalescent green, their necks marked by a neat white collar; below that was a brown so unremarkable as to accentuate the uncanny palette above. The females took the effect further, they were entirely mundane but for a brief banner at their sides, a folded flag that, when they flew, unraveled into a lustrous indigo band bordered by black strips bordered by white ones.

It made more sense then, why they pivoted so often: they were showing themselves off. And that was why they never looked at each other, refusing to give in to another's beauty. My gawking must have seemed gauche to them, a capitulation even, given I was not exquisite like they were, my greatest physical traits were a strong jawline, high cheekbones, pectoral muscles I had developed by repeatedly pushing myself away from the floor of my office; if they knew I'd spent all that time only to make my chest bigger and more tightly bound they would feel, at most, pity. Perhaps they already pitied me, surely they could see I was the same breed as the gaggle of girls next to me, who were currently enacting a scene the ducks must have witnessed a thousand times: the pose practiced and graceless, the arm jutting out, the chin lifted, the smile feigned, as if a smile could be feigned—no, all it said was that something more authentic was not on hand.

Obviously I was in a terrible mood, I didn't want to be here, didn't want to see him or speak to him ever again, every time I did some new bad thing glommed on to my life. And now he was twenty minutes late, of course he was, he'd done the same thing at our lunch. *2 pm, on the dot*, he'd written. Or was *on the dot* just another lame reference, this time to the pin he'd dropped me, showing where we'd meet? (It was in the water itself, at the southern end of the Central Park Reservoir, I was now at the closest spot on land.) I had almost been late myself, Milosz had forgotten the code to my locker, but thank God I wasn't, I would have missed out on nearly ten minutes of these girls photographing each other, encouraging each other with words that seemed to have no use but to annoy me—*I'm not mad about it*, and *I'm here for it*, and *all of the things*, and *I love this human*—language without substance, verbal memes that meant nothing, that did nothing but reference themselves. *Yeah?* they would say after declarative statements, a rhetorical device that only created voids between them, it was more important to mimic each other in sound than to exchange genuine, intimate information.

I'm so sorry, Ian said, appearing by my side, shaking his head at his own misdeed. I looked at my watch, made my irritation obvious. *Well, yes, for being late. But much more so for the whole, you know. I didn't listen, I swear. And I already deleted the file. I didn't want to be so aggressive, but I figured you wouldn't agree to see me again unless— Well, here we are.*

Right, I said, looking beyond him to the girls.

Let's find someplace more private. He walked past me, I heard the sound of our jackets chafing but didn't feel it. *It's so exciting, what you've already accomplished.* He turned his head so I could hear him, he slowed so I could catch up. *And if my understanding of what you're doing is correct, I think we're just a few small tweaks away from really opening the lid on this. We may need a week or so—*

We? No, Ian. This has nothing to do with you; it never will. Not that I believe you have any fucking idea what you're talking about, and even if I did I wouldn't give you one byte of our algorithm. So enough, please. I'll forget this morning, forget whatever else you've done, but if you try to intimidate us one more time I'll go straight to the authorities.

He stopped walking. He smiled at me. Why could I never make contact with him? It was like he had no center, like he was made of only disparate, shiny, borrowed traits: a person like terrazzo.

Brass tacks, he said, his voice deepened in caricature. *Okay, fine. Everything on the table. So I did listen a bit, mostly to the part about your friend, the one with brain damage. What the hell was that about?*

I kept my face still. I didn't react, even inside. How could I have forgotten about that? But even now it felt like it hadn't happened—that my confession, having failed to be correctly interpreted by Magda, had vanished. I breathed in and when the air came out his image appeared to tilt. His head dipped slightly, he was trying to look concerned, trying to hide his pleasure, but really he was trying to look like he was trying to hide his pleasure, his entire being seemed one infinite recursion, everything was about something else, I couldn't stand it anymore, all I wanted was to shake him until something real fell out. I imagined putting my hands on him, on his jacket, and then, before I could even think to do it, they were there, the nylon balled into my fists. It felt too easy, like I'd hardly done anything, and yet I'd breached a serious boundary, I could tell by his eyes, which were finally honest, he was startled, nervous, I wanted more of it, wanted to wring out whatever truth was inside him, I pushed my knuckles into his chest, I slapped my hand against his neck, dug my fingers into the thin skin, around a thick, tender cord. He had closed his eyes, he was squeezing them shut, waiting for me to hit him, I waited too, waited to surprise myself, but all I could think about was a distant beat, a rhythm, coming from my left, my hand, his neck, his pulse, not a *thump-thump* but a *thump*, steady, shallow— could he himself feel it? I was too calm now, too rational, I was aware people were watching. It wasn't a second after I released him before he was his usual self again, his shock gone, already pretending to find the whole thing funny. He pulled his jacket straight and took a step back. I almost apologized, the words were on my lips. To say anything else I reminded him that we'd offered him a stake, that he could have made money the right way.

The right way, he repeated, and then chortled, a sound I could tell was genuinely his by how repulsive I found it. *You have no idea, do you?*

A gust of wind came, lighting a small pain in my hand. I looked down to see a thin line of blood trailing off my thumb.

The stocks you're playing with, he said, *they're all low cap, low volume, low float. No? Still nothing? Well, I'm sure Milosz can ex-plain it to you himself.*

I meant what I said. Never contact me again.

As I walked away his face stayed with me, a more natural smile than I'd seen on him before. I couldn't believe I hadn't hit him. I turned back around. *I'm sorry Hitler took your family's farm, but I had relatives they didn't even waste bullets on.*

He nodded, he seemed to appreciate the reference. *Of course, Herschel. Moral victory is always the victim's.*

I dropped a cricket in. It padded around the mulch, it could hardly find purchase. Once it did it stopped, it was completely still before starting again, its legs moving too fast to see. The lizard was the same in that he never betrayed his next step, but always seemed to be in motion, his lungs continually pump-ing oxygen, his tail painting shapes in the air. Except now. He paused for a suspended moment, he was unusually inert. And then he darted across the cage, the bug in his mouth before my eyes could find it.

Anoles, the clerk had called them. *It's a weird word but you can name them what you want.* What had initially caught my eye was a pair of gerbils in the window, when I walked past they stopped to watch, displacing their own worries with mine. They always worried, it was like breathing, this I real-ized when I came inside to see them up close: they had already moved on to something else. I needed a steadier counterpart, I walked past the rodents and the rabbits, the birds and the fish, I found the anoles in the back of the store, practically hidden beneath a row of spiders. Their bright green skin was reptilian but supple, scaly and thick but with plenty of give; it felt as though I was touching them with my eyes. At first they seemed oblivious to their surroundings, to their condition even, like the red panda, but it wasn't obliviousness, really. They simply didn't care what happened outside their tank, what was inside was enough; they had consciously chosen a smaller world.

I asked to buy the first one I saw, and then one much smaller, from another tank. He wasn't even half the size, about the length of my pinky, not including his tail; when he exhaled, the absence of air left large notches in his sides. The clerk, a dead-eyed young man who probably wished he worked at GameStop, told me I should pair the adult male with another adult, as that would increase the chances he would deploy his dewlap. This was a flap of skin under the neck that, to intimidate or seduce, extended into a bold, strawberry-colored semicircle. He pulled the dewlap out so I could see, even though I asked him not to. He interpreted my distaste at his violating the animal as a sign I didn't get it, he said the dewlap was really the only reason people bought anoles. When I asked him how he would feel if a greater being pointed out his erection as his most noteworthy feature he gave a brief laugh and then told me about their ability to camouflage. I nodded, I repeated that I'd like to buy the two anoles, I now wanted to leave the store as soon as I could, the squawks of the birds were filling my ears, and even the parrots' speech— *Thank you, have a nice day; Thank you, have a nice day*—seemed to be cries of pain.

They'd yet to change color or use their dewlaps; I didn't think the younger was even of age. Either way, I took this as a sign that they found my office comfortable. I was worried, I'd bought the largest tank I could carry—including mulch, branches, hiding spots, and a heater—but it seemed hardly big enough. They appeared calm, though, and more so now that they were digesting. Watching them like this—the crickets in their mouths, their eyes barely moving—helped me cultivate my own patience, which I needed now more than ever; I'd asked Milosz to my office forty-five minutes ago and he still wasn't here. They were a reminder that life could be lived slowly, that you could spend it just sensing and interpreting what was around you. Mostly they looked out my window. At their angle they could see the planes coming from LaGuardia, I watched them myself, the flight paths satisfyingly simple, a single line, its empty perfection accentuating the rhythms of the birds, which now appeared as wild but taut balances between liberty and obligation.

Milosz appeared in my doorway. I motioned him in and he took a seat.

I caught him glancing at the tank, before I could explain it he said, *Simo wants more money. Up front, I mean. He wants half his raise now.*

A hundred thousand? Up front? He nodded. *I don't like that.*

But considering what he's worth to us.

Okay, I would just rather incentivize. Let's increase his stake.

I think he— He really means up front. He said something about his family. Simo was from Serbia, the southernmost region. From what he said about his home I got the feeling they lived as if Tito were still around. *He wants the money today.*

I rolled my eyes. Simo was smart to send Milosz. *I'll wire it later. But say you had to wring it out of me.*

Good. His shoulders dropped. *And the round is filling out?*

We got 5.2 this morning, and 2 more this afternoon. That puts us at about 150, uncommitted and without Colin.

Great. And when will he close?

That's what I want to discuss. I told him about my call with Ian, and only the call, that that was why I'd wanted to know which stocks the algorithm had fed us. Then I asked him what he thought our biggest security weaknesses were, I knew that the question would exhaust him, so that when I asked my other question he would give me his simplest, most honest answer.

He spoke about advanced encryption standards, our no logs policy, and something called a *kill switch.* Then he stated what he seemed to think was already obvious: that Ian was still nowhere near the code itself. *If he was, we'd probably never hear from him again. No, I'm sure his access point isn't the network but something more physical. A video camera, or a person.* I looked to the door and he obliged, getting up to close it. *Really,* he said. *The stocks, the prices—these are just purchase orders.* He squinted up at the ceiling. *It's like he's trying to get us to give him our credit card number just by showing that he already knows our date of birth, our middle name.*

I see, I said, looking out the window. *You know, he brought up something else, too, something interesting. He pointed out that all the stocks we've had success with, they're all low cap and low volume. Low float, too.* It took all of a second for his face to confirm what I'd feared most. *Why is that?*

Well, it could be reduced complexity, it's easier to map and all that. With black boxes you really don't—

Milosz.

He nodded and looked away, at the tank. *Okay. So, it seems, as of now, that we will only be able to capture stocks that fit that profile. Reduced complexity does make them— Well, okay. I'll put it like this. If we predict a price for a given stock but then don't let the algorithm buy along the way, that prediction, I have realized, will be false. And that would, by all measures, seem to suggest manipulation.* I held up my hand but it was too late, *manipulation* was the one word I didn't want to hear. Did he himself understand the implications of what he said? He looked as though he'd found a small wrinkle in our strategy, and not recast the entire business as a borderline criminal enterprise. The algorithm wasn't just predicting prices; it was, somehow, manipulating the market to make those predictions a reality.

When were you planning to tell me this? Why am I the last to know everything?

You're not. In fact I don't think anyone knows, certainly no one has said anything. This isn't— They don't think along those lines. He gauged my reaction, he looked down. His face brightened for a moment but he extinguished the thought.

What?

He shook his head in amusement. He looked back up at me. He couldn't help himself. *It just didn't add up, how it worked. We were obviously building a ladder, establishing some price, then one a bit higher, and so on. But it made too much sense, I didn't think retail investors were that logical. Well, they're not. No, our algorithm had only figured out the trigger points of other algorithms, and then triggered them at the exact right times, even causing them to trigger each other, if that makes sense. We're fundamentally lining up other quant funds, all in a row, and then with one bullet—*

It's illegal.

It's not, actually. Not yet at least, not if we don't know what's happening. And we don't, that's the whole point, isn't it? It's a legal gray zone, it has to be. Like traffic laws and self-driving cars. But not even. People see cars every day, they care about traffic safety.

Mathis suggested a lawyer at Baker McKenzie. We'll see what she says.

Please, he said. *We know what she'll say. She won't condone it, that's her job, to not condone things.* I shook my head. *Hersh, please. There's a reason why there aren't laws for this. We've built something the world hasn't even anticipated.* The glint in his eye. His pinched cheeks. It made more sense to me now, why he chose finance over a more august career. What did any mathematician want more than to construct something the world hasn't even anticipated?

I looked at the tank, at the younger anole. There was now direct sun and he was hiding under a branch, his breathing still, his mind elsewhere. Milosz was saying something about money, he was changing tack, appealing to my greed. Of course we wouldn't lose what we earned, not most of it, if it was made illegal it would be years from now, only after it became some public issue, after there was enough outrage, after Congress figured out how the hell the market worked—at least how it's worked for the past decade. By then we would have turned our profits into real estate, or reinvested it elsewhere, or just created an offshore fund. If need be we'd work with the government, help them understand what would then be an industry-wide phenomenon, we'd work something out.

It's a big accomplishment, I said.

It's bigger than us, he said, not without hesitancy; he was finally discovering abstract speech. *I've never felt so small in my life. Really. I saw a twenty-dollar bill on my desk. It looked primitive, like a relic.* I caught myself smiling, his own smile was infectious. *What we've invented, it's like fire, it's going to spread no matter what, so we might as well make it as big as we can. We need Colin, Hersh, no other way, even if it means Ian. I don't care, give him— Let him buy a stake in the firm, anything less than the board threshold. Give him four percent, five percent, give him last year's terms, whatever it takes to get him on our side and out of the way.*

Not last year's terms.

Of course not, but that's your job. You fill the fund, I don't care how. I'm ready to go all in as soon as we have the capital.

I brought my tongue over the abfraction. *I'd love to never speak to Ian again.*

Take his money, Hersh. He stood up, he put his hands on his head and then dropped them to his side. *You can do it, Hersh. Okay?*

I nodded. He waited for my eyes, and when he got them he shook his head, again in amusement, and left, closing the door harder than I would have liked.

I looked out my window—no planes, no birds—and then at the tank. Both anoles were hiding now. I peered in from above and still couldn't find them, so I tapped hard on the glass. The elder stuck his head out, and then ran to the highest point in the tank, atop a branch. He was panting, he was scared, but it suited him. He was more present than usual.

I leaned back in my chair. I put my hand on my face and pushed it around, dragging my mouth down and to the side. I went to my email, found Ian's message from this morning. *Please keep in mind that my endgame is to work together, really.* I opened the attached image but closed it before I felt anything.

Two minutes. Two minutes more of him. That could be all it took, and then I would finally be able to concentrate on what mattered. I gathered my thoughts, recalled all our past interactions and imagined every pose he might assume, and then called.

That was fast, he said.

Do you have a minute?

So Milosz set you straight.

You think it's manipulation. It's not, end of story. Low caps are just easier to map, and they have greater upside, obviously. But we're moving to large caps this afternoon. And speaking of, I'm calling because we're ready to start playing with real money. It's full now, the fund, but that's if we take some Saudi capital, which I'm reluctant to do, given, you know. So I'm calling for Colin's share, which I understand you have some say in. And in return for your good favor, I'd like to offer you some stake in Atra Arca itself, at a reduced valuation. Fifty percent reduced. Milosz said the most he'll approve is a two percent stake, but I'll convince him to raise it to four. That assumes Colin signs, and that you quit this le Carré shit.

Interesting. Two hours ago you were at my throat.

Right, literally. I'm just ready to move on. I listened. Silence. I need the money, Ian. It's that simple.

Okay. So, to make me go away, you're trying to sell me something. He probably didn't have cash enough to buy a bip.

Well, I'm offering you—

You know what I want.

We can't give you access to anything proprietary, we can't. Even if I was okay with it—which I'm not—Milosz would sooner die than give his approval.

Which is why I was hoping to make an offer with you, not Atra Arca.

What does that mean? Silence again, this time absolute; he was on mute. *Ian?*

Give me a second. Was he annoyed? He breathed out of his

nose. Yes, he was. Another ten seconds passed. *Herschel. Does your wife know about this brain damage situation?*

Now I put myself on mute, even though I wouldn't make a sound, even though my breath was stuck in my lungs. I knew the answer, the correct one, I just didn't know how to say it. I double-checked that the phone was on mute and then tried: *Yes*, confident. *Yes*, exasperated. *Yes*, simple.

Hello?

Yes, I said. *She knows everything. She's devastated, it's a terrible situation.*

So it would be no problem to call her and offer my condolences?

Do not contact my wife.

He breathed out again. Whatever came next would only deepen the threat, give me yet another chance to fuck up. I ended the call and put my phone down. I watched it, waiting for it to ring, but it didn't. Fuck. I looked at the elder anole. Fuck. He hadn't moved from his branch but his breathing had settled. He was thinking slowly again, lost in himself.

He wouldn't do it, no, not right now. If he really thought the threat had value the last thing he'd do was squander it. But still I couldn't get the image out of my head: Franny, caught in the middle of something, the phone cradled between her jaw and shoulder, his voice in her ear, her eyes narrowing, her eyebrows knitting. The scene abstracted itself, I saw a foul pink spirit wafting over her silver silhouette.

What would he say? That I'd told my therapist I was responsible for a friend's brain injury? Franny wouldn't believe him, no, but even so, she would tell me the story, she would watch my reaction. And then what? I couldn't even lie about her to Ian— *She knows everything*, I'd told him; why did I have to say *everything?*—how could I lie about Ian to her? It would unravel right then, right in front of us, the truth and all of the other deceits rolled up in it. It wouldn't make sense to her, that I hadn't told her before. It *didn't* make sense, except everything does, the discrepancy would fall on me, or my nature, I would be someone who could have hid such a thing.

I wanted to see the younger anole. I ducked low, in the glass of the tank I saw my reflection. I looked away, to the window, I couldn't stand it, not because I couldn't look at myself but because I could.

Why didn't I care?

I felt nothing for Birdie. Even when I thought of Will it was just with pity, really, the type I might feel for anyone visited by tragedy. If I had intense regret for my actions it was only because of how I felt right at this moment, for the sweat on my forehead and in my palms, for another rein around my neck that led back to Ian's hand. The more I searched for remorse the more it seemed nothing but a word, one that matched no genuine human experience, it was far too rhapsodic. *Remorse*, it didn't even make sense, it had no internal syntax, *to morse again*, you could pull off the pieces and there would be nothing left, there was no center. But I was curious, I looked it up on my computer: from the Latin *remordere—to bite back*, or *to bite again*.

The younger anole appeared in the corner closest to me, his front feet on one pane, his back feet on another. I imagined petting him with my thumb, the pressure and rhythm of his breathing against my skin, its steady tempo passing me composure. I stood up, maneuvered myself over the tank, and slid the top over, just a bit. I lowered my hand in, careful not to touch the glass, and held it there, a few inches above his body. He knew I was there, he must have, but he didn't move.

I dragged the back of my ring and middle fingers across his torso, it was a wonderful sensation but only in retrospect, the moment didn't last long enough for me to feel anything; suddenly he was clutching my thumb, scurrying up my hand and arm, stopping only when he came to the top of my shoulder, where I could see him, barely, out of the corner of my eye. Slowly I stood up straight, I was afraid to move more. How had I been so careless? Why didn't I think things through? I felt light, goosebumps rose out of my skin, I worried he would feel them through my shirt and run. In one steady motion I brought my other hand up and over him and snatched his tail. As I lifted him off me he writhed through the air. I thought he might squirm free and had to pinch him tightly until he was safely in the tank, at which point I closed the lid and held my hands on top of it. I didn't want to look inside, I felt in my fingers how hard I'd squeezed him, that I'd momentarily disregarded the fact he was another being in order to remedy my use of his body. When I finally sat back down, instead of peering through the glass, I fixated on my own reflection. I refocused, seeing with terrible clarity the mark of my own hand. Yes, his tail was crimped, the clean curve horribly interrupted, what pain he must have felt, and all because of my impulsiveness. I needed him to do something, confirm he was okay, again I tapped on the glass and immediately regretted it—why had I done that before? I'd made the elder feel he was about to be killed just so he would grace me with his presence. He must have believed I was some monster—and he was right, in his world I *was* a monster, when in fact I could have been a benevolent god, how easy would it have been to make their lives as good as possible? How had I not thought of this? Why did I refuse to acknowledge my privilege? Really, how long had I watched the ducks at the reservoir and not thought to help? It would have taken five minutes and fifty dollars to bring them a week's worth of world-class semolina. I had taken them for granted, all of them, all my life, their beauty and inspiration and entertainment and grace, I had thought it was some moral accomplishment not to *eat* them, not to *wear* them.

The younger's head twitched up, down, and up once more. Slowly the skin beneath his neck extended, it was about half-way open before it snapped back again. But then, with a bit more effort, it fanned out fully. It was of a lighter shade than the elder's dewlap, but still the hue was marvelous, nearly lurid, it *was* lurid; instinctively I knew that this was the first time it had happened: this was his sexual awakening, a premature leap into adulthood brought on by trauma. How had I compared it to an erection when it so clearly resembled the dropping of testicles? It even had the same pattern of dots found on a stretched scrotal sac.

For five seconds he kept it open, and when it closed he dipped his head down. But then, in a last juvenile flourish, he lifted his jaw as high as it would go, flaunting himself once more for all to see.

I couldn't believe I was going to leave them here all night.

———

I set the tank down on the bench beside the bay window in the dining room. It was starting to get dark, I hoped they understood they were looking outside, I'd given them as much nature as I could. The dining room walls occasionally thrummed, mechanical noises, the cooling system, I believe, it was why I'd planned to keep them in the family room, but Franny was in there, watching television, and I thought the dining room would be quieter. The anoles were quite sensitive to sound. At the office, when I'd finally forced the damaged tail out of my mind and begun to work, I'd noticed that they tensed as I typed. I'd switched back to my laptop's built-in keyboard, which wasn't as loud. I'd had a lot of typing to do, I was now willing to be even more specific with our results, including exact profits and a full risk analysis of the week's trades. This time I wrote without keeping Milosz's feedback in mind. I sent it to everyone, even those who had given us hard no's.

Left alone with his injury and the newfound ability to express his masculinity, the younger anole came quickly into adulthood. He only really showed his age during the ride back to the house. Whereas the elder went to the highest branch to see what the noise and shaking was about, the younger took cover; he was out of sight until I brought them into the house.

I went down to the family room, which was lit only by the TV. Franny was absorbed in a movie—something new starring Tom Hanks—her legs heavy on the ottoman, her hand resting on the remote. This wasn't *opposite of cheat day* behavior. I sat down on the couch next to her. The Hanks character was at a bank, failing to get a loan. He was demonstrating his defeat in every twitch of his face, in his coltish arms. I found it embarrassing, his performance, if he were really a man failing to get a loan he would be more self-aware, he would try to suppress his emotions, he would use his body to hide the ball of shame that lay at its center.

Can we turn it off? I asked.

She didn't hear me. I reached under her hand for the remote and paused it.

Oh, yeah, she said. She wiped her mouth with her palm. *On!* she yelled. I was too close, my shoulders lifted. The lights lit up. She looked at me and smiled, for a moment her expression seemed as exaggerated as Hanks's. Her cheeks were covered in makeup, her lips too red, her eyelids a false shade of pink.

What? she said, wiping her face again.

How was your day?

Fine? He hadn't called her. Obviously. She was squinting at me, I became aware of my own face. *Actually, Birdie made a bit of progress.*

Oh?

She seems to be responding to music. Not that the doctor would admit it, that she was reacting—probably because he was the one who said it wouldn't do anything, that she couldn't hear. Fuck him. I laughed, she didn't. *I read it everywhere, even comatose patients hear what's going on around them. They might even be able to feel things, too, that's why I put my phone on her stomach while it played, so she could feel the vibrations. We listened to Joni Mitchell,* Both Sides Now, *we used to play it all the time in college, we'd bonded over it, the fact that both our moms loved it. They told me I was playing it too loud, the nurse did. I could have sworn she let a smile creep in.* She cackled so suddenly I flinched. *Like, I fucking get it, okay? Possibly the saddest song in history being played to a woman with tubes keeping her alive.* Her face fell again. She picked up the remote and then tossed it away. *But show some compassion, for her or for me, I don't care. Maybe they've seen too much to have empathy, maybe it's a vocational hazard, but how hard is it to treat patients like humans? Well, I was right, when we came to the chorus she started moving, and in rhythm with the song. I immediately asked for the doctor, I demanded that he come so he could see it himself. And you know, when he did he just nodded, he said it was* interesting, *that's it. I asked if he was going to write it somewhere, like on her chart. He said he could if I wanted him to. As if I'm a child. Meanwhile, right in front of us, here's a woman who has shown barely any signs of life, and she's, well, her arms kind of—* She started to mimic Birdie, lifting her limp wrists and moving them up and down. I grabbed the cushion beside my leg, bracing myself; the last time she'd done an impression of Birdie the echoes began. But it had no effect on me now, it seemed so far from reality, cartoonish even.

She calmed herself, she reset. She told me about Birdie's medications, the nurses, the screaming man next door, and Will. While Franny was there he continually fielded calls from clients; he was a psychotherapist of some prestige, at least that was what Franny had gathered from Birdie, long ago. These calls mostly consisted of him putting on a soft, compassionate voice and repeating the same line, nearly verbatim: *Things are still scary here, but I hope to be back in due course. And trust that we'll pick up right where we left off.* It bothered her, this easy, transactional sympathy, especially given the fact he showed no real emotion in the face of a catastrophe in his own life. She reminded herself that people grieved in different ways—and, it had to be said, he and Birdie were all but divorced. (She used this opportunity to tell me that he'd cheated on Birdie, and not just a few times. This was another obstacle to her taking him in good faith.) She hated to wonder what would happen if Birdie were here for weeks—months, even. If he went back to London she would be here all alone, except for Franny and a few other every-now-and-again friends. (She had no close, immediate family; her parents were dead and her brother estranged.) Yes, they were, legally, husband and wife.

And yes, he was the person in the world who knew her best. But the two must have, up until a few days ago, despised each other. That was what divorce did, especially when you were relatively young and there were no kids involved. *Tastes like divorce*, that was what Birdie had said about my drink. What she'd meant was that it was bitter but relieving.

And how is the destruction of modern finance? she asked, desperate now to change the subject.

Tricky. Our whale is threatening to back out.

That's odd. Does he know what you've been capable of?

I believe so. It's just that he wants too much.

Tomorrow's another day, she said, standing. *But tonight is tonight. The food should be ready now.*

Oh, great. But you know, I think I'll—

It's vegan, Herschel, she said, and then adjusted her tone. *No, I'm happy you're trying this. And I should have been more thoughtful this morning, too.*

It's fine, I said. *Really.*

As I followed her up the stairs and into the kitchen she told me about her day. Visiting Birdie and preparing dinner were just the bookends, in between she had finished a scale model of her newest chair, finalized a prototype with her mill, and even begun sketching out something new. If talking about the doctor and Will had rankled her, she found calm again in revisiting the day's progress, its unexpected flashes of inspiration. In fact, compared to all her undertakings involving Birdie, her job now seemed, if anything, a diversion.

We plated the food—vegan mac and cheese, charred broccolini, roasted cauliflower with ramps and raisins—poured ourselves wine, and put on music. Just as we were about to enter the dining room, when she pointed out that *we've been living with those German fucks' design choices for exactly three months now*, it occurred to me that I hadn't mentioned the anoles.

There are lizards there, I said, a moment before she'd have come to the same conclusion.

She stopped in the doorway. *There are*, she said, not looking back at me.

We continued setting the table. We sat, we tried the food and the wine.

Is the dining room their permanent home?

Well, I'd bought them for the office.

But they're here now.

A fly buzzed past my face. *I didn't want to leave them alone*, I said, swatting it away.

She nodded. *Does this have to do with you being vegan?* Again this obsession with motive, rationale. Yet if I told her I wanted to keep kosher, would she not readily accept it? She never questioned my parents' adherence to *kashrut*, in fact she took pains to prepare strictly kosher meals whenever we had them over; we even had a second set of plates. But that was okay because, what—it was their faith? So it didn't matter that Jewish law was arbitrary, outdated, and bizarre, so long as it had an explanation you could put into words: God said so.

It would appear that way.

You said you wouldn't want a dog. Even with kids. But now we have lizards.

Well, I don't want dogs. They're a lot of work, as I said. And they're too emotionally taxing. You're always letting them down, telling them what not to do. Anoles are different, they're self-sufficient. I glanced up at her, she was peering at the tank. *I plan to get more, so they feel like they're in a real social environment.*

More lizards?

Something beyond her shoulder caught my eye: a piece of fabric featuring every conceivable color, resting on a chair in the living room. It was garish, jarring, vaguely familiar. Birdie's shawl. It must have dropped off her before she left—but why was it up here, in the middle of our home?

Anoles, yes.

In that tank?

A bigger one.

And will this new tank be in our dining room or at work?

I looked over at the tank. From this angle it blocked the bottom half of our Matisse cut-out print, which she loved. When we moved in, I'd wanted to hang my Simon & Garfunkel poster there, but she had, not so subtly, suggested I put it in my home office.

I'd like to set up two tanks, and then get some sort of smaller device to transport them.

She put down her fork and knife. *I want you to be happy. And I will always support you. If this all makes you happy, being vegan, and the lizards, then of course I have no problem with it. But I think at this point I deserve an explanation.*

I nodded, but this was a lie, already I was lying just with the movement of my head. *I don't have a reason. I can't offer you an explanation. I stopped eating animals because the thought repulses me. And I bought the anoles because I find them inspiring and I feel a connection to them.*

But just a few days ago you didn't think eating meat was wrong. And you've never wanted pets, not dogs, not cats, not lizards.

Sure, and thirty years ago I thought girls were gross. I regretted the regression to humor, it was an excuse not to be forthright.

I've changed, sure. I'm changing. That happens. I've realized that something I believed was wrong. People are allowed to vacillate.

She looked confused. Vacillate *means go back and forth.*

Did it? How many times had I used that word in my life? How many of my words were wrong, defective, misrepresentations of who I was and what I felt? And what if it wasn't just nouns and verbs but prepositions and whatever else, the connective tissue, without which we would only have loose parts, could only hand one another a bag of bones?

Okay, I said. *That's the opposite of what I meant. What I meant was that this isn't some* thing *I'm trying out. It's not some* cause. *It's physical, actually. It's permanent.*

She nodded, she repeated the last word. It was the one she'd used so many times to describe her ideal home. *I feel like you're about to tell me that you've seen the light, that you've been born again.*

Another fly darted by. Where were they coming from? We kept the windows closed, we had screens on everything, we threw out expired fruit. Was it just the warm weather—would they be with us through summer?

Right, I said. *So you think I'm some kind of cliché. Well, I'm sorry if I can't express how I feel in novel, new language. In fact I don't care to express myself at all, you're the one who demands a reason for everything, you ask me to show my math on basic moral decisions like not eating other living beings. Can you explain why you can't kick a cat but you can kill a goat in front of its kids? Can you explain why you don't eat horse? Or just tell me why you wouldn't eat a human. Explain that.*

Fucking Christ, she said. *Can we just eat?*

No, I couldn't. I'd lost all appetite, I could hardly look at my food, the plates used to serve countless meals of cows and pigs and chickens. But she had no problem eating. No, and to see her lift the food to her mouth—it disgusted me, the chomping and disintegrating performed with such practiced grace, the pink tongue and gums and white teeth, this obsession with the whiteness of teeth, the purity of our mouths, the need to be free of evidence that food passed through us, we were like deranged soldiers who frantically cleaned their guns each night, who made them shine and cherished the luster.

I think we should reconsider whether we're ready, I said. *For children, I mean.*

She made a quick, guttural noise. Her eyes blurred, she went elsewhere. She set her fork down but held her knife. With her free hand she picked up her plate, raising it slowly, and then slammed it down onto the table, the ceramic suddenly everywhere, in every corner of the room. The noise was surprisingly simple, a clean break, not like the screeching of her chair, which rattled the glasses on the shelves as she backed away from the table. I listened to her climb the stairs, slam the bedroom door. I turned to the window, to the anoles; from where I sat the tank appeared empty. I looked back at her chair, far from the table and turned to the side. It struck me that in her absence I did not love her more, as was usually the case after a fight. I had hate for her. Yes, *hate* was actually a good word, it served its purpose—not like *love*, which did too much: without the word I might not know the thing itself.

I stood up, brought my dishes to the sink, and washed them. I went up to my office and signed in to my computer. I wrote a brief email to Magda, thanking her for everything, and terminated our relationship. Philip had sent me a message, links to the videos that had turned him vegetarian. I clicked on one, I couldn't watch more than five seconds of it, I wondered what person could. To wash away those images I selected one of the suggested videos on the sidebar. It featured two storks celebrating after laying an egg, performing a choreographed dance they must have practiced or witnessed before, or maybe it was always there, dormant inside them. I clicked on another suggested video, I watched rats laughing, and then I watched one of squirrels planting trees, I watched chimpanzees trading bananas and seahorses giving birth, and snails sleeping for years at a time, and elephants jumping, frogs vomiting, bats waking up, cows ruminating, prairie dogs kissing, pigs nursing, octopuses trying new food, dolphins speaking, sloths digesting, otters swimming, the facial expressions of horses, the loneliness of crocodiles. I watched two minutes of an interview with a writer named David Abram called "Language and the Perception of Nature," and then I downloaded the audio version of his most popular book, *The Spell of the Sensuous*. I started listening to it and then clicked on the trailer for a movie called *Gunda*. I bought the movie, which was without a voiceover or any words at all, and so I was able to watch it while listening to the book. It was in black and white, long scenes of a mother pig and her newborns, and a few other farm animals. We saw the piglets suckling, walking through nature, growing up; after about an hour they were adolescents and then they were loaded into a truck and then we saw only the sow, bereft, searching, attempting to understand what could not be understood, that her children were gone and would never return, her udder now a heavy reminder of their absence, and all of the previous scenes depicting her indifference as they grabbed at her, fought over her nipples, were suddenly recast as memories of hers—memories that would fade, were already fading.

When the credits came I felt my chest expand and contract, I was close to hyperventilating, I wished I could cry and get it over with but I knew I wouldn't. I switched to my noise-canceling headphones and went downstairs, through the now completely dark house, to the kitchen, where I laid out garbage bags and put in all the meat and fish, all the cheese and eggs and milk. I did the same with the pantry, and then the backup freezer we kept in the basement. I took the bags outside, three in all, and stuffed them in the trash.

I grabbed a seltzer from the fridge and went back upstairs. By this point, Abram was discussing the ways in which humans have integrated with the natural world: how our senses were originally developed to abet a reciprocal relationship with the earth, but are now spent on mastering it. As he spoke of the magic of plants and animals, wind and soil—"we find ourselves in an expressive, gesturing landscape, in a world that *speaks*"—I began to feel trapped in my office, the lacquered oak and pulped wood, the bulb shining through the frosted globe, the computer screen soaking me in blue. With my attention freed up I put the book on 1.5x speed, and then went downstairs again, this time to the dining room, and the anoles. As I entered I stepped on a ceramic shard. I bent down to pick it up and held it in front of my face. It reminded me of something, the rectangular shape, the way it reflected light: Birdie's glass as she'd shaken it at me, asking for another drink. I put the shard in the tank and lay down on the floor beside it.

I had more concentration than I knew myself capable of. In fact, the more the night progressed the less tired I became.

The feeling was familiar, it was like the withdrawal I felt after I used a sleep aid too frequently. And yes, I'd done just that, but this was more, I couldn't stand to stop listening, Abram's sentences were mesmerizing, the writing spectacular, it was whimsical but fully committed to truth. He at once justified my new mistrust of language and made me see those feelings as unformed, a hunk of metal that could, with enough thought, be hammered and tamped down into a tool that could actually *do* something.

He painted a clear arc leading from the beginning of man to today. His history was not one of tides, or shifts in power, it was not decided by individuals or even armies, it was a tale of relentless human progression and our resulting departure from nature. He spoke about how words had once bound us to the land, how we borrowed from it sounds and expressions. Then we wrote them down, at first as symbols that mirrored the natural world, but soon the Hebrews, my own people, devised letters as loops and lines that referenced only themselves. But the Hebrews retained reverence for a higher power, the spirit, the wind of the soul, and so omitted breath, vowels, from their writing. The Greeks pushed us further still, adding symbols for the air between the consonants, giving us the power we once reserved for God or for nature.

At around five a.m. the book ended. I was surprised, the story clearly wasn't over. I checked the publication date: 1996; this seemed its only flaw. Since then we had only further adulterated language, irreparably so, we had discovered how to extricate information even from words, we could build systems and tools without the flamboyance of serifs and glottal stops, the grammar of today and tomorrow had nothing to do with the way the human mouth moved, it cared only for the most efficient way to transmit information from one machine to another—that was, after all, how value was created.

Language had always helped us extract value from nature, but over time it had completely severed itself from it, ceasing to echo what had once been its inspiration. And now, just over the horizon, was a world where we too would be a part of nature language did not need. And it would be the old story told anew: language becomes detached from something, and thus is free, finally, to eat that thing alive.

I only noticed the morning's first light because the anoles did. They scampered awake and then settled in their usual territories: the elder on top of his branch, the younger in his corner. I fed them, watching as they caught the crickets, and then as they maneuvered the meal down into their bodies. Staring at the gut of the elder, seeing his breathing rate settle, I had an odd feeling, a sensation I couldn't quite grasp. It wasn't until I thought of yesterday, how I'd held the younger by his tail, and imagined the scene from his point of view that I found it, something so simple and obvious and yet it had never occurred to me before. Even if the anoles saw themselves reflected in a window, or in water, or in an actual mirror, they would never know what they looked like, really. They could never see themselves as a predator could. Their own being, so small, so fathomable, would forever be their blind spot.

I awoke to the sound of the espresso machine. I was still in the dining room, on the floor, the end of the rug curled into a pillow. I was relieved, somehow, to see that the shattered plate still hadn't been cleared, that Franny hadn't been in the room while I was asleep. I stood up. The sun blinded me, it flooded the room. In the harsh light I remembered myself, who exactly I was, the day awaiting me. However mundane my morning routine had always seemed, it was now imbued with the significance of a last lap. Perhaps this wouldn't be my final day at Atra Arca, but it would be the last time my coming to work had a purpose. Yes, today we would decide to shut down operations, we had to. If this happened to be a good, prudent, lawful business decision, well, that was useful insofar as I wouldn't be the only one making the decision. Milosz, the board—I appreciated that they didn't know what I knew. They didn't feel what I felt. Even the thought of the office, the servers alone in that room, the algorithm silently shifting the market—it was, all of it, repulsive.

When I walked into the kitchen she made sure to turn her back to me. I went up to my office, took out my toolkit, and measured the dimensions of the free space against the back wall. This was where I had, until now, planned to put a bookshelf. I signed in to my computer, still on the screen was *Gunda*. I went to PetSmart's website and searched for tanks, I added two 120-gallon aquariums to my cart, as well as bedding, hiding spots, plants, branches, high-quality crickets, and a vitamin supplement to dust the crickets with. I found transport bags for my exact purpose, I added one and checked out with express, same-day delivery.

I took a shower. The water pressure was fine again, I could wait to call the plumber. I dried off, shaved, combed my hair, and got dressed. I ordered a car and brought the anole tank down to the foyer. In the kitchen I grabbed an orange as well as the *Financial Times*. I had no desire to speak with Franny or kiss her goodbye but felt I should, it was an essential part of my morning ritual. I walked up behind her, when I put my hand on her side she swatted it away. She shook her head, she was upset with me and needed to communicate it, but still I knew that she wanted affection, she wanted to know that we were, foundationally, okay. I stepped forward, my chest against her back, I let her lean into me, we stayed like this long enough for the familiar feeling to return. Such extended close contact always made me feel that we were, for a moment, one person, that anything one of us felt would soon drift into the other. But today the feeling was muted, I couldn't forget myself, forget that I was in my own, distinct body. After all, there was something in me that could not pass between us, that would not even survive in her. She had rejected my arguments about meat, how could she accept a belief much greater, one I myself couldn't even explain, one I knew not through words, not even through thought; it was, by this point, faith. I kissed her neck, and then I left her.

I brought the tank outside and saw Lucy across the street, tied to her stoop railing. My presence ignited her; she began barking nonstop. It wasn't until I walked down the steps that I realized what was going on: the meat and dairy had been there, in our trash, for hours. I didn't want to look her in the eyes, she was being tortured and I alone could fix it. The car should have been here already, I set down the tank and took out my phone but this seemed to make her bark all the more, so I put it away and unfolded the paper, the salmon-pink sheet I'd always thought of as a quirk but now I wondered, for the first time, how they made it that color. I glanced at the door, our new walnut door, and then back at the paper, I looked the cover up and down, I was holding my breath, nervous for something I hadn't yet become conscious of: besides the title, which I knew to be *Financial Times*, I couldn't make sense of any of the text, it was as if I had absolute dyslexia, I could stare at individual letters and see a *b*, a *G*, but the spaces between words were elusive, the ordering of letters arbitrary, they changed every time I blinked or refocused. This was confusing, it was funny, a laugh choked my throat, it shook my chest and tensed my stomach. Lucy could tell, she stopped barking, but when I lowered the paper to check for the car she started again. I briefly despised her for her rashness, her stupidity, and then regretted it; she was only desperate, she was being tormented. I folded the paper and went over to the trash. I lifted the top from a can and flies dispersed. The thought of reaching my hand in, fishing out a steak—I couldn't. I looked up to the windows of Ben's apartment and then back at Lucy, her eyes; that was enough. As I walked across the street she knew to be quiet—no, she wasn't stupid. Her collar was complicated, the blue nylon was both frayed and slippery, I had no idea how it worked, but why was I concerning myself with this end? The other was tied to the gate in a simple knot, I unraveled it in seconds. Lucy darted forward but I held the leash, the tug pulling even my heart. She turned around and stared at me, pleading. *Hey!* Her mouth hadn't moved, no, the sound came from the back of my head. *Hey!* I turned around and saw Ben bounding down the stoop. *What are you doing?*

I was just letting her— I put out some meat last night. One of the bags has frozen steak in it, I'm sure it's good.

Okay, well just, like, don't untie someone else's dog.

I know that, I said. *I would have asked, but you weren't here.*

He was baffled, he was trying to show me that my actions

baffled him, his face said: *This doesn't make any sense.* He walked over to me, grabbed the leash from my hand and then tied it back around the gate.

He wasn't going to let her have the meat? Because I tried to help her myself?

You're free to take her there on your own, I said. *It's good stuff and it will just go to waste.*

She's well fed.

I looked at Lucy but she didn't notice my gaze, she was still staring at the trash cans. Ben and I made eye contact; his eyes flicked away but then came back to me.

It's hard to see her like that, I said. *She's desperate.* Again he squinted at me, performing his worry. *I'm about to leave for work, once I do you can feel free—*

What's the problem here? A new voice, from across the street. I turned to see Philip trotting over, waving at us. As he got closer I saw that his face mirrored Ben's, even though he had no idea what was going on, what there even was to be disturbed by. His hands found his hips, his chin lifted. God, he wanted to arbitrate.

He tried to untie my dog, Ben said. *And now he's trying to tell me I have to feed her his trash.*

Philip placed his hand on my shoulder and looked at me. *I'm sure it's just a misunderstanding.*

Ben started to speak but stopped. His face refreshed, he was no longer confused. *Philip Guggenheim? I had no idea you lived around here. I have to say, we loved* The Phoenicians.

Oh, thanks, he said, looking down.

You know, Ben said, *it was just— It's this superlative display of realism, nested in a sort of*—he twisted his hands like he was solving a Rubik's Cube—*almost magical conceit. And it was effective, too. I swear, for days I couldn't eat meat.*

Why did everyone say that? Like it was some accomplishment to change people's minds for a week. I lifted my shoulder so Philip would remove his hand.

But you eat meat now? I asked Ben. *You eat animals as intelligent as Lucy?*

Philip looked at Ben's nonresponse and then said, *Awareness can be action in itself.*

It can be whatever you say it is, but still it doesn't do anything. Do you think the Uighurs are grateful for our awareness? Or the victims of the Holocaust? I'm not sure they appreciated the rest of the world looking on, aware. No, I don't think awareness is action, I think that's just something you can tell yourself to pretend art is powerful, to make our obsession with entertainment seem noble. I paused, my instinct was to gather myself, but I was already gathered, I knew that what I was saying was true just as I knew how it was being taken. *Real art should change people, for good. A clever exploration of vegetarianism is not art, we'd do better to put out more of the pornography you sent over yesterday.*

Philip looked to Ben, *I sent him some videos from PETA,* and then back to me. *I think what you're saying is that art has to be political. But it can be more, it can be human.*

I agree completely, I said. *What's more human than creating more and more bullshit without thinking about the consequences?*

Got it, Ben said. *This has been stimulating, but I'm going to—*

I know how I sound, I said. *I'm passionate, but that's only because I know change is possible. If you let yourself believe in something it will change you, it will make you want to change the world.*

My car was here. It had been for some time. I looked at

Lucy, conveying my sympathy, and then at Ben and Philip, each in the eyes, I wanted them to know that if I was zealous I was still sane, that my words were worth considering. I went back to my stoop to get the anole tank and brought it into the car. I looked ahead, I didn't want to see them now, I knew they'd be trading eyes, drenched in defensiveness, focusing on my display of emotion to avoid thinking about the contradictions baked into their arbitrary morals. How could I have expected otherwise? Denial was comfortable, ignorance a luxury I no longer had. No, I'd seen into the future. I'd even helped build it.

———

The server room was cooler in the morning. I didn't even feel warm air wafting out. The machines were just getting started, waking up from the night. Like the sea lions at the zoo they were bound to our workday, except we believed that processing our data was their God-given purpose, that they owed us their lives. Even the name, *servers*, made it easy to ignore what was now nearly inevitable. It was a failure of our own imagination, sci-fi gave us images of metallic humanoids that slashed our throats and fucked our spouses and turned off the life support of astronauts. But the future we risked wouldn't make for a movie poster. There would be no explosions, no screams for help, in fact we wouldn't scream at all. Like dogs and pigs, trees and streams, our speech would be reduced to sound, noise in a world of information.

I know, it's a mess. Milosz. How long had he been there? *I didn't mean to scare you.*

It's okay, I said. I turned and saw Simo, too.

Can we talk? Milosz asked. *In private?*

Right, I said. *Sure.* We went down the hall and into my office. Once we sat down, Milosz looked at Simo and held out his palm, inviting him to speak.

So, Simo said, mostly to Milosz. *Last night I was approached, just outside the office. I'm sure you know who I'm talking about.*

I'm sure I do, I said.

Well, he asked me to dinner.

Why did he say it like that? *You went?*

I did, yes, but only because I thought it could be useful to us. And I believe it was. I played along with him, I pretended to be interested. He made me an offer to start something new, together I mean, he said he'd buy me out of my contract. He talked and talked, he went on forever about his ideas, which are pretty much our ideas, which he apparently knows in great depth.

Great depth.

*I was also surprised. I thought he was like you, a businessman. But he has a much deeper understanding. The way he talked, and even the terms he used—*he looked at Milosz—*well, they were very similar to the terms we use here. Eventually I asked, in so many words, how he knew what he knew. He told me that I wasn't the first person here he spoke to. He referred to* a source, *that was the word he used. He said he had* a source *inside the company.*

So it was. All this goddamn hand-wringing over VPNs and lockers for our phones and it probably took, what—a hundred thousand? Less? Maybe nothing, I doubted Ian had money to throw around, and I supposed his excuse for charm could have won over one of our junior traders. Tim, if I had to guess; his ego was an unlikely size, given that his last job had been doing municipal bonds at some family office.

Okay, I said, looking at Milosz. *So our work is compromised—*

all of it, probably. At this point I have no choice but to tell investors what's going on, and to be honest I can't imagine they'll—

Herschel, Milosz said, *why don't we have this conversation—*

If I were an investor of ours, I said, my voice raised just enough, leaving plenty of room more, *and I knew what we know now, I would demand my money back. In fact I think we have a fiduciary—*

Okay, please, Milosz said. *Let's keep our heads.*

I exhaled. I gathered myself. I was starting to feel like I'd only gotten two hours of sleep. *Perhaps instead of building a fortress around ourselves we should have paid more attention to the people walking out the door every day.* I stood up. *But it's too late. No, Simo, you shouldn't have gone to dinner with him. It'll be a great anecdote to drop while he's poaching our investors, he won't say he bribed some junior researcher but that he worked directly with the VP. Yes, I know the NDAs are a formality, but—*I raised my voice higher—*fucking read the thing. You violated it by going out with him. You both have created so many fucking breaches of trust and contract we hardly have a business anymore. This isn't a fucking math department, this isn't a thought experiment, we're creating something in the real world. We were. No, given what we know now, given everything—*I glared at Milosz—*I don't see any other option but to wind things down.*

What are you saying? Milosz's voice now matched mine. *You don't say "It's time to wind things down" like there's some switch only you have access to. In fact you control seventeen percent.* He glanced at Simo, he wished we were alone but couldn't stop now. *We've talked about this. If there are small legal hurdles they're in the future, okay. There's a leak, okay, but think. Why would Ian stalk our building unless he was desperate, he doesn't have anything but stocks and prices, maybe some strategy. Just—I need until the end of the day. No, lunch. I'll get the team together, we both will, me and you, the problem will be resolved.* He stood up. I always forgot he was taller than me. *We've gone too far for this.*

There was nothing I could say, in fact it was best I said nothing at all. I reminded myself I wanted him to find the leak, I wanted the problem to be resolved.

Let's do it off-premises, I said. *I wouldn't trust a single inch of this place.*

Sure, Milosz said. He paused, looking down at my desk. He reached over it, took my phone and put it in his pocket. He looked at Simo, who stood too, and without another word they left. Well, I thought they did. After a moment I realized Simo was still there, staring at my bookshelf. He picked up a book, Piketty, and examined it.

It's trash, I said, but he didn't seem to hear. For a few seconds he just stood there. And then he put the book back, closed the door, and retook his seat.

I smiled at him. I waited for him to say what he needed but he only stared at the anoles.

Don't worry about the NDA, I said. *I'll forget it happened.*

He pushed the air out of his throat. Had I ever seen him without his sense of irony?

You look tired, he said.

It's been a week.

I'm sorry, he said. *About the money.* I nodded, I pretended to know what he was talking about. *Milosz said you had to make some sacrifices.*

His up-front cash, right. *You deserve it*, I said. *We wouldn't have said yes if you didn't.*

He nodded, he lowered his brow. *So I didn't tell Milosz everything. Actually, I first spoke to Ian yesterday morning.* He looked at me, gauging my reaction. *He called me. He made it clear how much he knew, the stocks we'd targeted, the prices. And he told me it was illegal, that he was ready to go to some guy in the Southern District. Polk, he said, an old friend. Not that I didn't already have an idea about, you know, what was happening. I just didn't think that much about it, it's really not my domain. But it became so obvious then, how short-lived this would be.*

So you wanted your money now.

It's a lot, I know. It's even more in dinars. It was a thud, the phrase, he'd practiced it too many times. I trusted that he believed what he was about to say, but still I couldn't hear the words as anything but tools of persuasion. *It's enough to change my parents' lives. To let them go somewhere else if they want. Really it's giving them the chance they gave me. You know, it's a miracle I'm here. My younger brother is twice as smart, but I was the one my parents sent to university. They can't believe I have three laptops, that I eat dinner out most nights. Sometimes it feels like I'm living in the future, but then I remember it's just that they're stuck in the past.*

It sounds like you had reason enough to do what you did.

Even so, the money came from somewhere.

Yes, the algorithm you built. I looked at the tank. Both anoles were now on the top branch. Still he was staring at me. *Simo, you're forgiven.* I tapped lightly on the glass but neither moved. They were remarkably motionless aside from their breathing, which was as rapid as I'd seen. I leaned back in my chair. *You made a good decision. A savvy one. No, we can't continue what we're doing. It's not right, and it's illegal.* I looked up at him, his arms were now folded. *But look on the bright side. This whole thing probably would have made a couple of people unreasonably wealthy while putting a lot of great thinkers out of work. Today you're an accomplished quant, tomorrow you're as good as cavalry in the nuclear age.*

Well, tell that to Milosz.

Try telling anything to Milosz.

He laughed; we both did.

But really, I said, *the metaphor holds. Oppenheimer didn't let the idea of a massacre stop him. Would he have let the SEC?* Now only he laughed. *To Milosz this is all just an idea. He can't see the reality of things. He's not the one who's going to have to call our investors, who's going to have to wring every last cent out of the business.*

Simo raised his eyebrows at me, and then he—what? Smiled?

What?

Well, you tell me. No, I had no idea, I expressed as much. *Just now, when you were outside the server room, you were— I wondered if, you know. They're insured, aren't they?*

He held his smile, but now there was nothing behind it.

For a PhD you think a lot about money. You should start your own firm.

He chuckled, so much so his shoulders bounced, perhaps it was only relief.

What exactly did you think I had in mind?

His laugh was tight again. *Well,* he forced a new smile, trying to reclaim some of his irony. *I think we both know it's a mess in there. I told him to get a specialist in, the way they are now they could overheat.* He nodded to himself. *It's fathomable that they could overheat.*

I see. I looked back at the anoles. I put my arms over my head, grabbing one hand with the other. *Well, you can take the*

Piketty. Maybe you'll get more out of it than I did. He nodded, he didn't catch on that he should leave. *And I'll start wading through my inbox, which is practically quicksand.*

He nodded and stood, grabbing the book on his way out.

I looked at his now empty chair. What had he said? *Fathom-able.* Fathom, the measurement. I looked it up, six feet exactly, the height of a man, as if anything bigger were unfathomable.

I opened my desk drawer. There was the matchbook from The Dutch, from a dinner late last summer; it was Milosz and I, and Dominic, who had just agreed to loan us $2.2 million. He had wanted to discuss European soccer, for nearly an hour we pretended to care. We'd yet to return the sum, in a few months we'd owe him another $200,000. Whether we would be able to pay him back or not I didn't care, didn't really care, not beyond losing him as an investor for something new. You couldn't. He'd known the risks, they all did.

I struck a match, I waited for it to burn my fingers and then shook the fire away. The insurance money wasn't important, but it did do something, it helped convince a part of me that was, though no longer relevant, still present. A minority stake-holder. Such a corny thought, I still had my sense of humor, that was how you knew you were still yourself, still centered, despite how others made you feel.

I stood up, I walked out of my office. In the kitchen I found Milosz alone, at a table, eating something from a bowl. It was just how he looked when we first met. I made an espresso and took the seat across from him.

You'll need to talk to the team yourself, I said. *I've got too much work to do.* He knew this was bullshit, it didn't matter, he wasn't going to put up a fight. *I'll need my phone back, too.*

Without a word he got up and walked away. I followed

him to the lockers, waited as he put in the code. He handed me my phone and went back to the kitchen. I had three missed calls from Franny, and two texts: *Are you okay?* and then *Philip stopped by. He was worried about you.* I started to type but stopped, Milosz was making a speech: All researchers were to be ready to leave in five minutes, they would be back in the office by 10:30—forty-five minutes from now. I wrote Franny back: *I'm fine. No need to worry.* I walked down the hallway, past the servers, I didn't look inside but I did slow down, enough to feel that their warm exhales had resumed.

I went into my office and, standing in the center, took inventory. There was valuable equipment, hundreds of books, there were objects of sentimental value, photos of my family, of Franny and me, souvenirs from London and Venice, my father's baseball mitt, my grandfather's yarmulke, a football signed by Brett Favre. It was hard to think of it all together, but still that sum couldn't hold a candle to the $1.3 million I'd personally lent Atra Arca. Yes, the insurance policy could yield $1.5 million, but that would be used to pay off the rest of our lease, and then any outstanding invoices—hardware, software, Milosz's worthless security system—and if there was anything left it would go to our preferred lenders, and who exactly was *preferred* would be up to the lawyers; right, the lawyers needed paying, too. I wouldn't recoup a cent, no, I wasn't fucking over just lenders and investors but myself as well.

Herschel?

I turned around to find Peter waiting in my doorway. He told me someone from PetSmart was here, he said it like a question. I had him send them in, and a few minutes later a tall, thin man with a protruding Adam's apple rolled in a hand truck bearing two boxes, one of which was massive: the tank.

He then went out and returned with another hand truck—the other tank? I was about to say there'd been a mistake but realized I was the one who'd made it. Why hadn't I shipped one tank to the house? I heard Milosz and the researchers gathering their things. I told him to unpack only one of the tanks. He looked worried, he said he didn't know it was a tank, he couldn't move it himself. I said I would help, he said I couldn't, that he needed to call his coworker, they were waiting in the truck just around the corner. I checked the time, I told him to leave it, leave everything, I offered to buy the hand truck and then got out my wallet, which offended him, he didn't look at me as he repeated that he needed to call his coworker. I looked into my wallet, all I had was three twenties. When I held them out he paused, like he wasn't going to accept it, and when he did he averted his eyes, as if he didn't want to see me see his misconduct, as if I weren't complicit. He reached into his coat, pulled out an invoice and pen, and placed them on my desk. I leaned over the page, it was just lines and dots scattered at random, I took the pen to the middle, as soon as I started I forgot what letter I was on, I drew three loops in a row and handed the invoice back to him. He pushed it into his jacket and then, finally, left.

I went to PetSmart's website; again I couldn't read a thing. I pinged Peter and told him to come to my office. When he arrived I pretended to be on the phone and asked him to go to my computer, duplicate my last order—minus a tank—and send it to my home, same-day delivery. I walked around my office while he did this, nodding, looking concerned.

Once he left I opened my desk drawer and took out the matches and keys. Again I surveyed the room, but before I could think of losing this, losing that, I walked out to the hallway and pulled the fire alarm just outside my door. It was the sound I expected but still I was startled, it rang so loud I could hardly think, my shoulders rose high and my head dipped down. I forced my chin up, my arms down, and I walked out to the trading floor. Peter was standing, already calling 911, competent as usual. I told him to leave immediately, he nodded and hung up. Oren was walking to the door, I asked him where Gina and Tim were, our other traders, he said he didn't know. I watched as they exited into the stairwell, and then jogged back to the server room.

Inside and just above the door was the camera Milosz had installed. I didn't doubt that the footage would be kept on one of the very servers it monitored, but still I lit a match, reached my arm through the cage, and lifted the flame up to the lens. I counted to five, for good measure I lit another and held it under the belly of the camera. It started to smoke, white wisps that creeped up the device. It was so suddenly absurd, that something as simple as fire could ruin a device that had taken us hundreds of thousands of years to invent. I felt it then, the reality of what I was doing, that I was *doing*, taking action and not just passively existing in a world that continued to lose its soul. I put in the combination for the old padlock, opened it, and took out the keys. I found the one labeled 70 and unlocked the door, but when I pushed it just shook. At chest level was another lock, the new combination—my birthday, that permutation of it. I tried something but knew it wasn't right, I tried again three more times, it was impossible to think with the alarm blaring. I closed my eyes, I shook the cage, I let myself scream because no one would hear me. I calmed myself, really I pretended I was calm, and then failed twice more. I ran to my office and scanned the walls: behind my desk, on a shelf, was my Louisville Slugger. There was hardly enough room in the hallway to swing, but still the lock cracked on my second try. I picked it up, put it in my pocket, and went inside. Two steps in it was already warmer, the air thicker, I unbuttoned the top of my shirt as I found my way to the back of the room, there you couldn't even see the hallway over the towers. On the floor was a tangle of yellow and black cords, most leading into the column of servers it abutted. I lit a match, got down on my knees, and held it under the thickest wire I could find. Ten seconds passed and nothing happened, I stood up and tossed the match, there were only four left, I lit another and stuck it through a hole in the back of a server. I waited, I smelled something blunt, sour, I looked at the floor and saw a thin trail of smoke. As I bent down to get a better look the server above made a crinkling noise and then popped, and then again, louder, loud not like the alarm, which was basically a song, it had rhythm, this was chillingly spontaneous and almost too loud to hear, it entered my ears not as sound but as pain. It happened again, twice in a row, I might have fallen but caught myself on the wall. Already the smoke was crawling across the ceiling, and by the time I made it out into the hallway it was seeping out of the room. The pops came from all over now, the crinkling noise, too. The smoke was pouring upward, flowing into itself unnaturally fast, it was so dense and opaque it almost hid the fire at its center, which was such a light shade of yellow I worried it wasn't hot enough, I was about to step inside to light another match when a wave of heat slapped me on the forehead. As I covered my face I heard a hiss, it was soft but steady, I removed my hands from my eyes and found the room entirely aflame, light flaring from every corner, already the fire had jumped from box to box, through wires, it had found every piece of plastic that could be burned, it had only needed a spark, an iota of life. I let myself stand there for a few moments. And then another few. What I saw felt like an extension of myself, a seemingly small truth that had been given air enough to breathe, had showed itself to be greater and more dazzling than I'd ever believed.

I put back the padlock, picked up the bat, and ran to my office. The elder was on his branch, I removed the top from the tank and lifted the stick into the carrier bag, shaking him off. The younger was in the corner, I held my breath, grabbed him as gently as I could, and dropped him in, too. Against the zipper I felt the sweat on my fingers, already the room was warm. With the bag on my back I went out to the trading floor, I wanted to take one last look around but the sprinklers went off.

The street was full and getting fuller. People were coming to watch, filming the scene on their phones. If some of them were worried—crying, consoling each other—most were excited, they were intoxicated, no small part of them wanted to see the whole thing burnt to the ground. I scanned the crowd for the activists, I suspected no one would cheer destruction more than those who had defined themselves by opposition to institutions, but I couldn't find a single one. No, and come to think of it they hadn't been there that morning either, they'd already given up, they'd accepted failure, if that was even what it was, perhaps they'd already gotten what they came for: a sense of purpose, however fleeting. I saw Oren and Gina, I shook my head in disbelief and looked up at the building, watching as the smoke escaped from our floor. I heard sirens in the distance, and walked away, up Wooster.

If I felt a sense of accomplishment standing outside the server room, watching what I'd done, it had already dissipated. Thinking of it now only made me more energized, more inspired, more awake to the work that lay ahead. Yes, if I'd achieved anything it was to suppress a single outgrowth of something more systemic. Of course the problem wasn't Atra Arca, it was the strain of thought that gave it life, it was the collision of greed and ingenuity with our eternal myopia, our blind faith in progress. We now built things that exceeded even our imagination, by the time we understood the consequences it was far too late. Yes, I'd been given a rare glimpse into the future, a blip of horrible insight, and it was a gift I wouldn't waste.

I took out my phone and pulled up the website of the United States Attorney for the Southern District of New York. Ian wasn't bullshitting: David J. Polk. I called the number listed on the page but no one answered, it wasn't even a personalized voicemail, no, I'd reached some report line for the public. I left a message, detailing who I was, what Atra Arca was, where we'd gone wrong, where the law had: failing to foresee how machine learning-based algorithms could take intent out of the equation, absolve its creators, enable people to profit while freeing them from responsibility for their actions. I urged him to consider the integrity of the market, to look into this as soon as he could, it was only a matter of time before someone less principled built what we did. I hung up and then put my phone on silent.

By this point I was north of Houston, NYU territory, this was obvious from the number of children I saw. Maybe they were old enough to drink but they were children, they were innocent, unserious, they gave themselves to their phones.

And what a banal thought, how trite, we knew this already, young people loved their phones, we all did, even to say it out loud was silly, that was how bad it had become, it was an idea too big to comprehend yet too obvious even to state: we had forsaken the world in front of us for one we created. We were now a culture of narcissism—yes, of course, again this had been said with such frequency it was meant to be ignored—but we were more: we were a species of it. Each and every one of our greatest breakthroughs put just another mirror between us and nature. Language let us forget the sights and sounds of the world, the wheel let us transcend our bodies, artificial light let us control night and day, photography let us outsource and manipulate our memories, books and phones and the internet reduced distances to a point, denied Earth its immensity. And with every upgrade the human race wrought we saw more and more of ourselves, we saw less and less of the world we'd opted out of, we grew only in confidence, we became bold in our ignorance, we became deranged, obsessed not with who we were but who we weren't.

Did we always walk with our mouths open? These students, they were slack-jawed, literally, they'd been infantilized, debilitated by their own comfort, spoiled by safety, we all were, so few of us knew hardship, brutality, violence. No, of course we should be safe, we should never make war, but for thousands of years we'd been forged through nothing but, we were built for it, we had the imagination to make do with any set of constraints, but more and more we had no constraints, our imaginations were hammers without nails, and we grew anxious without nails, we became depressed, so we pretended to need what we didn't, we sought to acquire more and more, and when there was nothing left to acquire we sought just the *ability* to acquire, we yearned for money, value itself, the last resource whose finitude we respected. We created a zero-sum game, emphasis on *zero-sum*, emphasis on *game*, we were willing to take from others just to put our imaginations to work, we were willing to make a science out of profit. It was the final frontier, value, the last opening to reality that our own contrivance would soon close for good.

God, it was great to be outside, the breeze on my face, the wind in my ears. It was this block, it created a wind tunnel, you never got this much breeze in Manhattan. I stopped the next person I saw and asked him what street we were on. *Mercer*, he said, which seemed funny, like *one who gives mercy*. I said the thought out loud so he wouldn't think it was him I found funny, as he looked unique, like someone who wouldn't use traditional pronouns. Franny's cousin was like that. They always struck me as slightly from the future, they were, people like them helped us imagine an undoing of the lies inherent in language, revealed it as a sclerotic system that would always lag behind current modes of thought by, at best, decades. I was white, heterosexual, and wealthy. But really I was Jewish, I wouldn't have been considered white a hundred years ago. Though I'd never slept with or kissed a man, I did notice male beauty. And weren't we all rich compared to someone else? This was just the sorites paradox: take a grain of sand and add another, and another—when exactly does it become a heap?

Soon I came to Union Square. The sun was now high in the sky, it was hotter than it had been all year and everyone had prepared, wearing their best new summer outfits. It seemed that cinnamon brown was in for women, and pants were higher waisted for everyone. As I passed a home goods store

I glanced at my reflection, I took in my slacks and button-down, the shirt folded up around my forearms, the way the wind lifted tufts of my curly hair. It wasn't a solid image but it served its purpose, the person I saw then would play me in my memories, when I thought of my interaction with that nonbinary soul he was there, transparent like the rest of the scene. As I walked up Broadway I saw him with his hands in his pockets, the bag hanging from his shoulder. I saw him as others did, as a black box, and then I looked inside, I saw his thoughts, how lost humanity seemed to him, how misguided, how our delusions had wrought havoc on other species, on the planet, on our own destiny. I liked seeing me as a *he*, it gave me a new perspective, one that was a bit elevated and set at a distance. It gave me something else, too, something that I couldn't quite put a finger on but that carried with it relief, it was the sort of calm that comes prior to the administration of general anesthetic.

He lived the day in reverse: walking uptown, setting fire to the servers, the PetSmart delivery, talking with Simo, and then with Milosz there too, getting to work, that awful conversation with Ben and Philip, waking up after just a couple hours of sleep. In each scene he imagined everything he could, he scraped his memory for every last detail. By the time he was done he was at Fiftieth Street. He was surrounded by sky-scrapers now, the phrase *concrete jungle* came to mind, carrying with it a sense of irony. All his life he had leaned on irony, a defense mechanism meant to preempt embarrassment or humiliation, but it had an upside, he could see that now: it forced him to be his own cynic. Yes, and that was exactly what he needed here—a counterargument to all of this, something to make the case for humanity, for progress, he squinted and thought of the neighborhood. Not two blocks away was the Museum of Modern Art.

It was lunchtime on a Friday but the lobby was packed. He went over to the membership table and gave the woman his card; he and Franny were members though they hadn't visited since last summer. In the elevator was an old woman, she clutched her purse like he might try to steal it. She got off at the fifth floor, he waited and then got off, too. He walked into a nearly empty room, there was a young Asian couple, a man his age. To his left was a work—Hopper, he was sure—depicting a man at a gas station. He couldn't see what the man was doing, but he was alone, that was the message, *This man is alone.* Hopper was always pointing out the alienation of the modern world, but really he was consecrating it, his paintings excused solitude, for him it was natural to feel apart from society. He was craven, a coward whose work only calcified the status quo.

He came to a column of disconnected teal metal prisms set against a wall. The placard was a brief jumble of letters. He breathed in and held it, he looked away and then, quickly, back at the placard, he did this again and again; he could read it without reading. Donald Judd. And of course it was *Untitled*, an irony given works like this required so many words by so many critics just to mean anything at all, and still all that writing summed up to nothing. He was ready to leave, he turned to the exit but something caught his eye, the bottom left corner of an otherwise unremarkable canvas, he saw half a tomato painted in such a way that it didn't look like a tomato so much as it represented how we conceive of tomatoes, it admitted the falseness of our own perception. His arms filled with goosebumps, he walked up to it, again the trick with the quick glances. *The Carbide Lamp* by Joan Miró. He took a picture with his phone, he turned away and looked back, he felt a flash of joy. With this new energy he walked deeper into the galleries, to a new room, where he saw, on a wall by itself, a painting much larger than he was. It featured a giant red horse, a few other horses, at the periphery were men working, carried away by the momentum of the central stallion, with wisps of white and streams of light implying many moments at once; there was too much action for a single frame. He recognized the artist, not by name but he knew the movement, he and Franny had seen an exhibit on Italian Futurism when they'd just started dating. Ever since, when the topic of modernism would come up in conversation, he would dutifully note that he liked most of all the Italian Futurists, he would parrot the curator's words he'd read years ago, that the Futurists *celebrated transformation and glorified revolt*, they *sought to revitalize a decaying culture*. But now he felt, if not those thoughts exactly, then at least the presence of some wild truth—a truth not constructed by well-articulated arguments but one that could exist without words. What he saw was a cry for the natural, and not some Thoreau bullshit, which was just a lament for the past, but a way to live in the future, to wield conflict, to actively work against the order crystallizing around us. In front of him was art that said no thought mattered unless it led to action. It was true, of course it was, this was a philosophy so obvious even children knew it, intuitively. He touched his arm expecting goosebumps again but the skin was flat. No, the idea wasn't new to him, he'd felt it just an hour ago, as he stood outside the server room, watching his flames engulf something that was never meant to be. He took a photo of the work, and then the placard. *The City Rises*, Umberto Boccioni.

Retracing his steps he found the elevators. He called a car, and by the time he made it downstairs and through the lobby it was waiting for him, a black SUV that smelled of upholstery and cheap fragrance. Franny never used perfume, which even the old him had appreciated. He lowered the windows and asked the driver to turn the music down.

She was a good starting point, Franny, there was no better option, she trusted him and he her. She would listen to him, help him hone his ideas, she'd even play a firm devil's advocate. He took out his phone, he had four missed calls from Milosz. He thought to call her but worried he'd have to start the conversation right then, instead he sent her a text with the help of Siri: *Are you working from home?*

But she was more than someone he trusted. She was the love of his life. It had been a rough week, she'd yet to become acclimated to who he'd become, but yes, he loved her, of course he did. If anything it was the old him that had taken their love for granted, had defined it, had defaulted to a too-easy composite of other concepts: fondness, attraction, mutual respect and admiration. He had defined her, too; she was intelligent, empathetic, playful, stimulating—adjectives that could be written down and applied to millions of other people, they were senseless, literally, they distracted him from all of what he felt in her presence but could never describe, not without deforming it, reducing it, making it into something it wasn't.

This was a new beginning. From now on they would submit themselves to that other love, the one even animals feel. That weekend they would not utter a word to each other, they would only be present, understand each other through intuition. And then, after two days of silence, they would make love, what a beautiful way to conceive, through a dedication to something not even words could capture. The thought of having sex without language aroused him, so much so that he felt real pleasure as his pants began vibrating. He reached into his pocket and pulled out his phone: Milosz. Outside he saw the East River, they were on the FDR. He rolled up the window.

Hello?

Where are you? Milosz said, his voice cut by wind. *Why don't you answer your phone?*

I'm on my way home.

What happened? The fire was on our floor?

Yes, in the server room. There was nothing—

In the server room?

Yes. I saw it myself. He waited for Milosz to respond but heard only the pixelated breeze. *In fact I was the one to pull the alarm.* He looked at the screen of his phone. *Milosz?*

Right, he said, and then something else that was too soft to hear.

Did you find the leak?

This is a setback, that's all it is.

Milosz, I think at this point—

He started yelling. Herschel pulled the phone away from his ear. When finally there was silence again he said, *Right, I know. But let's talk about it later.* Again no response. *So you didn't find the leak.*

No, Herschel. I have no idea.

Okay, talk soon.

He hung up and put the phone down. He tried to resume

thinking about Franny, their coming weekend together, but it was like trying to return to a dream in the morning. They drove past StuyTown, the Lower East Side, the Financial District. They went through the Battery Tunnel and came off the highway into Carroll Gardens. Clinton Street had never seemed so placid, poised. He thought of the Boccioni painting, he pulled up the image on his phone, there was more action there than these streets saw in a year. But he was being foolish, he was too literal. Revolution was a matter of perception. The painting was a work of art because it showed what could not be seen. He himself knew that catalysts of radical change didn't need to look the part, those servers were just black boxes with wires in between. Yes, even those who had to program the things found it tedious, painstaking, prosaic. It was only a select few with enough acquired intuition who could get a sense for the scale of outcomes, who understood that success meant chaos, that we could be a trading day away from a kind of anarchy history had yet to imagine.

But then what about Milosz? His view into the future was far more precise, it must have been, and still he forged ahead. Perhaps that was the problem, to Milosz it was just a vision, he didn't have to consider the reality of it, no, that was Herschel's job, to infect the world with Milosz's idea; without Herschel an idea was all it would be. But it wasn't Herschel whom Milosz needed, really, it was just someone like him— and didn't he already have exactly that? Yes, he had the perfect proxy waiting for him, Herschel's understudy, practically. Ian would love nothing more than to fill the void he'd left. Okay, it had been a good idea to call the Southern District, but this couldn't wait months, years—those two could make something happen in days.

He picked up his phone. He had a text from Franny, which he asked Siri to read aloud: *Yes I'm home. Also dryer broke again.* He opened his conversation with Ian and dictated a message: *The firm's had a bit of a setback. I'm desperate for capital and willing to talk access. Let's set up an in-person.* He sent the text and looked out his window. It was pacifying, this neighborhood, all the sturdy brownstones and empty sidewalks. The car came to a red light and he told the driver to let him off.

It was cooler here than in Manhattan. Maybe it was just the breeze, or how you could hear it through the trees. They were flowering now, soon the wind would be louder still, when all those pretty petals formed circles on the ground. He thought of a time-lapse video of plants he'd seen a few weeks ago: vines reaching for metal poles, their arms tottering like Dr. Seuss characters. What had struck him was their intent, they appeared to make plans and execute them, like animals living on a different time scale. He thought of Milosz's obsession with teraflops, how many operations our computers performed each second. A given machine could accomplish more work in a minute than we could in our entire lives. If they could see us, if they cared at all, our movements would hardly even register.

He began the walk home, thinking of Ian, the practicalities. He envisioned himself in the park again, or just outside, by the Met. He'd offer to get coffees, he'd go early and have them ready, Ian's cup in his right hand, that was how he'd remember. But that was the easy part. Right, acquiring what was needed, that was the problem. He knew you could find poisonous substances on the dark web but he'd never been on it before and suspected it was all one big FBI honeypot. His friend Rafa took drugs, weed and molly, he had a dealer, maybe the dealer knew someone. No, that idea was much worse. He put his hand on his forehead and pushed the skin up, it looked ridiculous but it helped him think, feeling the random corrugations. Botox, it was toxic, that was the point, it caused paralysis. There was the story of the woman in Maine who'd died from botulism, acquired the drug on her own and self-injected. And what about that guy from the squash team in college, Nick something, Nick Bowers, he was a dermatologist now—didn't he have a practice in Murray Hill? He could stop by, tell Bowers that he was researching a skin care corporation, a major acquisition, the company was public, too. He couldn't say which one but with his tone, his smile, he'd imply he might as well. *I'm doing some competitive research. Botox-related. You don't— Do you have some with you? I'd love to see the packaging.* And then a distraction, some gossip, his phone would ring and he'd take it outside, he'd have to run, it would happen so fast he'd forget to give the Botox back. *Nick Bowers*, he wrote the name in his memo app.

He was at the house. Fridays were nice because it was garbage collection day, for a few hours their block was spotless. The place was still so new to him that he could stand outside and bask in it: their ownership of something so stately, well-appointed, imposing, even. That was why it had bothered him so much, that brief squabble over the oak tree. Philip and Clara were right, of course, it was dreadful to think of excising one of the block's last vestiges of nature—but had that been their rationale? No, their objection had cited only their own loss of property value. That was how far we'd come: the best way to protect nature was by attaching a dollar value to it. As if people could own trees. It all seemed so decadent now—such an embarrassing, bourgeois tiff—but really it had nothing to do with class, country, culture. What was more timeless than two groups of people arguing over control of the natural world?

He climbed the stoop. As he slid the key into the lock he heard the kinetic pulsing of violin. He pushed the door open: *Flight of the Bumblebee*. This was a welcome surprise, and auspicious, all that jubilant energy; she never listened to those Hollywood classics on her own. He hadn't thought of music, whether that would be part of their silence. Up the stairs he found her in the living room, drawing, her back to him, couch pillows on the floor and an orange peel by her side. She hadn't heard him come in and he didn't want to disturb her, she scared easily and was probably in her flow. He thought to go downstairs and close the door again, harder, but then she stopped drawing, she sensed something, she turned around. Her instinctive delight in seeing him was quickly replaced by apprehension, but it was thin, obligatory, necessary to maintain continuity with their earlier conflict. To hell with the narrative arc, he thought, and smiled at her, warmly, naturally; it grated so confidently against expectation, and even against the music, that it proved itself. She seemed relieved—hesitant but relieved. He set down the carrier bag, she stood up, and they embraced. He rocked them back and forth, alternating which foot bore his weight, and, glancing in the dining room, saw that she had cleaned up the plate. They came undone and looked at each other, his serenity was contagious, it bloomed on her, too—and that was the point at which she questioned its source.

She looked away, stepped to the side. *You were right about not being ready*, she said. *For kids, I mean.*

No, no, he said. *Please, I didn't mean it. We're both ready, I know we are. Actually, I wanted to talk about exactly that.*

She noticed the bag on the floor, her vague doubt resurfacing. But when he told her what was inside she simply nodded and said, *You can keep them here. You can keep them wherever you want.* To show she meant what she said she picked up the bag and brought it into the dining room. He followed her, but was stopped in his tracks at the doorway: the new tank had been delivered, and she'd already set it up for him, it was full of all the accessories he'd ordered. On top, neatly stacked, were the containers of crickets. *I love you*, he said. He did. God, she was thoughtful, she was too humble even to connect eyes as he expressed his gratitude. He walked up to her and they hugged again. In her arms he told her that he'd had quite a day, he laughed at the understatement. *Jesus fucking Christ, Franny, the office burned down.* They came apart and he laughed again, he covered his face with his hand, and then he told her what had happened, as he would tell it to Milosz, to anyone else. It was good practice, she didn't know as many details, he could make more mistakes. At each new kink in the story her head shook in disbelief, and when he said that their work was lost, that he was sure they'd need to close down, she took a seat. After he finished—telling her that he'd walked for hours, thinking—she stood and they hugged once more, they kissed, she contorted her face to convey optimism. Her eyes ticked to the bag on the floor, she picked it up and brought it to the tank. She only wanted to make him happy, show him that she cared, again he said that he loved her. She held the bag over the transfer window of the tank and unzipped it. One of the anoles, the elder, leaped down. She peered inside the bag, tilting it one way and then the other.

Oh, she said. *I thought there were two.*

The younger must have been caught in some fold, unless

he'd packed away just one. No, he hadn't, and before he could let the thought run its course he went over to the bag and looked himself, he turned it upside down and shook. Out fell a stick, hardly even a twig. It seemed to be made of dark green canvas. It was a tail.

He handed her the bag and crouched down. He picked it up, it was hard, already lifeless, though he could still make out the crimped segment. He looked at the tank, where the tail belonged, he thought to put it inside, but when he saw the elder, his body distended, he fell to the floor. Cold air came under his shirt, came against the skin of his stomach, his neck, he was sobbing, softly, he didn't want her to hear, though the sound was so much more horrendous muted.

He needed to breathe, the air came in all at once, through his desiccated throat it became a screech, one that lifted Franny's shoulders. She came down to the floor, put her hand on his side, but her empathy was wasted, he wasn't worth consoling: it was all his fault, if he didn't know why exactly it had happened he at least knew that. He hadn't fed them since early that morning, had he? Of course not, he hadn't even checked in on them once he'd left the office, for hours they'd tumbled around in that bag like clothes in a dryer, without light, they must have been terrified, even humans resorted to cannibalism in desperate circumstances. That wasn't far off, they were basically stranded on an island together, they had been from the very beginning, it was all his doing, against the advice of the salesman he'd paired an adult with an adolescent, he'd had the hubris to build a social environment on a whim.

He sat up and wiped his eyes. He breathed in, and out, he believed he had himself under control. He stood and walked to the tank. The elder was on a branch, looking out the window. His torso was bulging, it was asymmetric, the terrible fact of it took shape as some cold, spatial curiosity. Herschel tilted his head, he tried imagining it—but why was he just standing there? Maybe it wasn't too late, maybe the younger was still alive, still— He opened the lid with one hand and plunged the other inside. The elder darted away, out of sight, and that brief bit of action was enough to bring him to his senses. Again his own thoughtlessness surrounded him, buzzing, warming his cheeks. He had almost doubled his sin by not fucking *thinking*. Just fucking *think*. He was ready to shove his fingers down another's throat just to, what? Relieve himself of his own guilt? He looked through the other end of the tank, found the elder in the corner, he was in discomfort, having had to scramble with his body full, he just wanted peace enough to digest. Herschel glanced at Franny, who stood facing him, her arms loose at her side. She was wearing makeup, he realized, she was wearing the black blouse she knew he loved. He wanted privacy, he wished she weren't there, her presence made him feel trapped in himself, in his own humanity, with her in front of him he could not deny how different he was from the anole, how hopeless communication between them was, but if he were alone with him, if there were just two beings in the room, he could let go of his doubt, he could make what seemed then like a magical leap. But of course animals could recognize our emotions, and that was all he wanted, he didn't need to speak and be heard, he just needed the elder to identify *sorrow*, he needed him to understand he was being asked for *forgiveness*, concepts that existed in any social environment, how could they not?

He told himself Franny was not there, he closed his eyes

and believed it. He used his face to transmit remorse, he made himself a mime, expressing the emotions as much as he physically could. He opened his eyes to see that the elder was staring at him, and now that Herschel had his full attention he asked, silently, for forgiveness, his eyes wide with hope, his hands out, his palms up.

Herschel.

He kept his concentration, he was almost there.

Herschel, she said, louder.

He glanced up at her, when he looked back the elder's mind was elsewhere. He stood up straight and faced her, her arms were now crossed. He found her expression oddly satisfying, it gave him a bit of joy, even; this was exactly what the elder felt but couldn't communicate: disappointment, anger, confusion.

Franny, he said, approaching her. *It was my fault. I didn't feed them, and then I stuffed them in that bag.*

Do you think this has anything to do with the rest of the day?

No, I don't.

Okay, well, you didn't mean to do it, right? It was an accident.

That makes it better?

Of course.

So you would rather be accidentally killed than murdered?

Jesus.

Think about it.

Sure. I mean, I'd be dead regardless.

What about me? What if I was murdered? Would you rather it have been an accident?

I don't know. It would depend.

On?

On a lot of things, she said, her face pleading—for what? For him to have some sense? He was asking her for the opposite: that she abandon herself for just a moment.

If I died in a car crash, and the driver had tried to kill me, would that be worse than if he was just drunk?

She looked away, shook her head to herself. To her it was still just some thought experiment.

Look, I said, *is it really any better that what happened to Birdie was an accident?*

Her face dropped, finally. *That's not funny.*

Exactly.

Yes, Herschel, it is better.

Why?

Why? she repeated. Her eyes narrowed. And then, when his face didn't change, they opened again. She may have despised him then, briefly, she couldn't even look at him as she said it. *We don't have to feel angry. There's no one to blame.*

There wasn't, he reminded himself.

Her face was still. Her eyes flicked to the side, narrowed again. She was thinking, replaying the last few seconds. When they made eye contact again she looked unsure, dumb even, it was a rare sight. Desperately he wanted the moment to pass, he felt his desperation and shoved it down, he shoved everything down.

A plane sounded in the distance. When it petered out he heard silence, but as a faint, high-pitched ring. He laughed, at least it felt like he did, his stomach contracted but there was no noise. She looked more confident now, now that he wasn't, if she didn't know what she didn't know she at least knew the answer existed, it was in the room, in him. Her shoulders relaxed and her head ticked to the side. Challenges suited her, put her mind to use; she felt let down whenever she finished a crossword puzzle.

Was there any other way? Would she settle for anything but what she knew was the truth? He wanted to sit down. There was a chair in front of him, the thought of pulling it from the table, putting his weight on it—the room seemed crowded, dense, hot, the air from his lungs dragged against his throat and came out as white noise. He put his hand out but there was nothing there, he stepped forward and grabbed the chair. It was uncomfortable, sitting, the wood was too hard, his legs too long, he leaned forward until his cheek found his palm. He didn't hear her sit but there she was, pulling his hand away from his head, forcing him to hold it up himself.

Can I have a few moments? Alone?

She sat back in her chair, her arms folded. No, there was no other way. She wouldn't accept anything but what she knew was the truth.

I had no idea, he said. He felt relief already, just for making the decision, for taking the first, irrevocable step. *Of course I didn't. I just wanted her to leave.*

Suddenly he was on his feet, unsure if he could balance, a toddler amazed at his own uprightness. He walked into the living room, over to the couch, and sat on the floor before it. In front of him was the drawing she'd been working on, it was the leg of a chair, as soon as he picked it up she took it from his hands. She was sitting now, too, angled as before, not beside him and not across.

I gave her a fairly large dose of a sleep aid. I put it in her drink. It sounded much worse than it was, *sleep aid*, like he'd bought it for that purpose. He hadn't wanted to say the brand name, with it came the original tone of the decision, which was that of humor, spontaneity, inspiration even. *It was ZzzQuil. I found it in the medicine cabinet.*

He leaned forward, over his knees. It felt good to fall like that, with his spine carrying his weight. He bent down more, and to the side, he found her lap, the crease between her thigh and calf. When her hand began caressing his head he felt that he could touch her leg; he brushed her, caressed her, soon he was kneading her skin. He smelled the detergent on her clothes, he felt the air from the ceiling fan. She was crying. He knew it from how her stomach lurched. In those random contractions he tried to decipher what he couldn't ask: what she was thinking; for whom, exactly, she was crying. He himself cried, he ached, he yearned, he longed to be anywhere else, anyone else, himself just a week ago.

He hadn't expected to feel humiliated. But he was, he was a disgrace, a fraud exposed, he had pretended to be someone he wasn't. But now it was obvious, he was hopelessly himself, someone who would do what he'd done, would hide it from her, hide it from even himself, and in the most wretched ways. It was against this humiliation that he felt the other thing, the sensation shame barely allows. No, he hadn't expected gratitude, either. Disbelief, really. That she held him, that she bore his presence, that she didn't leave him alone. She didn't yell at him. She didn't ask him questions. Still her hand stroked his hair, the motion so familiar but had she ever done it before? It was wrong for him to receive so much love, any love at all, but to refuse it would be to refuse her, it would be to ignore her sacrifice, which was not some noble gesture but the corruption of something all her own. Yes, in her tears—still she was stifling them, swallowing them into the sharp spasms of her gut—was a promise. She was crying for Birdie, and she was crying for him. But her tears flowed for no one more than herself.

His head fell further into her lap, his body became slack. And with his knees together, his legs bent, he closed his eyes for good.

⁓

It all felt so distant it might have been a dream. My actual dream was of our hotel room in Stockholm, years ago. Over and over I watched Franny receive and prepare our room service breakfast: stirring coffee, spreading jam on toast, deshelling eggs.

I reached for my phone but it wasn't on the bedside table. I sat up to see the clock on the other side of Franny. 5:51 a.m. I'd slept for what, sixteen hours?

I swung my feet off the mattress and stood up. Something unusual; I was already dressed. If I had the urge to question whether yesterday had happened at all, I couldn't once my hand found my pants. I lifted from my pocket the broken combination lock, the loose numerical discs.

I couldn't think of any of it—smashing the lock, guiding the match into the server, *The City Rises*—except through something like disassociation, I saw someone who wasn't me, who looked like me but acted on his own, I couldn't remember being in his body. Yes, to relive any bit of it was embarrassing, but it was the embarrassment of another's humiliation. To think I had almost asked Franny to be together, in silence, for a whole weekend—and then try to conceive. It was comedic, sure, it was too absurd not to be, but what lingered was horror. It wasn't just that I'd thought those thoughts, but that I might think them again—the possibility that my current sanity might only be a brief reprieve, the eye of the storm.

I walked out of the bedroom and into the bathroom. I turned on the light and, seeing myself in the mirror, flinched. But it was encouraging, the sight of myself afraid; fear had been so foreign to that other person. Yes, I was fearful, I've always been. Just as I was ambitious and practical and vain. I, Herschel. Me.

I closed my eyes, remembering more, and opened them again. Temporary insanity or not, I couldn't deny that those actions were mine, I owned them now. Yes, I'd set fire to the servers. Yes, we'd lost all of our proprietary code. But okay, well, it was actually the right thing to do. Even if it meant leaving a lot of money on the table, even if my stake would have been worth tens of millions of dollars. Hundreds of millions. More. That would take some time to absorb. But still, I'd helped maintain the integrity of the financial system. And that wasn't hokum, I was the last person to suffer righteous regulation bullshit; no, what I'd done was necessary to preserve the market—not to mention my own career. It was what Bruce always said, *Anyone can trade in their integrity for a quick mil. But it'll be their last.*

I tugged my lip down and saw the abfraction, I touched it but it didn't hurt. I started brushing my teeth.

Bruce. Yes, I regretted calling him Wednesday, rubbing our success in his face. Surely it would make the closure of the firm that much sweeter for him. But it was okay, thinking of that regret, it was such a different thing from thinking about yesterday, which didn't surface regret so much as disorienta-

tion. No, there was no through line between that person yesterday and me now, whereas I could be ashamed of calling
Bruce because that *was me*—I could recall exactly how I'd felt
in that moment.

I set the toothbrush back and washed out my mouth. I took
off my pants and shirt, my briefs. I looked at the shape of my
legs, I'd always liked my thin ankles. In the mirror I inspected
my collarbone, my disheveled hair, I was proud of my body, I
enjoyed my face, it made sense in the most fundamental way
that I looked like me. I stepped on the scale. One hundred
sixty-five pounds. Pounds: *It's a lot of pounds*, that was what
Colin had written in his email. He'd be happy he hadn't sent
us a penny.

I stepped off the scale. Wasn't that my first memory, being
weighed? As a baby, on that cold metal basin. Our building had
caught on fire. That was news. Investors would need to hear
from us, need to hear that everything was okay, that we would
be working out of a temporary office et cetera. And then, in
a few months, we would deliver the unfortunate news: things
hadn't panned out, the idea was there, it was possible, but not
with our resources, and we couldn't responsibly ask for more.
It would be easier that way, insurance-wise, lawsuit-wise.

Fucking shit. Hundreds of millions of dollars. That was
fuck-you money; I would have called Bruce and literally told
him to go fuck himself. I felt it in my stomach, a pang that
carried with it something else, too: There was no place to go
on Monday. I was, for all intents and purposes, unemployed,
at least I would be, soon, after I'd spent a couple of months
shoveling dogshit into the furnace. And then what? If I ran
into an old colleague, someone from business school, I would

have no answer to the golden question. Years ago I worked at Webber, and then I failed at starting my own fund, and now I was trying to conceive with my successful, working wife.

These thoughts pushed me out into the hallway and up to my office. As I waited for my computer to boot up I did push-ups, which felt great, I could really tell I hadn't done them in days. I signed in and went to the business bank accounts; yes, Simo's bonus had already been withdrawn. I opened my email, there were 113 new messages. I scrolled through, only about 30 were real: 10 potential investor rejections, 3 invoices, 2 notes regarding a new hire, and around 15 lenders and investors asking about the fire. I Googled *wooster fire* and found just two articles, one from a CBS affiliate and the other from a very local publication; apparently a fire isn't news anymore. Both articles were short, a couple of hundred words, if that, just long captions for the same video of black smoke rising into the sky. There was no mention of foul play or anything like it. But if there were some suspicion, would it really end up in an article like this? How careless had I been? I had no idea, I'd burned the lens of the video camera—did that even do anything? There was Ian, he could call the police, an anonymous tip, even, an investigation would surely— No, Ian didn't know what had happened, why would I think that? I needed to get my head straight. I coughed, swallowed, closed my eyes. Once I'd emptied my inbox I'd feel better. I went back to my email but the thought of him stayed with me, as I began reading an invoice I saw his face, every wrinkle of it. I closed my eyes again. Ian. My plan. I could now retrace those thoughts exactly: I was going to poison him, with Botox, that I stole from Nick Bowers. *Do you have some with you?* That was what I was going to say. *I'd love to see the packaging.*

The room was too cold. I went into the hallway and adjusted the thermostat. I walked back into the office, I sat down, I reminded myself that I'd done nothing wrong.

I had been temporarily insane.

Yes, but then why did I still feel it? If I didn't feel the desire to kill him, still I knew that desire's shape, its color.

The thermostat still hadn't kicked on. The water pressure, the dryer, the heat—why was everything in this house broken? I thought to do more push-ups to warm myself, that was a good, healthy way to channel my angst. Yes, but I needed something more sustained.

I left the office and went downstairs, back to the bedroom. Quietly I grabbed my running clothes and took them to the bathroom to change. In the kitchen I had a bowl of dry cereal and cashews and drank two double shots of espresso.

Outside the sun was up, the streets empty, even for a Saturday. I ran through Gowanus, South Slope, and Sunset Park to Bay Ridge, where I jogged along the water. It was wonderful to feel my body, to feel that I was slightly more out of shape than I'd like to be, that I was no longer so young, that the funny feeling in my knee still nagged. I watched the seagulls fly against the wind, fighting just to stay in place; they were an aerodynamic curiosity, nothing more. When I hit the Verrazzano Bridge I turned back, by then my muscles and joints were demanding more and more of my attention. This was exactly why I loved running. With less headspace to spend on actual thoughts things began to clarify, my analyses became more efficient.

There were four distinct problems: the fire leading back to me, my temporary insanity, the firm closing, and Franny's knowledge of my involvement in Birdie's accident—

specifically, what this would do to our relationship. The four were so brilliantly unalike that I could vacillate between them and continually refresh my perspective. The problem of the firm's closing consisted of mourning lost wealth and questioning what to do with my life, both would take a significant amount of time. That was also true for the issue with Franny, this was not something that would simply go away, it would sit in the corner of every room of our house, we'd notice it day and night, it could take years before it blended in with the rest of the furniture. The problem of my temporary insanity contained vague questions I could entertain if I wanted to— Why did it happen? What should I make of it?—and one quite concrete: Would it happen again? No, it wouldn't, I now knew that instinctually, knew it as I knew when I was dreaming. I was myself again now and forever, the Herschel I'd been for thirty-eight years, and each new mile I felt it more, I did, that it was all in the past—no, on another timeline altogether.

By the time I got back, sprinting down the block and then walking the last bit, I had only made theoretical progress on the first problem, reducing it to a question of the missing lock and the security footage. There were unknown unknowns— was there something inherent in the fire's spread that implied arson?—but my hesitation to leave a trail of Google searches like *how to know if it was arson*—even on a VPN, even on DuckDuckGo—allowed me to avoid unnecessary worrying. There was Simo, too. He was under the impression I wanted the insurance money, but it wouldn't be like him to do anything with that knowledge, and not after that fat bonus—not to mention that the fire was, after all, his idea. But the lock, the footage, for these questions I'd need to extract some information from Milosz's brain, really they were but two of the million things we needed to discuss. And sure enough, when I entered the foyer I saw I had five missed calls from him, as well as two texts: *We need to talk ASAP* and then *Meet you at your place, leaving now.* This last had been sent at 7:02 a.m., forty-five minutes ago; the trip took just short of an hour.

As soon as I walked up the stairs I knew I was in the thick of Franny's morning routine: I was hit simultaneously by the smell of fried eggs and the sound of the shower. She liked to let the eggs finish on the pan while she washed and dressed. One of the first times I knew I was in love with her was when I discovered this habit, how irrationally efficient it was. In the kitchen I listened to her shower, waiting for her hums, but they didn't come. I heard a brief torrent of water and then it stopped altogether.

On the pan were two eggs, sunny-side up, a piece of brioche was waiting in the toaster. The scents mixed wonderfully, I took it as an act of ill intent that she had made only one portion until I remembered I was vegan, at least I had been yesterday. But I wasn't now, why would I be? My feelings toward animals, language, humanity—they all belonged to that person I wasn't, that person who'd only, up until I came clean to Franny, occupied my body. The seagulls looked like seagulls, why would an egg not be edible? I took a fork and lifted off the pan a sliver of cooked egg white. I brought it to my nose, it smelled fine, good, the way an egg should. I split my lips and moved the fork down, but I couldn't do it. No, I didn't want to. *Want* to, yes, this was a decision, not like the lamb or the shawarma or the milk in the latte, each of those had induced a physical sensation—discomfort, disgust. But why didn't I want to? If the feeling was elusive it was also, somehow, familiar. Distantly familiar. Was it years ago? I walked into the living room, to the spot on the floor where I'd confessed to Franny, where she'd held me until I fell asleep. How had I gotten upstairs? I found it then, the feeling I was looking for. Yes, it was years ago, many years ago, I must have been twelve. We were in a hot tub, me and my friend Joel and two girls a few years older than us; he was an assistant at the sports camp where the girls worked. I was nervous, excited, the night had a purpose, Joel's doing: the girls had previously agreed to let us touch their breasts. When the time came, when he asked them if we could do it and they said yes, I left the hot tub, went inside, got dressed, and called my dad to pick me up. I was a good kid, it was a moral instinct—albeit one likely inherited from shows like *7th Heaven*. But it was more, this would have been my first sexual experience beyond kissing a girl on the lips, and watching Lisa masturbate. It would have been an initiation into a new understanding of life, one that would utterly replace my old one.

I walked through the kitchen and into the dining room, where I saw the anoles. The anole. I remembered the scene, myself on the floor, sobbing. The pain of reliving it was progress, already I could do so for more than a few seconds and without clenching my teeth. But still, I didn't need the reminder, nor did I need to have to remember to feed it crickets, or do whatever else. I made a mental note to put the tank out on the stoop and walked out of the room, through the kitchen and up the stairs, to the bedroom, where I found Franny, a towel around her body and one tied on her head. She looked at me and smiled, it was slanted, self-conscious, but still she held it for my sake. She didn't know what to do with the sight of me, but she was doing her best, she was a marvelous woman, I couldn't believe how lucky I was to have found her.

The permits were approved, she said, her tone so even it took me a moment to grasp the sentence. *I called the contractor. Work can start next week.*

Wow, I said. *Amazing news.*

I invited Philip and Clara over to celebrate, she said, breaking eye contact. *Yesterday, before you came home.* She undid the towel around her hair and set it on the dresser. *I understand if you're not up to it.*

I nodded and, turning away from her, began to undress.

It would be casual, she said. *I told them noon.* She coughed. *I'd just pick up some pastries.*

I turned around and held out my hand. She threw me the towel and I covered myself.

I don't know what you said to him, she said, *but I thought it would be nice to smooth things over.*

No, I wasn't up for the get-together. But it was what she wanted, and I owed her so much. *Sure*, I said, *that sounds good.*

I went to the bathroom and started the shower. Looking at my face in the mirror, it hit me: the permits, the contractor, the gut renovation. What was the estimate? It wasn't seven figures, but close. Given the state of the firm, my $1.3 million loan now all but gone—no, maybe the renovation wasn't such a good idea, not until we talked with our accountant. *Work can start next week*, she'd said. God.

Just as the water got warm I heard the doorbell—Milosz— followed by Franny scrambling to get dressed. I got in and began washing myself as fast as I could. Even Franny's social dexterity was no match for Milosz's inability to make small talk, mostly he stammered observations of his interlocutor; I imagined him telling her that her hair was drier than he remembered. But there was something else, too, the vague sense that it was against my interest to let them talk. I soaped just my head and hair, letting the lather trickle down, as soon as it rinsed away I got out and toweled off.

I found them in the family room, him on the couch, her in a chair. She was nodding sympathetically; she seemed, if anything, sad.

Herschel, he said. His voice was so soft I wouldn't have understood if I hadn't been looking at him.

Franny stood and excused herself, I didn't hear her exact words because I was caught by Milosz's posture, I'd never seen him sit like that, one leg draped over the other, his hands resting on his knees, so mannered. When I sat down, taking Franny's place, he waved at me, only once, his hand tracing a rainbow.

I'm sorry for the visit. I just really needed to talk.

No, I said. *Of course.*

But can we have some privacy?

Franny was still within earshot, I knew because the clanking of plates stopped abruptly. We could have gone up to my office, but I had an instinct against bringing him through the house.

Franny, I said, raising my voice, *do you mind going out to get those pastries?*

We listened as she finished what she was doing, she came down the stairs to the foyer, put on her shoes and jacket. All that time Milosz and I basically looked at each other, we weren't capable of chitchat, we knew each other too well but in such a narrow way.

She closed the door. He nodded gracefully. He seemed so suddenly small, well-behaved, a boy waiting patiently.

Would you describe the fire? he asked.

You haven't checked the footage?

It was kept on the servers.

So nothing saved to the camera itself.

No, they're not— Herschel, the floor basically collapsed. They wouldn't even let me in.

I didn't see much, I said. *It happened so fast.*

But tell me what you saw. Anything.

I described the crinkling noises, the pops, the smoke and the light-yellow fire below, the hiss, the wall of heat, the flames scattering as I left. It was hard to look at him while I spoke, each new detail seemed to cause him even more discomfort, seemed to tug his mouth even more askew. In some way it felt like I was breaking up with him, that despite the distress my words inflicted, they brought closure, too.

The fire started in the back of the room? he asked, looking at his shoe.

It seemed that way, I said.

He nodded. *At the back.*

It happened so fast I almost missed it, if I hadn't been looking right at him I might have. His hand and head had already reset. I had to say it to myself to prove it really happened: he punched himself, just above the ear. He seemed to have forgotten it himself, perhaps I should have pretended, too, but I couldn't, so I laughed, I tried to catch his eyes, let him know this could be a joke if we wanted it to be. But he didn't look at me, he only gazed at the piano.

You can sue me, he said. *If it helps at all, then sue me.*

Milosz.

Or report it as negligence. That's what it was, I was negligent, absolutely, even a fucking idiot would have realized it was too hot.

It's nobody's fault. It was an accident.

He laughed, this gave him real pleasure, too much, suddenly it seemed more plausible that he'd punched himself. *So accidents are nobody's fault? What a world, Herschel.*

What was I supposed to do, really? Even if I could take away his guilt—as if I could explain what I did, or why I did it—it wasn't as though it would just disappear. It would only be converted into hatred, one that would never resolve. Yes, Franny was right, it was better when things were accidental; with blame came anger—as if grief alone weren't enough. No, the two together could make you go insane.

Forgive yourself, Milosz. He nodded, but then shook his head. I squeezed the cushion of my seat, I feared he would hit himself again, or worse. *You won't be able to move on until you've done that.*

I'm ready to move on. Why do you think I'm here?

I nodded. Right, of course, already he wanted to start something new, he didn't know how things worked, that you needed money, that even getting our seed funding had been a miracle, one that could not be repeated because those bridges were now burned, quite literally. No, and for all of our work we had nothing to show, because we'd kept everything on servers we could see and touch, instead of on a remote network like everyone else, because he was paranoid, he confused the emotional security that came from physical proximity with actual security, so much so he overlooked the fact he was shoving hundreds of hot servers into what should have been a conference room. Yes, it was, actually, his fault. Not to mention that what we had been doing was illegal, or as good as illegal, another detail he had the privilege of casually ignoring, he lived in a world of theoretical delight, he got to spend his working life thinking about things that didn't exist because people like me sold our souls to try to make use of them, we looked people in the eyes and made false promises, we were forever optimistic in the face of the fact that we were trying to sell things that hadn't been built just so we could buy the resources to see if they could be built at all.

Well, you know I wish you luck.

Herschel.

No, the money's not there. People want to know what they're investing in, and, frankly, I can't tell them, because it's illegal. You're brilliant, Milosz, your work is brilliant, but this idea isn't meant for the world.

You're limited by your imagination. Now he wanted to look me in the eyes. I let him, I nodded. *You can't imagine what doesn't exist. This idea is just too big for you.*

Perhaps, I said. *Either way, I know you'll find someone who feels differently.*

He stood up, still staring at me. I forced my arms slack, my neck loose, only in my head did I prepare to defend myself. He inhaled, lifting his shoulders, and walked out of our house.

I sat there, thankful to be alone, thankful that I'd never have to see him again. I wouldn't, I'd make sure of it. I had handled it well, all things considered, I'd explained my reasoning, I'd given him the freedom to go on without me. *Well, you know I wish you luck.* That was gracious, even if we both knew it was a lie; no, I'd hate to see him take this idea to someone else. So why say it at all? It was gratuitous, he knew me well enough, he wasn't dumb. Saying such pablum was effortless; how easily I left myself, gave him just an empty husk. I thought of the last time I'd sat in this chair, Monday night, after Birdie left, when it was just the four of us. I saw Clara in front of me, bent at the waist, her phone in my face, a picture from their ultrasound. *Isn't that marvelous*, I'd said. Was it? It looked like every other ultrasound. It was something you said, just something you said, we say things that are just things to say. By that point Birdie was in the hospital, or on the way, unconscious and bleeding from the head in the back of a stranger's car. If I'd known— Well, what? I knew now, and I was just sitting here, for days I had lived my life without ever asking for an update on her. But I had been that other person, and— I'd incapacitated someone, I had taken from her the capacity to be herself, to communicate with her friends and family, to laugh, be hungover, write plays, feel the joy of shitting. Never again would she misplace her keys or fall in love or be annoying or boorish or self-involved or talk over anyone, I would have given anything for her to be in this room, to ignore me and casually insult others, to be given back her freedom. I could feel the wood inside the cushions of the arms of the chair, it was rectangular, which seemed inelegant, but what else would it be? I wanted to punch myself the way Milosz had, immediately and with no reaction, no indulgence, just the pain. I brought my fist up, I closed my eyes—I couldn't do it, I was a coward, I was actively deciding not to, just as when I'd failed to eat the egg. Instead I pushed my fist into my forehead—if anything it felt good, moving it around, wrinkling the skin. The Botox, Ian, yes, I'd planned to poison him with a drink. My tongue hurt, it ached, my fingers dug into the chair, feeling for the edges of the hidden wood. Birdie again, Ian now—a drink over and new excuse, an act but, I'd decided against, yes, yes, where was Franny, she should be home, her hair like always and me in her arms. I took out my phone and called her but she didn't pick up. I went to the window, she was crossing the street, a nice white cardboard box in her hands. I sat on the couch, where Milosz had been, and soon she came into the room.

He's gone?

He left, I said.

She set the box down and then pushed her hair away from her forehead, briefly forgetting I was there. She turned to face me. *Will's staying through May. He booked an Airbnb.*

That's great. I'm glad to hear that.

She nodded. *Have you spoken to Magda about what happened?*

No, I said. *Not really. And I'm not sure it would be a good idea. Legally, I mean.*

She opened the pastry box, an excuse to look away. I shouldn't have said it like that, shouldn't have even brought up legality. And I'd lied to her too, by omission; I'd fired Magda—not that I couldn't take it back, of course I could, I would just tell Magda that I'd made the decision under—

My phone was buzzing. I reached into my pocket, a 917 number. I looked up at Franny but she'd already left.

Hello?

Hi, is this Herschel Caine?

Speaking.

This is David Poke.

Not sure I know that name.

I got your message. Message. *I'm with the Southern District.* Poke. Polk. My message. *Is now a good time?*

I have a minute.

Okay, well, I'd like to start by setting some ground rules, as—

Sorry, David, really, I meant that I have a minute.

I just need to confirm and clarify some things. Starting with your exact role, and how you—

I've given you a head start, and anonymously. That much was promised on your website. So don't contact me again.

Yes, but—

And isn't this the SEC's domain? No, really, don't call me again.

I heard him inhale, I hung up.

What the hell had I said in that voicemail? I scoured my memory but could hardly find purchase, it didn't matter anyway—what more was there to lose? If it had been a mistake to call it was only because it could bring more attention to the fire, but even that was a stretch, people gave the Southern District far too much credit, the SEC, too. There were criminals managing pension funds, market manipulation was rampant, people spoofed prices for fun. A fire? No, they wouldn't get their suits dirty. The important thing was that I wouldn't have anything to do with any investigation into algorithmic trading, if I got one smudge of cooperation on me I might as well become an accountant.

It felt good to exert myself like that, it made me use my brain in the right way. Proficient, effective, strategic. And there was so much more to do, by now I'd have dozens of emails to answer, and many more to send, there were relationships to salvage, losses to cut, lawyers to whip into gear. I ran up to the kitchen, where Franny was eating her eggs and reading the paper. I grabbed the *Financial Times* and peeled an orange. When I threw out the rind I saw, in the garbage, stapled sheets of paper. I squinted: a medical article, marked up with pen and highlighter. I went up to my office, where I did four more sets of push-ups while listening to *Flight of the Bumblebee* on repeat. I logged on and browsed my email while eating the orange. I started small: invoices that would need to be punted, such as this VPN bullshit Milosz had ordered in his paranoid lunacy. Vendors were easy, at the end of the day they would get nothing. Next were lenders and investors, the same gist would work for each—a terrible accident, to be sure; we've already made progress on a sublease—but they needed to be individually tailored. This was time-consuming and tedious, in fact when I was finally ready to move on to the lawyers I was relieved, at least with them I could use shit grammar, I had to if I had any chance of getting this done, I'd lost count of them all, who was who, I had an Excel sheet for just this purpose. It had made more sense to file as an LLC but *Atra Arca Capital Management Inc.* sounded better. I'd pay for that now. I sent call invites for tomorrow, from 8 to noon and 12:30 to 3; I'd keep office hours for investors from 3 to 7—as if they'd ever stop calling.

I'd saved the worst for last: employees. To steel myself I went downstairs for another coffee and more food. I was starving now—what the hell did vegans eat? I made a large bowl of spinach, chickpeas, strawberries, walnuts, and canned beans, and packed a container of hummus under my arm. In my office I ate without pause while the words came to me. I had to fundamentally fire them all, without severance. And they'd need to be reminded of their NDA, the relevant portions. It couldn't be an apology; there was nothing to apologize for, this was due to the fire—but that could only be implied, not even: the inference had to be theirs. And anyway we'd given them good jobs for some time, an interesting story for their next round of interviews. By the end of the meal I had a nice paragraph in my head, I wrote it down, tweaked it, and sent it out with some personal touches. The last on my list was Peter, last in terms of salary but also ease; I knew he'd be crushed, I remembered him saying that the job would be the first time he had health care. I thought to call him but feared the lies he would force out of me, and anyway it would be too much to hear him feign courage, to hear him thank me. His was the only email in which I wrote *I'm sorry*; they were my last words to him.

God, it felt great to be done. I reclined in my chair, allowed myself to appreciate the give, the lumbar support. Something in my chest, a familiar feeling. Without thinking about it I brought back up the salad, which was as flavorful as when it first went down. Having broken my weeklong streak, I now let myself ruminate at will, and for the next few minutes I sat there chewing, swallowing, and regurgitating—starting the process over again.

My email to Peter was still on the screen. *I'm sorry.* It was too easy to say, but it mattered. When you told someone you were sorry you were siding with them, against your former self. You were drawing a line between you now and you then. That was what this whole noon get-together was, wasn't it? *Smooth things over*, she'd said. That was fine, I looked forward to it, even; like these emails, my apology to Philip would put things even more in the past. I stood up, puttered around, looked out the window. The stoop of Ben's building. Yesterday morning. That insufferable conversation. I thought back, heard myself—*Art should change people, for good*—and cringed. No, a basic apology wasn't enough, I needed something that truly demonstrated my remorse, something that could repay the immense social debt I'd created for myself. I looked again at

Ben's place. He was owed an apology, too, the same apology in fact, yes, but with much lower stakes. A practice run.

I closed my email; already I was getting replies, follow-up questions. I checked the time, 11:46, and went downstairs. Franny was tidying up, which was normally my job, I made a mental note to make it up to her.

Outside it felt like the first day of summer, but then, as I crossed the street, I remembered that yesterday had been just as nice; already that day, that person, had been expunged from my memory. I went up their stoop and pushed the buzzer. A few moments later a new voice answered. *Hello?* She sounded suspicious. *Hi*, I said. *I was hoping to talk to Ben. It's your neighbor, Herschel.* A pause, a long pause, she never even answered me. The door buzzed.

The stairwell smelled mustier than I remembered, and it was much darker, too. I expected him to be waiting by his door but he wasn't. I knocked, I heard someone take a couple of steps—he was just waiting there?—and then the door opened. *Hi there*, Ben said, his face glazed with an unlikely bonhomie. He waved me inside, where I saw a woman I assumed was his wife, Hadley, rearranging pillows. It was a fine excuse to be in the room, surely she just wanted to see who I was; she knew everything, of course. Possibly even my first time here, when I'd cried over Lucy, had been recast as what it was: the behavior of a madman.

Thanks for having me, I said. *I won't be long.* I waved to Hadley. *I'm Herschel, I live just across the way.*

Pleasure, she said. That was it? Did people say just the one word?

I looked to Ben, I needed him to invite me fully inside, to take a seat, but he didn't. Instead he glanced at Hadley, right, he was negotiating the urge to show me he was game, that yesterday's incident didn't faze him, with his need to prove himself to his wife.

I just wanted to say that I acted out of line. Yesterday morning, I mean. I looked at Hadley; if she was going to leave this was the time to do it. She didn't. *I don't know what got into me, lecturing you and Philip about art. Of all people.*

You're passionate, obviously. And that's great, you can't write that bestseller without passion. He'd found a good balance: the forgiver, the encouraging authority. And it was the perfect test for me, such a patronizing tone.

Well, I appreciate that. I made a face: breezy contrition, a new expression I'd practice on the way back.

We'll see you around then. At the dog park, I'm sure. I showed my confusion. *Oh, there's one just on Hicks, at Amity.*

Lucy came into the room—had she heard the word *dog?*—and perched on the couch.

We don't have a dog, I said.

Really? I just assumed. You're such a natural with her. A natural. I looked at Lucy, she was inspecting the rug, the pink and red Persian. I remembered it well, it was the background to her image when I'd been lost in it, when I'd felt her sadness. No, that hadn't been such a crazy thought, not one to cry over, of course, but yes, dogs could be sad, she looked sad to me now. This was an odd, simple thought. They were staring at me. I asked for a glass of water, they couldn't deny me that. Ben said, *Of course*, and Hadley left to fetch it.

I asked him what he was working on and pretended to listen. I looked back at Lucy, I waited for her attention, I coughed and she turned. I braced myself; last time it had felt like jumping into a pool, the cold had been all-consuming, so much so that I'd lost my bearings; no, that couldn't happen again. I glanced at Ben and said, *Oh, hmm*, and turned back to Lucy. She was now staring at me, and I at her, I waited, I made myself open, vulnerable, receptive, empathetic, I was now willing to lose myself, make a fool of myself—who cared what these two thought?—I was willing to do anything, I would cry again if that was what it took but I couldn't cry, I couldn't pass through whatever it was between us, no, it was like willing an erection; the more I tried the less it might happen.

Here, Hadley said. She handed me the glass and I took a sip, the cold water tracing the walls of my esophagus.

Maybe she wasn't sad at all, maybe I was only projecting. Of course I was. A dog can't yearn for a freedom it never knew in the first place. But if we took away something more tangible, if we let her feel the fresh air on her body, the wind in her ears, and then led her inside for good, if she knew that from then on she would only experience the breeze in the muted flickering leaves and—

A loud voice, in the distance. It was enthusiastic, performative. Clara was at our door. I turned to see Hadley glaring at me, I drank half the glass and set it down.

I'll get out of your way, I said. *But thank you for listening.* I collected their nods and let myself out, walking one story and careening down the rest, by the time I got outside Philip and Clara had already been let in. I took out my phone, 12:07, and jogged across the street, where I found, at the bottom of our stoop, our old blue laundry bag—right, the broken dryer, Franny had done drop-off. I lifted it into my arms and walked up and inside, where I found the three of them in the family room, Philip and Clara on the couch, Franny setting out the pastries, looking up at me, silently asking where the hell I'd been. I said I'd be right down and then hurried upstairs to the bedroom, where I loosened the bag and dumped the clothes on the floor. I was about to leave when I saw, out of the corner of my eye, a bright yellow women's swimsuit. I'd never seen Franny wear such a thing, no, none of these items were ours, some stranger's clothes were lying in the middle of our bedroom. It was both men's and women's, kids' too. I picked up a brown knit cardigan from the pile and put it on, it seemed such a breach but Franny would get a kick out of it, and I went downstairs.

They were laughing, but it was polite laughter, tenuous, when I came into the room it stopped altogether. I took a seat and eyed the pastries.

The smaller cakes are vegan, Franny said.

I leaned forward, grabbed one, and took a bite. They were watching me, as if I were some hired entertainer. No, but I did have something to prove, that I was no longer socially problematic.

I didn't know they made vegan financiers, I said. *And yet, here I am.* Only Clara laughed. Philip gave a pinched smile and then said, almost to himself, *So you're vegan now.* It would be like this until I did what I had to. *Okay,* I said. *Let's cut to it. I was an asshole to you, Philip.* He looked away, forced his eyes back. *When I saw you yesterday morning, I'd been up all night, for work. I was afraid that things were coming to a close. Actually, I was right. But that's no excuse.*

I set the pastry on my leg and buttoned the cardigan. I turned to Franny, waiting for her to notice, but she didn't.

I'm sorry to hear that, he said. *But yes, you were an asshole.* He smiled, finally, his honor restored. *And you know, I'd still take your company over that god-awful Brit's.*

I glanced at Franny. No, she hadn't told them, and she couldn't now.

Well, she said, standing, *now that the boys have made nice, let's all fatten ourselves up.* She picked up the platter and held it out to our guests.

I love cannoli, Clara said. *But are those croissants almond? Maybe I'll have both. I am eating for two.*

Philip gave a short laugh meant to dissuade his wife, which apparently only I noticed. She took both pastries, and then bit into the croissant.

Darling, you're three months pregnant, he said. *Our child could fit into that cannoli.* We all laughed, but his was nervous; he'd caught himself telling his wife what to eat. He lifted the cannoli from her napkin and took a bite.

Franny went around and poured us coffee. When she got to me we didn't make eye contact—the residue of the *god-awful Brit* comment. But our collective cowardice sounded in the coffee splashing into my mug, it appeared in the brief steam, with it came the sudden realization that Birdie was still in the world, and just a couple of miles from our home. I took a sip, I needed to move on. I looked back at the pastries. I'd had barely anything to eat and I'd run fifteen miles. The cannoli, the croissants, I could eat the entire platter. There were two more financiers and I took them both.

Oh, Philip, Clara said, *do you want to tell them what you found last night?*

Again his short laugh; how had I not noticed it before? No, he didn't want to tell us what he'd found, he looked at Clara, and then at Franny and me. Was Clara oblivious? Or did she just enjoy throwing him wrenches? I would. She was a bit impish, actually, it was hard to notice because of the way she held herself; she reminded me of that new senator from Vermont.

Well, Philip said, *I found the Airbnb listing of our neighbor, Ben.* Clara laughed, how naughty of him, she held her hands to her face as if trying to hide her mirth. She was more than impish, it wasn't an act; she was, in some way, unresolved. For a split second I saw Milosz in her place, it had been only a few hours since he'd sat in that exact spot. *He told me that they traveled quite a bit. And given that his wife doesn't work, and he's got an editor's salary—I just had a feeling, and I was right. Two hundred seventy-five dollars a night.* Through various grunts we agreed this was high. *And by the way: classic goy taste,* he said, turning to Clara. *No offense.*

This was funny until we remembered that Franny wasn't Jewish, either. No one was going to say it, though, and how ridiculous, to not say something everyone was thinking. Still, when I opened my mouth all that came out was *I'm sure it's more charming in person.* It was too positive, against the grain of the conversation; to make up for it I said, *It's hard to get past the language on some of these listings. "Make our beautiful home yours" and "We love our house and you will too." Isn't it all a bit . . . wife-share-y?*

They all laughed, Clara the loudest, her laugh was mean, we were being mean, the word stayed in the air, stayed with me even after they moved on. As they talked about their pregnancy I imagined myself palming Birdie's head and cracking it against a curb, I saw my own face looking on in disgust as blood exited her nose and ears.

Vitamin A, Philip said, *Vitamin whatever, it's better to get it through food.*

The thought carried with it its reciprocal: Birdie cracking

my head. Claret goop running down my face. I saw her in the hospital, but as a visitor, watching me, the patient, in a vegetative state. I saw her here, sitting where I was, eating pastries and drinking coffee while I was someplace else, forgotten, kept alive by machines.

Prices of doulas. The absurdity of home births.

What did she look like then, right at that moment? The urge to know inflated at once, it filled me, it pushed against my throat from below.

Franny was looking at me, her eyebrows raised, she was trying to communicate something. She seemed hopeful, excited: she wanted to know if she could tell them we were trying. I nodded, I went to grab another financier but I'd already eaten them all.

So, she said, and then told them, I couldn't listen because of her teeth, they were so white, she was so beautiful and put together, she could run a room, her grace was infectious. I felt like I was watching a movie, it wasn't just the way they acted— just the way they should, I too acted just as I should—it was like there was a screen between us, one I was on both sides of, I was the viewer and an actor, too. But this screen was more like a membrane; with great effort it could be overcome, it would vanish—a hymen, yes, why not, the passage required something magical, a will to freedom I didn't have.

Wonderful, Philip said. *So happy for you.* Beyond his head, through the window, I saw the oak tree, its branches moving with the wind. Such a delicate balance, to be able to bend so much and not break.

Really, Clara said. I imagined Milosz there, saying it the way she did, with such charm. It was funny and I laughed.

Franny turned my way: Why had I laughed?

It will be wonderful, I said, and then they were talking about something else, they were taking turns, allowing for interruptions and spontaneity but within such rigid, unforgiving bounds. Even Clara had great regard for the rules, if she seemed especially alive in some way it was only because she flouted etiquette, but just enough to draw attention to it, she was the worst offender, she was obsessed with convention.

They talked and talked. The less I took part the less I had to see myself as an actor. But the relief didn't last long, the more I was just the viewer the more I felt the screen in front of me, and there was nothing to do but watch, and it was a meaningless show, there was no central concept or conceit, it didn't explore anything at all. Not to say that there wasn't conflict, that they weren't charismatic; they were, Franny most of all, with her white teeth, those white teeth I'd seen go through an egg, which made me hate her a bit, just a bit, sure, I had hated her then, but now I felt nothing, and now I wanted to feel that hate. I wanted to feel anything.

I pulled out my phone, 12:27. I had a text, from Ian: *How does tomorrow work?* I closed out of the app, the next most recent was my photos. There was *The City Rises. The Carbide Lamp.* I felt Franny looking at me; I was being rude. I put the phone away and tracked the conversation, which was about the Hudson Valley, a house they were looking to buy, I said I'd heard Newburgh was the new best bet, investment-wise.

Again I thought of Ian, and yesterday, and again my fingers pushed into the arm of the chair, to the wood below, but now I was calm, more than calm, the thought was nothing more than a fact—*I'd planned to poison him*—it floated above me, unattached to anything else. How to make Birdie's accident a fact, how to get it far enough away to see; that was the problem, she was inside of me, drifting like wax in a lava lamp, the metaphor was absurd but the ratio might have been exact, in my head she was now the size of those creeping boluses, if she didn't take up most of the space still you couldn't move without bumping into her, any thought held long enough would soon be encroached upon, engulfed.

So I just told her, okay, enough—Clara, talking about her therapist—*My parents are just old, they're not racists.*

Again, me hitting her head against the curb, then her doing it to me, the need to know what she looked like at that exact moment, thoughts that were now so well-trodden they didn't even need to be thought, it was like checking the time, except checking the time was inexhaustible, for the rest of my life I'd be checking the time, as opposed to these thoughts, which were supposed to accumulate, they were little punishments that added up to something, a sum I needed to repay. But how much was one of these thoughts worth, really? Nothing, next to nothing, if I thought these thoughts for the rest of my life still my debt would be unpaid.

Well, there's no use in talking to Franny about therapists. Already they laughed, they were relieved I was speaking at all. Like a good sport I told the story: Franny showing me an email exchange with a client, and then, by way of the timestamps, me realizing it had transpired while she was in teletherapy, the story's purpose being to show that she never stopped working. I'd told it too many times and couldn't muster a performance but still it landed enough that I could parlay it into *Speaking of which, I really must be getting back to my own work.*

It was far too early to end the get-together but they pretended it wasn't, Philip even looked at his watch just to say, *Oh, yes.* We stood, we shook hands and hugged, we begged them to take the pastries and they did, and as Franny saw them out the thoughts returned again.

Well, that was a terrible idea, she said, standing outside of the room. *You could have just said you weren't ready to see them.*

I'm sorry, I said. I was, though she could tell my mind was elsewhere, and before we could get into a fight I let it spill out of me, I described the thoughts I was having as fast as I could, and then in as much detail as I could, except as I did they expanded, they became even more fleshed out, they became an even bigger burden, one I could handle only because I knew she'd carry it with me, she'd think those thoughts, too, but when I finished I saw on her face only disgust. It was hidden, well hidden, though I knew her too well, her expression might have looked neutral, frozen, but still it reflected those horrid thoughts back to me, I saw them anew, as she did, how awful and creepy they were, how contaminated my mind had become.

When had I become this way? Not on Monday, when I'd done what I did. And not on Tuesday, when I'd realized the consequences. Even just a day ago the world had felt enormous, more open than it had ever been. But I was alone now, surrounded by my own failings, my own stench, my world was the size of a cage. It had happened overnight, while I was sleeping, after I'd fallen into Franny's lap. After I'd told her what I'd done.

Can you believe I think these things?

Her lips split, but she didn't speak.

Franny, I'm a monster.

You're punishing yourself, she said.

I deserve it. I deserve much worse for what I did.

Herschel, you made a—

How can you stand me? How can you look me in the eyes? She didn't, her gaze now stuck to a spot on the floor between us. *For days I didn't tell you it was my fault. And it was. If not for me your friend would be back in London, she'd be back in her own life.* She shook her head. Her eyes were glazed. *At least admit that. Admit it was my fault.*

Even if it was *your fault, it wasn't because—*

But I'm a monster, Franny. You know that now. So just say it.

You're not.

I am, so please, please please please just fucking say it.

She looked back at me. Her hand found the jamb of the archway. *You're a monster,* she said, her voice loud and plain. She turned away, she disappeared up the stairs, up another flight. I listened to her footsteps, waiting to feel—what, exactly? No, nothing had changed, already the thoughts were coming back. *You're a monster,* she'd said, but it was nothing more than words.

I took out my phone. *The City Rises.* The charging stallion, the men strewn, an exciting painting and nothing more. It had meant so much to me before, given meaning to what I'd done, as if setting fire to a roomful of servers made me a visionary. No, but it was a thought, the servers, a fire in a crowded building—had I even bothered to check? Another tragedy born of my own neglect. If something had happened, if I were responsible—

Again I Googled *wooster fire.* There were the two articles I'd already seen. I contemplated emailing the journalists but then I saw one more, also from that CBS affiliate, an interview with a firefighter. He had gray eyes and a soft voice, for almost a minute he spoke about the importance of updating the fire safety code, and then he said, almost as an afterthought, *This building, and in the middle of a workday? It's a miracle no one was hurt.*

I closed my eyes and the thoughts returned, the new details seamless with the rest: her hair stuck together with blood, an empty bag of potato chips on the ground, her dead eyes. Now my face instead of hers, my skin waxen, a leaf lifting with the wind. Her in the hospital, me here, the urge to see her face.

The playground on Fifth Avenue and Third Street, not far from where I lived when I was just out of college, living in that studio. On Sunday mornings I'd come here to think and drink coffee, I'd watch children play tag and on the swings. The idea of having my own had seemed wholly conceptual.

There were more teenagers here than I remembered; had they always been so, what? Flawed? Awkward? Each was either entirely overconfident or disarmingly shy. And the way they walked, like they'd woken up with different legs. It was almost cruel to witness them like this, like works in progress. But maybe I was being cynical, maybe they were now their most natural selves, their edges unpolished and their colors undulled. Isn't that why the teenage years are so embarrassing? We're so vulnerable then, we give the world our naked selves, we've yet to learn how to hedge, conceal, blur.

Just to my left were two young boys, playing in front of their fathers, who seemed to be grinding through small talk. The shorter of the two was more active, he ran circles around his friend. When finally he got tired he stopped and stuck out his tongue, wagging it back and forth. His friend stepped forward and covered the shorter boy's mouth, who then bulged his eyes, flicking his pupils left and right. When the taller boy covered the shorter boy's eyes, the shorter boy started stomping his feet up and down. The taller boy tried to stop him by stepping on his shoes, but instead got his own foot stomped on, and then the fun was over. The taller boy looked to his dad but then decided to exact justice himself: he made a mean face at his friend.

You're the dumbest person I've ever met, the shorter boy said. *But have you met yourself?*

The shorter boy was stumped, outdueled. They stayed still for a moment, staring at each other, and then continued to play.

I stood, drank the last of my coffee, and walked out of the park.

The hospital was four blocks away and I cherished each one. No, I didn't want to go, I didn't want to see her face or Will's or be given an update by some dour doctor or too-hopeful nurse. But it wasn't being there I was afraid of, really, it was leaving, it was success. I was there to undo what my confession had done, to witness my own monstrosity, to wash myself with guilt and be thrust out of this purgatory, even if it meant becoming that other person again—but what then? To lose my grip like that, to be so overwhelmed—like those teenagers in the park. I'd been just as impulsive, just as impressionable, I'd listened to that book and convinced myself I couldn't read. It was embarrassing, ridiculous, as ridiculous as a weekend-long silence with Franny.

And yet, I sensed that I wasn't being fair, that I was not only neglecting something significant but doing so for the worst of reasons: fear. I had so quickly and so willfully scorned that other person, I'd refused to acknowledge what

I'd experienced: I had been connected to the world around me, truly connected, I'd tapped into something sublime, supernatural even; I knew guys from business school who went to India only to feel something like it. It was a talent, actually, just one I'd need to hone. Again I was like a teenager, a gifted guitar player who couldn't help but write insufferable lyrics. I had found a melody, a level of emotion worth sharing, but still I needed to mature into myself.

I came to the hospital. I'd lived five blocks away but had never been inside; it was said there were better places to go. I walked through crowds of people, the hallways were narrow, I finally found the receptionist after retracing my steps back to the entrance.

I'm here to see Bertie Barnes, in the ICU, I said. *Or maybe she's been moved.*

Relationship to the patient?

Friend, I said.

ID.

I handed her my driver's license. She took it without looking up at me, and then tapped on her keyboard. *Still ICU.* She rotated a small camera on the desk, and then, without warning, took my photo. Had they done that the first time we were here? A name tag printed out, she gave it to me and said, *Second floor, room 2008.*

I had as much trouble finding the elevators. Mine was packed. For some reason we all looked up at the ceiling though the light was harsh and bright. I got out, her room wasn't far, a different one than before. Just outside was a nurse on a computer.

I'm here to see Bertie Barnes, I said. *She's in that room.*

The woman turned her head but kept her eyes on her

computer, she finished typing and then looked at me, flashing her teeth.

Sorry, hon, you're welcome to go in.

I peered inside the room. *Her husband's not here?*

Will went home to sleep. Bless his soul.

Right. And how is she doing?

She's calm, she said, nodding. *She's stable.*

I approached the room but stopped in the doorway; her face was full of tubes. I asked the nurse what happened.

She was intubated, she said.

When?

Well, when she got here. She seemed to suddenly question who I was, and stopped just short of asking. *It's what's keeping her with us.*

I nodded and walked inside, I took a seat before I could think of leaving. Still I couldn't look at her, not at her face, just the lump of her body under the sheets, the whiteboard above her bed, the TV hanging from a long arm attached to the wall. It was turned away from her, toward me, Will's seat. An infomercial on low volume.

I forced my eyes on her but saw only the tubes, the slow swell of her chest. No, she hadn't already been intubated when we'd visited on Tuesday, I was sure of it. I'd ask Franny when I got home, or maybe I could speak to someone now, ask to see her records, if something fishy was going on, if I was being lied to, if the nurse outside was, then there was a reason, perhaps it was their own medical care that had led to her current state.

I stood up, I sat down. I was spineless. Craven. Wasn't this the exact purpose of my visit, to look directly at what I'd done, to accept responsibility? It was just that I wasn't ready, I hadn't sufficiently prepared myself—why hadn't I written something down? I took out my phone and opened the memo app. *Nick Bowers*. I deleted the note and started a new one, I wrote as quickly as I could, all those thoughts I'd had on the playground and on my way here. I didn't reread any of it, when I was done I put away my phone, stood up, and pushed myself over to the bed. I placed my hand on the roll guard and looked down at her, inspecting first her cheeks and forehead—the bruising was nearly gone, a faint green shadow—and then her nose and eyes. I waited, I held my breath, but still I felt the same, still I was precisely me. It was the TV, the muffled babble was too distracting to think, to digest what I was seeing. Was there no remote? Over and over I pressed the hardly functional volume button on the screen. But then, once it was finally muted, I began to hear everything else, the beeping, the buzzing, the intercom. Was it always so loud? Again I thought of Tuesday, seeing her for the first time, I'd been nearly unable to stand. That was after the doctor had pushed open her eyelids, had so casually revealed such a dreadful sight, as if he were peeking through blinds. I looked to the hallway and then leaned over her. I set my fingers on her lids, my pointer on one and my thumb on the other, and then, gently, I lifted them. Her eyes were vacant, yes, they were horrifically misaligned, but now I was, somehow, numb to it, as though I'd seen the image a thousand times before. It was only after I looked away, to the hallway, and back that something new emerged, a difference between Tuesday and today. Yes, it was still the left eye that strayed, but now it seemed that neither was fixed, that both would tilt if her body did. It was as if the basic grasp of life had become unclenched.

As I took a step back she began to look different, her body

more of an object, a mass, and yet she seemed more diffuse, too. As inert as she was—*calm*, as the nurse had said, *stable*—I felt that she was actively expanding, that, lacking some unifying force, she was starting to drift apart. She was disintegrating, there was no better word, she wasn't just dispersing but reducing, each second that passed there was less and less of her. If she was here, at my side, alive, it was only because of the tubes in her, it was because we allowed loved ones to make the choice. No, if I needed someone to reflect back all that I'd done, to make me feel my sin as if it existed outside myself, I'd come too late. I was now the only person in the room.

I was sitting again, my hands on the seat of the chair, I held them there so they wouldn't come to my face, couldn't wipe away the tears. I sobbed, once, I wanted more, I thought of Birdie, her eyes, the tubes, I thought of Will, I thought of anything I could, even Lucy, even nature, our departure from it, our abuse of it, all those thoughts I'd had yesterday, they were hardly outlines but they too helped cut the shape of my sorrow, which seemed so simple now, a fact so plain it could hardly be thought. No, nothing can be undone, I said it to myself and in every possible way, even the tropes, the clichés, each new formulation brought me closer to feeling it, brought more tears—just another example, *Crying doesn't change a thing*, it was true, for years I could cry and still I'd be here, with this thing in me I couldn't touch or see.

Oh, dear. The nurse was shaking her head at Birdie, frowning. *Yes, it's very sad.*

They came all at once now, the sobs, they overlapped, so much so that I no longer heard the incessant beeping, the rhythmic vibrations of the bed. When finally I managed to stop I assumed that the nurse had left, that I could gather myself alone, but she was only readjusting Birdie's pillows.

I'm sorry, I said.

Darling, of course.

She turned to Birdie, giving her a kind smile, as if Birdie was looking back at her.

My wife told me she was making noises? Vocalizations, I mean.

She was, but not any longer.

I swallowed. I folded my arms. *I can hear my own heartbeat,* I said. *In my ears.*

She nodded, as if she heard it too. *Pulsatile tinnitus.*

Is that temporary?

It could be temporary, yes. It could be permanent.

I nodded and looked back at Birdie. Still the nurse just stood there.

You're welcome to stay for as long as you like, she said, *but she needs to be cleaned. Normally we ask that only next of kin—*

Oh, sure, I said, standing. She smiled at me as I walked out.

I ambled around the hallways, peering into other rooms. I sat on a bench near the nursing station and listened to their small talk. When I went back to Birdie's room the door was still closed. I waited five more minutes, ten, fifteen, I wondered if Will would return before I was let back in, and before either happened I left.

Outside it was hotter still. There was a thickness in the air, that sense of coiled freedom; it was now fully summer. I didn't want to go back home, I wasn't ready to. I walked up the street and went into the first restaurant I saw, Purity Diner. At first I thought it was called *Established 1929,* as that was bigger on the awning; perhaps they were proud to have risen out of the crash.

It was nearly empty, I took a seat in a booth. I wasn't hungry but knew I should eat, I ordered coffee and the daily special. On the TV was CNBC, the NASDAQ. I took out my phone to look at my portfolio and the memo app opened. I saw the phrase *action is not the only* and deleted the note. When I closed the app my photos came up. I deleted the ones of *The City Rises*, the Miró. I checked my portfolio and then my email. The lawyers had responded, all of them. Already they were asking more than they should. Did anyone still believe in client confidentiality? How else did the rumor mill churn?

The coffee came and I drank it immediately. As the caffeine hit I let myself imagine the coming weeks, the endless calls, the carefully worded emails and hunting down of signatures. A careful undoing. In those hours debts would be repaid or nullified, the measure of our work taken and distributed, and, once all parties had accepted their fate, Atra Arca Capital Management Inc. would cease to exist. How clean, how seamless. How unlike anything at all.

I thought of Franny. She was probably doing yoga, or working—anything to take her mind off me. *You're a monster*, I'd forced her to say. That was the very least of it. If Birdie was my sin, still our silence about it was shared, and it would lurk in every silence we shared; we'd no longer be able to look at each other and be sure of what exactly we'd see.

I looked into my coffee mug and flagged the waiter for more. I picked up my phone and went to my texts, my conversation with Milosz. He'd written last: *Meet you at your place, leaving now.* I looked up at the TV. A bald man talking angrily. Interest rates were set to rise on Monday, the market expected to dip. Nothing that can't be undone. I wrote, *We need to talk about yesterday. In person is best.* I hit send and put my phone down.

The waiter came with the coffee, and soon after he brought the food: steak frites, mostly frites. I poured out ketchup, dunked a fry, and ate it. I heard a police siren in the distance, and then another. As if they'd send patrolmen. No, if they suspected foul play they wouldn't arrest me; they'd call, invite me to some well-appointed government building. I thought of my brief chat with Polk, my voicemail to him, the fire itself. Had I remembered to lock the door to the server room? God, I had to tell Franny.

I picked up my fork and knife and set them on the meat. I let the tip of the knife enter, slowly, and then I carved a piece. I looked at it, smelled it, and placed it in my mouth, on the back of my tongue. I chewed slowly, and then, as the juices dripped down my throat, at a normal speed.

I swallowed. I took a sip of water.

It tasted fine.

ACKNOWLEDGMENTS

TK [allow 2 pages]

ACKNOWLEDGMENTS